"In *Isinda: Fallen Dagger*, Rhett Bruno stages a fantastic universe awash with myth and wonder. Bruno's gripping story of Zano, an emancipated slave, is served by the author's vivid descriptions of the splendors of the land of Isinda and by memorable accounts of the history and mores of its inhabitants."

—Jean-François Bédard
Assistant Professor
Syracuse University
School of Architecture

"Isinda, Fallen Dagger, the first in Rhett Bruno's trilogy of a hero's struggle to bring peace to his war torn land, is a masterpiece of the imagination. Rhett's wonderfully creative and evocative writing transport the reader to another realm: one in which the battles are fierce and grueling and the characters passionate and multidimensional. His first work should be celebrated as a gift to the fantasy genre, and readers are certain to devour it in a sitting. One word of advice to Rhett: don't keep us waiting too long for the sequels!"

—Dawn Lynch
English Teacher
Hauppauge High School

"It was so easy to get lost in the world Rhett has created, I was hooked by the opening paragraph. You find yourself in a completely different time and realm driven by love and war, the perfect escape from reality."

—Alyssa Arcieri
Student at the Fashion Institute of Technology
New York City

ISINDA
FALLEN DAGGER

To Sina,

Thank you for your
support. I hope you enjoy.

A NOVEL

ISINDA
FALLEN DAGGER

Rhett C. Bruno

Tate Publishing & Enterprises

Published by Tate Publishing & Enterprises, LLC
127 E. Trade Center Terrace | Mustang, Oklahoma 73064 USA
1.888.361.9473 | www.tatepublishing.com

Tate Publishing is committed to excellence in the publishing industry. The company reflects the philosophy established by the founders, based on Psalm 68:11,
"The Lord gave the word and great was the company of those who published it."

Published in the United States of America

ISBN: 978-1-61663-305-9
1. Fiction, Fantasy, Epic
2. Fiction, General
10.04.22

DEDICATION

This book is dedicated to my loving
parents Lynn and Craig Bruno.

Without them, none of this would have been possible.

TABLE OF CONTENTS

PROLOGUE

Love ... It is a feeling that binds us all, and along with it must come its opposite, hate. Why are men bound by such emotions, emotions that when analyzed deeply are essentially simple? Such small words, with such loaded meanings; words worth fighting for; words worth dying for. Are we forever bound by feelings of intense like versus feelings of intense dislike? A beautiful woman can initiate a war, but so, evidently, can the loathing of another lord. By definition, the words are opposite, but are their effects any different? Can they not equally generate death and wickedness, or are they simply matters of interpretation as plain as good and evil? One thing is certain—these emotions are inescapable, no matter how swiftly you run. They are feelings so genuine, so intrinsic, that no mind can abolish them, and only few learn to contain them.

A History Written
in Blood

*"I dream of a day when a single
name shall echo across the land!
When there will not be Scaldor
or Humans, or any other race, but
Isindans!"*

The Battle of Futility, Zano Cynery

High above the unyielding ground, searing and blazing in its placid fury, the sun sat, suspended within a
canvas of blue. Its great rays illuminated everything
beneath, blessing the world with light where it would otherwise
be engulfed by darkness.

My story will be woven beneath this sphere of flaming gold,
in a place that will forever live on in the hearts of Isindans. It is
a memory that will linger on in this land named Isinda, in the
minds of its people and in the scars imprinted on the earth. It
will begin in the west where shin-high, amber grass rocked in
the morning breeze as far as the eye could see, across a flat field

with nothing more than a minute lump—not even a tree—to obscure the view. Various species of wildlife grazed across the grassland, and birds soared in the sky above without a care in the world safe for survival.

This is the beauty of the primitive mind that an animal possesses. There is no concern of love, or honor, or war. The only concern in the psyche of an animal is surviving to live another day.

The intellectually gifted races of Isinda had been there since the ancient gods birthed the land out of a rock in a barren sea. From the snow-capped peaks of the north, to the great southern desert, the gods erected all of this and also the organisms which inhabit these areas—from the creatures that cannot be seen to intelligent life forms such as the Scaldor and the Humans. This was the work of greater beings. Their names, as well as their stories, may vary among the different races, but it was in this way that Isinda was shaped.

At their inception, the races were as innocent as children, but their intelligence and also their capacity to destroy have never ceased to progress. Since the departure of the mortal gods, they have spiraled down a path of blood and iron. If you were to ask a resident of this land during the second age if he could remember a time when no race was at war, he would be unable to find such a period in the deepest recess of his mind. The history of this land has been written: each race forever in conflict, trying to conquer the others while ultimately failing. For ages, a stalemate of victories and losses existed, printed in the blood of the peoples of Isinda. It had evolved into a land of war that had every need for a peace that could not be found, and this was its history until a day of infamy arrived. A day in early Forunhor of 1027 G.D.—Bronze Empire years—on a field that would become known as the "Deadlands."

The amber fields continued to sway beneath a slight breeze, far below the great, glaring sun in its most dominant time of the day. There were no longer any animals strolling across the field and the birds had already scattered like flies from a flame. Silence pervaded in this moment. A baby blue sky was spotted with puffy, white clouds which floated along as slothfully as snails. The day was a brisk one, just cold enough to give your cheeks a chill or send a shiver down your spine with the gust of a strong wind. Perhaps it was the chill of death set upon the land by the Lord of Pregarus, for only a god could have predicted the devastation that would ensue. Death was nothing foreign to Isinda, but no mortal could foresee the magnitude of it that the infamous day would bear.

If you were to put your ear to the soil at that moment and listen, you would hear in the distance a steady rumble, like a weak earthquake, advancing from the west. A great army of the many races of Isinda marched at a fast pace, for the first time together as one—united. Most every race was present, united against the one race that had brought them to their knees. Awaiting this army in the Deadlands was the most daunting force in all of history: the great army of the Deimor.

The Deimor, by many, were considered demons due to their appearance and warmongering nature. These people, however, were far from the crude, immoral spawns of darkness as they were often depicted. Originating in the labyrinth of rock and black sand north of the Scaldor lands, the Deimor lived under harsh, abnormal conditions on nearly untamable lands. Their skin was thick and of a rusty crimson hue. Spikes and horns formed on their bodies in varied spots and patterns, predominantly on their heads and shoulders. Jet-black hair flowed down from their craniums, lengthy on both males and females. They all had flaming red eyes, which burnt with the radiance of an inferno, and with the same ferocity at that.

Unlike the other races, their way was not one of piety and prayer, for the only being a Deimor bowed to was their beloved king. They were a militaristic race, yes, but they were far from barbaric. These warriors were paragons of honor, and they believed it their duty to lose their lives admirably in battle, by the sword. Yet, peculiarly, the way all Deimor desired to lose their lives was not in battle with their enemy, but by the edge of love, by the blades of a people they adored more than any other. Peace in the afterlife was consummated by peace at death and to a Deimor there was no greater peace than dying at the hands of adoration. This was their creed: strength and glory in life, honor and love at death. It was this vigor and conviction that allowed them to sweep through all of Isinda like an unrelenting forest fire. That was so, until a day in the Deadlands where a wall of water halted them.

On the grassy fields of the Deadlands, the framework of a ruined castle rested, facing south, at the Deimor's rear. The origin of the castle was unknown, but within it, the throne room remained in untarnished condition. The walls were a dark gray stone, arranged in orderly blocks that rose twenty feet, and the same was true for the slightly-rounded ceiling. The space was that of a long rectangle, accommodated with pillars that rose up to the vaulted ceiling along the walls of the long side. Behind the pillars lay a few rickety, wooden doors, which led to what was mostly rubble and ruin. On one of the short sides was a large wooden gate that opened up to the grasslands, and on the opposite side, the throne. Perhaps the room was once more extravagant, with elaborate carpets unfurled before the throne and vibrant cloth draped down the pillars, but at the time of the Deimor conquest, the room was nothing more than an empty shell of rock. Slivers of light slipped through slits on the walls, giving the room a dim illumination, though not even a torch lit the aging hall.

Upon this forsaken seat of power sat an imposing figure, considered by many to be the most powerful man in all of Isinda. He was none other than the grand king of the Deimor - the illustrious Malum. The distinguished lord's glory years were far behind him. At the time he must have been at least into his sixth decade of life, though it was impossible to know his actual age, for the Deimor did not believe in keeping track. To them you lived until death claimed you, and everything between birth and culmination defined that death and its meaning.

The ruler's crimson skin was rough and wrinkled, weathered by war, the elements and age. Two petrifying horns rose up through scraggly, light gray hair and curved outward from either side of his head, each at least a foot long. A gangling, salty beard of prestige protruded from his chin, and his eyes held the appearance of dull rubies with their once-zealous color now sapped from them. A white robe draped down from his shoulders to the floor, laced with pure gold trimmings and black embellishments. Only one foot fixed into a sturdy iron-plated boot stuck out from the bottom of his robe and rested on the floor. His left leg had been severed years ago which, to his dismay, left him unable to aid his men in his war. A silver longsword with a golden, ruby-embellished hilt rested in his hand, serving as a replacement limb when he walked, and around his palm was wrapped a black cloth with the image of an emerald moon painted onto it.

Malum sat in deep thought, staring at the gate across the room. Before him sat his two sons, their legs folded. Their eyes were shut, keeping the flame from bursting out as they meditated. Quietly they concentrated their minds on the promise of forthcoming battle.

On the king's left was the man known as Unfordive the Sublime, the older of the twins. He was the most feared swordsman of his time, his skills on the field of battle said to be unparalleled. His swiftness and agility struck awe into every man he fought until the sharp blade of his sword met his foes' torso and sent them twisting into the abyss. Though strategy was oft not left to him, he was not incapable of drawing up the occasional tactic.

These talents allowed him to rally his men against all odds, without fear of failure or death. Though he was considered a prince, he never failed to join his men on the front lines—in the heart of battle and in the hearts of those he led. Legend has it he once held back a Scaldor army of 10,000 men with nothing but his sword. The most bizarre fact about him, however, was that he, along with his brother Seekoras, was not fully Deimor. Before his inception, the king Malum inexplicably fell in love with a woman of Suvrarian descent. Though this frustrated his people, his power obligated them to tolerate it and soon after accept it with open arms. The birth of Malum's sons sorrowfully resulted in the demise of the woman who became the queen of a race not her own. As noteworthy in history as she was, her name remains unknown to all but the deceased.

Unlike the rest of the Deimor, Unfordive and his brother each had only one ruby-colored eye. Unfordive's left eye was like a vivid emerald and the same was true for Seekoras's right.

The great swordsman Unfordive held a youthful and dynamic appearance, his frame as dexterous as any wild beast's. He anticipated the unexpected, as his eyes and ears were constantly vigilant. His sleek black hair fell down just past his clavicles, highlighted with streaks of jade. In spite of being a hybrid, his, as well as Seekoras', skin was the same crimson color the Deimor people shared. They both appeared dominantly Deimor, with flaws only evident in their eyes and hair.

As he sat before his father, Unfordive was fully-clad in a suit of painted white, boiled leather armor. The pauldrons extended down about three inches past the shoulder, with black pieces of fabric flowing outward from the ends. The leather cuirass was adorned with black, tribal spikes and designs, and had a red depiction of a traditional longsword painted down the center. On his powerfully-built arms and hands, he wore nothing in order to remain as swift as possible, while his thighs were protected by snow-colored leather cuisses, which covered a comfortable pair of close-fitting silk pants. His feet remained out in the open, toughened from years of exposure to the outdoors. Across his eminent lap laid an iron-bladed *katana* fixed into a hilt which was plated by gold. Embedded into the top of the hilt were small, diamond-shaped, flawless rubies. The handle was wrapped tightly in black silk for comfort, in such a way that each finger was gently cradled. His blade was perfectly curved and sharpened so acutely that it could rip through any mortal-made piece of armor. Finally, engraved just above the golden hilt, was an inscription in the calligraphy of Desthoroth—the ancient language of the Deimor—which read, "Eth Larka Mannoth," or in common tongue, "The Left Hand."

Seekoras, who accompanied his brother in meditation, was not the same blade-wielding warrior as his sibling. He assumed a more tactical role in the Deimor conquest, laying out the strategies needed to win battles. His martial skills were adequate, however, and he was able to hold his own on the battlefield. In appearance, he was identical to his brother in almost every way, except for his eyes, which were a mirror image of Unfordive's. His demeanor was calmer and more collected than his twin's feral and more energetic persona.

While meditating before his father, Seekoras was appareled in the same suit of leather armor, except the colors on his were reversed. He, like his brother, left his arms bare; however, he sheltered his feet and shins in black leather boots. Across his lap rested an iron bastard sword rooted in an ebony hilt. The grip was smooth and rounded, and entrenched into the upper hilt was an eye-sized, unflawed emerald. The blade was roughly three feet long and was easily maneuvered by Seekoras' robust arms. As on Unfordive's *katana*, a phrase of Desthoroth was carved into the lower blade. These figures read, "Eth Ralor Mannoth," which translated into, "The Right Hand." Most believed these phrases to signify the brothers being the figurative hands of their father. However, it could also have symbolized that together, the twins were so close they almost seemed to form a singular person. The actual truth implied by these Desthoroth phrases is unknown, but they represented how rigid the brothers' bond truly was.

Malum's blank stare was suddenly flushed with animation as he sat up in his seat of stone. "Rise my sons," he said in a soft, but dignified tone. His sons' eyes flashed open with the quickness of lightening. Their legs unfolded routinely and the weight of their mighty frames was put on their feet, the fingers on both of their right hands curling gently around the handles of their blades. Neither looked at their father; they simply stared forward with unrivaled intensity.

"I have grown weary during the course of our war. I stand here before you an aged man on his last limb. Our forces have been stretched thin across the land, but you must forget everything that has happened before this day, for it is in today's battle that the future of the Deimor lies," Malum stated, his eyes looking toward the ground and his voice nearly bereft of energy.

"We are strong, father. The weak will never conquer us!" Unfordive replied confidently as he prepared mentally for the thrill of battle.

"Yes … the weak. We swept across Isinda with such a force that the separate races we dominated have become one. We are their glue, but their bond is hardly firm. The slightest pin drop would send their limp confederation into disarray. These people that we fight are weak, indeed. They are engulfed by their hatred for us and their hatred for each other. They have yet to realize how strong they could be together, if only they would let the glue stick. We sought to destroy the weak, to bring the scattered races together under our rule. Now that we have taken them all separately; now that each race has fallen, they are forced to unite. They believe that we are the enemy. What they do not realize is that their true enemy lies within themselves. It was by their weakness that we Deimor stand where we are today.

"What will happen if we win? What will happen if we fail? My sons, I cannot tell you. What I do know in the depths of my heart is that if we fail the land will fall back to the way it always was. Their alliance will shatter, along with the power we now possess. With every bone in my body; with every breath of air I take I wish that I could fight alongside my people today. You know what you're up against, my children, and you know what you're fighting for." Tears swelled in Malum's eyes as he concluded.

"We fight for honor!" Seekorus shouted powerfully.

"We fight to rid this land of the weak and to restore it to strength!" said Unfordive with the valor of a roaring Tigress.

"To bring the land to its knees under the Deimor and let it rise among us!"

"So that our people may live on eternally to spread our way across Isinda, whose peoples so falsely refuse it!"

The weathered, but dignified king rose to his foot, leaning half of his weight onto the sword that had become his leg. He limped with a slouched back toward Seekoras, as though he were ready to greet death in his sleep. His blade scraped against the stone floor and his decrepit bones creaked as he halted before his strapping young son, who looked down upon him. They stared at each other compassionately, as a dying father should gaze upon the child who shares his blood. With all of the strength his old bones possessed, he reached out and placed a hand softly upon his son's breast. Seekoras bowed his head with reverence to the father who had taught him and raised him since he was but a mere child. He strained to hold back the insistent tears. Malum then lifted his frail hand and feebly limped his way toward Unfordive.

The king bit his lower lip, trying to blockade the liquid within the whites of his eyes. He then stood in the shadow of the vigorous, lithe body of a matchless warrior. Unfordive's eyes flamed with an undying passion and love for his fading father. When Malum reached out to place his hand, Unfordive heaved it around his back and embraced him vigorously. During this hug, they witnessed many years of life race past their eyes, as though it all had happened in mere seconds. Father and son unclasped, and Malum moped back to his throne. With a feeble twist of his body he slumped back into the seat.

The once-great king watched his sons, knowing it would be his last chance to behold them. His vision was cloudy, obstructed by a steady flow of salty tears. He gazed upon his sons, who had become the Twin Blades, with marvel, as an artist would look upon his finest work.

"Go forth my sons and let the Deimor live on. Strength and glory my children. Desara Norrath!" The lord of the Deimor yelled with the verve of a voice that had once transcended mortality.

His sons roared, "Desara Norrath!" in reply. These Desthoroth words had become a phrase used a great deal among the Deimor, especially between the Twin Blades and their soldiers.

The brothers took one last gaze at their beloved father and turned sharply to face the gate, coming to grips with their most likely fate. Their faces were intense, not a hint of indifference visible in their expressions as they walked rigidly, coming closer and closer to destiny until they stood, side by side, in the shadow of the hefty wooden door. They stared into each others' eyes, like searing fire into an uncontrollable jungle. Their heads nodded simultaneously as their hands came upon the grain of the gate. They saw in each other the importance of this day and grasped the inner love for their people and family. Together, as if opening a celestial gateway to the boundless heavens, they pushed it open, entering another world entirely.

Radiant sunlight ripped through the opening doors, blinding the brothers for a moment until their eyes could transpose from the dreary throne room to the sun's brilliant glare. Before them, like statues, stood columns and rows of Deimor soldiers in flawless formation. They wore heavy, iron strip armor cuirasses on their upper bodies, decorated with strands of black leather draped down from the trims. Across the chest plates were painted the Desthoroth symbol for strength in black—a symbol which resembled the eyes and teeth of a Tigress. On their heads they wore nothing, choosing instead to display their jet-black hair and variations of horns. Some soldiers had holes carved into the metal on their shoulders to allow spikes to slip through, which gave them permanent weapons.

The soldiers' legs were protected by iron greaves that were latched by leather straps over black cloth leggings and, unlike Unfordive, each soldier wore light iron boots that rose to just above their lower shins. On their hips hung sheathed, long katana swords. On their hands were hefty, wooden, rectangular shields about chest-high, which were bound by a frame of iron. Set onto the back of every Deimor, except for those in the second row, was a pilum of about six feet with a sharp iron tip. The soldiers in the second row held long, iron spears, which spanned more than eight feet, between the bodies of the first row. Every soldier was clad identically to further display the discipline and unity that instilled fear into their enemies.

This army was no mere Deimor force set to conquer a town or village; this was the grand force of the Deimor and, realistically, the last great army they would ever boast. It was a massive force of 150,000 regimented and courageous Deimor soldiers, each trained since they were no more than innocent children. It was part of the Deimor way to begin swordsmanship and military training from a green age. Each dedicated his life to the martial forces until he was incapacitated or relieved by a commander or the king. Unlike most other races of Isinda, the Deimor encouraged their women to fight—fifteen percent of their army was women—and gave them the choice of suiting up or living a life of housekeeping and farming.

Deimor society was incredibly militaristic, focusing solely on strength and the honor of battle. There were no great Deimor cities, nor were there noteworthy Deimor inventions or achievements. They were born with a sword in their hands and trained to use it for as long as their lives permitted. Any child who could not last the immeasurable rigor of their training succumbed to death. They lived in towns and villages along the Undaro Badlands, which circled outward from the large, but unspectacular, wooden manor of the king and his family. In their lands there was no tax or currency; there were no enforcers of government, for in truth there was no government. Emphatically, they followed their king with no need for policing or guards. The only laws they obeyed were respect for their fellow people and knowing what must be done for the maintenance of society and family. To the Deimor family meant the entirety of the race, and to safeguard them was a Deimor's utmost duty. Most civilizations would crumble with no strict guidelines or laws besides respecting and living, but it was this lifestyle of training, dedication, honor, and respect that allowed the Deimor, who were few in number, to conquer all the lands of Isinda.

The Twin Blades continued to pass through one hundred fifty rows of crimson Deimor, receiving a "Desara Norrath!" from each soldier they passed. History would consider their army to be enormous, though it paled in comparison to the force it would face that day. However, the Deimor did not need numbers to intimidate; it was their ferocity and skill on the battlefield that made them a daunting opponent.

Unfordive and Seekoras made their way toward the front line. Aside from the men they passed, the army was silent, staring forward with the focus of a pack of wolves on the prowl in a darkened forest. The image of slashing blades and clanking shields blitzed through their minds while they prepared to do what had to be done and focused on their duties.

Side by side, they stepped past the front line and out into the open. A field of gently-swaying amber grass was revealed to them. The sun was at full height, gleaming directly above their heads as the brisk air nipped at their hardened faces. Neither a rodent nor a bird was in sight, having all already fled from the looming battle. It was at this moment that the gallant eyes of the Twin Blades gaped in astonishment.

Across the peaceful, desolate field was anchored an army of epic proportions. This marvelous crowd, which consisted of the many races of Isinda, had gathered at the Deadlands, unified for the first time as a horde of roughly one million men. The force was titanic, stretching for well over a mile and spanning across the entirety of the eye's vision. The many races of Isinda were represented in this confederation that stood to oppose the Deimor. The aqua-colored Scaldor from east Isinda, the green Suvrarian of the southwest, the tanned Humans from the west, the colossal Sarnon of the north, and the dark skinned Arikarnan of the southeast. The Humans and the Scaldor accounted for the mass, planted in the center of the army with around 300,000 soldiers each.

The Humans lived in the temperate plains of western Isinda, an area carved with crags and valleys of sharp rock. Forests were scattered across the landscape but failed to cover any great vastness. The temperature there was moderate and seasonal, never too hot, and never too cold, with an occasional coating of snow in Frigusa. Humankind had always been a scattered race—torn into a vast number of separate kingdoms which were, more often than not, at war with each other and the races that surrounded them. The northern kingdoms often clashed with the mighty Sarnon, and the southern with the secretive Suvrarian. They were considered more civilized than the Deimor, since most of the Human kingdoms had established social classes and codes within their grand cities, but even so, they had no quarrel in slaying their own kind.

They held skin of fair tan, topped by scraggly hair ranging from blonde to dark brown, and eyes of brown. Considered the finest archers in all of Isinda, Humans were typically trained to fire down with precision from the lofty fortifications that surrounded most of their cities. Most of those present in the Deadlands wore light leather armor, and on their backs hung wooden longbows with a quiver of arrows. Their melee weapons ranged from iron short swords to longswords.

The Scaldor, standing beside the Humans in the center of the crowd, glimmered like sapphires beneath the sun's glare. Their thick, but sleek, azure scales covered their thin skin like a natural coat of armor. Below slick, black hair, which was banded with thin, indigo strands, sat eyes like churning oceans. They dwelled in the eastern lands of Isinda, east of the great Chasm of the Gods, in an area that was excessively bombarded by rain. Plains of vivid amber grass stretched over the land, embellished with occasional rock formations, and the vast Desolura Forest enveloped the northern section.

The Scaldor resided much like the Humans did, divided and aligned to diverse kingdoms. Their most powerful kingdom was the Bronze Kingdom, named for its abundant use of bronze and its incredible spire, which was plated in the shimmering metal. They came to this battle half-suited in thin bronze breastplates and greaves. They were armed with double-sided bronze swords, almost like short *naginata* with a blade on either side. The other half wore varied pieces of leather and iron armor with assorted weapons.

On the left flank of the alliance stood a gathering of Suvrarian, which amounted to at least 150,000 warriors, both male and female. If any race could be compared to the Deimor, it would be the honorable men and women of the verdant Suvan jungle. The Suvrarian lived relatively unified within the jungle, ruled by two kings: the Lord of the Wood and the King of Fur. Both had control over the many Suvrarian villages, which extended southward until the jungle halted at the bluffs of the Jade Sea. These people were master hunters and fishers who often engaged with the ferocious wildlife of the Suvan and even learned to tame species such as the brutal tigress. It is said that the green-haired, emerald-eyed men of the south had control over the very trees that towered within their jungle.

Before the dreaded Deimor they stood, clad in ornately-carved suits of wood, which were festooned with vibrant leaves and painted with outstanding colors. They adorned their faces and bodies with finely-detailed tribal paintings of a sticky green paste. Unlike the metal weapons of the other races, the Suvrarian fought with swords fashioned of the Beukilitus leaf, which hardened as strong as iron when heated and gave off a viridian glow.

Entrenched on the right flank of the army were roughly 50,000 hulking Sarnon of the powdery north. They resided deep within the Narsano Mountains and, unlike the other races which had an average height of roughly five-and-a-half feet, they towered at heights above seven feet and were as burly as bears. Sheets of slippery, slick ice covered their realm, which was glazed by layers of heavy white snow. Living in scattered tribes along the pallid mountainsides and valleys the Sarnon were often at peace. However, occasionally they warred amongst themselves with a barbarous intensity. Within the folds of the vast, white blanket of the north, they camouflaged with bulky, snow-colored fur and blue, leathery skin on their extremities and faces. Their small fangs were like bloodcurdling icicles and their eyes appeared like shiny black pebbles embedded in ice.

Considering their unmatched bulk, the Sarnon present at the Deadlands wielded massive stone hammers, clubs, and maces while wearing nothing but their own thick hides and the skins of slain animals.

The Arikarnan made up the final section of the coalition, resting behind the Humans and Scaldor. Their home, the great Akai Desert, was the most arid area in all of Isinda. It was coated with dunes of sand and dotted with oases, allowing the desert to be somewhat habitable. They were exceptionally tall, though not nearly as bulky as the Sarnon, and their skin was like charcoal stretched around elongated, lean muscles. Razor-sharp tusks extended from their protruding jaws, used for eating the thick-hided and shelled creatures that inhabited the sea of sand.

The Akai was spotted with unbelievable stone tombs and palaces to house Arikarnon nobles, both living and dead. Their adaption to the desert's incredible warmth kept them from parting from their domain, leaving them mostly on the defensive from Scaldor assaults and campaigns. Their staunch, tenacious demeanor derived from the strict mandates of their long-lasting dynasties. They arrived at the Deadlands wearing bundles of cloth over crude iron plates, which covered their vitals. They were eager to clash as they flaunted their jagged, stone-bladed spears and flawlessly carved stone-piercing axes.

On that memorable day, this great force—comprised of many races who had skirmished for centuries—joined together to face a common enemy and gain their independence. The Deimor had brought them together, but even the slightest dissension would tear them apart like sharp teeth into soft flesh. It was no great achievement of peace or unity; it was merely a feeble alliance of the weak who desired to guard themselves from the rule of others and from change. The races were well aware that the confederation would never endure past this battle and that the alliance was no more than a loose horde that refused to be conquered; a horde too naïve to realize that the Deimor had already brought them together. Unfortunately for the Deimor, they refused to accept assistance, instead making the decision to dissolve their figurative glue.

Unfordive and his brother stood in the middle of their army, a space of about forty columns of soldiers separating them. The warriors behind them stood erect, at paramount attention as they gazed forward. In their eyes not a hint of fear or anxiety could be spotted, despite the fact that across the empty grasslands awaited an army of one million men. It was a force that overshadowed any they had ever faced before—a number of people that none of them had ever witnessed in a single gathering.

The horde jeered at them, bending over and revealing their rumps, screaming malicious curses and slamming their swords against their armor. It is unimaginable how thunderous the Deadlands were that day, yet the Deimor were not shaken; they merely stared at this insolent throng with a hunger to engage in a long-awaited fray.

The many leaders of the alliance attempted to silence the

mass, which was accomplished after an endless period of raucousness. Military chants ordered the mob into alignment and called the Humans to line up across the front row.

"Well men, this is it. We have conquered Isinda, and today brings our chance to defend it. The weak have arrived to slaughter their conquerors, but we are the strong! You men know what we have fought for! There's no need for me to inform you of that!" Unfordive screamed out with command like no other, lighting a spark in the spirits of his followers.

"They come here with the belief that they can defeat us? Each of you is worth one hundred of them! My people, we have brought Isinda to its knees! They should fear an army of three Deimor, let alone this one! I say, let them bring their horde to our swords, and let the sky rain red with their blood!" Seekoras yelled out confidently, building that spark up into a flicker of flame.

"Here it is my people, my family! Our chance to accomplish that which has never been done before. I have been called the greatest warrior ever to live, yet I believe that there is nothing in this forsaken world keeping any of you from attaining what I hold—to fight how I fight. It all begins in your heart, in believing in those beside you. Do that and all else will fall into place. My brothers you have bled beside me; you have killed beside me; you have dreamt and conquered beside me! Now here today, we are one! Now, Deimor, let us die together!" Unfordive roared with authority, as the flicker of flame burst into a raging inferno, leaving his men salivating with unprecedented bloodlust.

"Desara Norraaath!" the Twin Blades and their followers erupted ferociously, pumping their arms in the air and slamming their fists against their chests.

The Humans made their way to the front of the horde, forming jagged lines, with their longbows at arm. The army of one million grew soundless along with their foes across the field. The eye of a hurricane loomed above, and once it passed, the calm would end, and the storm would rampage across the Deadlands, tearing apart all in its path.

Seekoras raised his sword and shouted, "Shell! Shell!" This signaled a defensive tactic honed only by the Deimor to commence. The front line dropped their weapons and entrenched their shields into the dirt. The next row followed by placing their shields over the ducked man in front of them at a perpendicular angle. This procedure was copied until the last line lifted their shields to an obtuse angle, compared to those in front of them, in order to guard from any far-flying projectiles. From afar, they appeared to have formed a shell of wood and iron—an impenetrable wall that implored arrows to pierce it. The only weak spot in the formation was the flanks, but these soldiers tucked tightly underneath to avoid protruding their limbs. Seekoras had disciplined his men to use this tactic against arrow volleys, and, though not the most comfortable technique for those involved, the *Turtle Shell* was nearly impervious.

The apparent leader of the Humans stepped out before the lines of his race and lifted a blade toward the gleaming sun, indicating for his men to pull an arrow out of their quivers and arm their weapons. They aimed their longbows toward the Deimor at an upward angle and pulled back the strings until they were taut.

With the downward slice of the Human leader's sword, tens of thousands of arrows launched from rest with a high-pitched crack, releasing a barrage of shadow across the grass. Like an irritated swarm of bees, they whizzed through the cerulean sky toward their targets.

Unfordive breathed deeply through his nostrils while he gently shut his eyes. Seekoras had fallen in behind the shields of the first row, now safely behind the protection of the great shell. As piercing iron blades tore through the air toward Unfordive, his eyes sprang open, revealing two wrathful torrents. He coolly caressed his sword's handle with both hands.

"Hold the Shell!" he roared, as he flourished his blade masterfully. The arrows crashed like thunder into the barricade but were halted completely in their tracks. Wood splintered, and iron tips were sent hurtling through the air. Others stabbed into the shields, wedging between the grains, while others still ripped through the shields, scattering fragments and blood onto the grass.

Unfordive stood amongst the onslaught of projectiles, twirling his blade into the oncoming arrows and felling them just before they met his flesh. The spectacle was inspiring. He stood amidst a swarm of death, but by the artful movements of his blade, remained unscathed.

The Deimor burst from the shelter of their shields as the last arrow coasted into the dirt, chanting and taunting with the clanking of metal and fists. Only a few hundred of them lay dead, cradled by the blades of grass beneath their corpses. As the living screamed wildly, the veins on their scarlet foreheads swelled like worms creeping beneath their skin. Seekoras smirked toward the enemy who believed their volley able to shred the will of his soldiers.

"Fall back!" he ordered, and the Deimor fell into the Shell formation as though they had never disassembled.

The Humans placed another round of arrows into their bows and readied them to be fired across the Deadlands. Their arms trembled in anticipation for their leader's blade to fall, and when it did, a second wall of shadow sped out across the field, the projectiles cutting through the air like eagles bolting toward their prey.

"Hold!" Unfordive bellowed as he gripped his sword, ready to cut through the ensuing volley. The Shell braced itself for impact and like incessant hail the arrows rained upon it, rattling the wood with cracks and thumps, and sprinkling splinters of timber across the Deimor Shell.

Finally the last arrow innocently struck the unfaltering blockade. Strips of wood and chips of iron lay motionless on the earth at Unfordive's feet as he stood, sucking air into his nostrils and snarling. His sword was secure in both hands, reflecting rays of light toward all who beheld it. Once again the shell dispersed, revealing a zealous force unscathed by the bombardment. The Deimor jeered barbarously, clanking iron and wood together and creating an uproar as deafening as they could possibly produce.

The Humans across the field placed their bows on the ground and fell back into untidy lines. The leaders of the alliance stepped out before their army and gazed across the endless Deadlands to see an unflinching group of Deimor lined up in opposition. They observed an army of crimson warriors who bellowed vigorously like wolves at a full moon, eager for the hunt. With a mouthful of orders, the leaders signaled their army to unsheathe their weapons and take in hand any object that could lead to the slim possibility of survival.

The vast horde broke out into thunderous clamor, creating an atmosphere in which it was nearly impossible to hear. The leaders flaunted their weapons and began to charge enthusiastically into the void of land. At their rear, as if set into motion by the ear-splitting noise, was an avalanche of warriors, tumbling mightily in pursuit. Grass was shredded and ripped from its roots in the wake of the force, spitting up heaps of dirt and unfurling a brown fog.

"We wait all of our lives, men!" Seekoras yelled as loudly as possible, desperately trying to overcome the earthquake that erupted across the field. The Deimor had grown silent, adrenaline pumping through their veins and replacing the blood that once had coursed there. The second row poked their spears between the warriors in the first row as Seekoras lifted his sword toward the heavens. The rest of the army pulled the pilums off of their backs and raised them up parallel to the ground as the avalanche closed in with colossal power, seemingly able to instantly wipe the Deimor away in a sea of blood.

"Hold!" Unfordive ordered, waiting to call for a release until the whites of his enemies' eyes were in clear view, when savage faces became discernible, with pupils dilated and tongues lashing.

"Release!" he yelled with a bloodthirsty roar and the angle of the Deimor's arms shifted quickly forward from their ninety-degree rest. Thousands of hands released javelins, sending them soaring across the sky and rippling outward from the center of the formation. The pilums darted toward the alliance like tiny bolts of lightning and, unable to halt, the immense horde sprinted directly into the onslaught. The Human and Scaldor front lines were decimated by iron blades, which tore through them like knives through fabric. Blood spurted onto the drowning grass as jagged blades carved into chests and skulls, and lacerated flailing limbs. The severed corpses tumbled into a pile that impeded the steady movement of the allied horde.

"Charge!" the Twin Blades yelled, signaling their dwarf wave to break out of stillness and explode into a frenzied charge.

Unfordive and Seekoras dashed toward the impending army with their own close at their rear. The alliance leapt over the mound of carcasses, only to meet razor-sharp spears at the base. Dirt and dust swirled around the colliding forces like two opposing fronts igniting a tornado. Bodies flew into the spears and slid down the shafts like skewered meat, only to smash into a wall of shields. The Twin Blades leapt upon the bloody pile, swinging and slashing at the soldiers below. Unfordive swiftly tore through any man who came within his reach, his blade twirling too swiftly to even be seen. The alliance force, however, was vast, and it encircled the left and right flanks of the Deimor, wrapping around them like a *U*. The sides of the Deimor army were squashed inward without the advantage of a heap of bodies, as the Sarnon and Suvrarian pressed hard against them.

In the center of the battle, the Twin Blades were engaged in a bloody melee, pushing onward over the corpse wall within a rusty miasma. The spear lines broke into an unorganized clutter of flashing swords and bashing shields, unable to be tamed by Seekoras's implorations as he continued to thrust forward with his brother into an endless wave of men. Through the Humans and Scaldor, the Arikarnan made their way into the bloodbath, where the only noises heard were the screams of men, the tearing of flesh from bone, and the popping of skulls.

Time pressed on, and the sun moved slowly across the azure sky above an unrelenting feud. The flanks of the Deimor began to deteriorate as the Sarnon and Suvrarian squeezed toward the center. The field of view within the fray dwindled, hazed by thousands of feet tearing at the earth. The Deimor army began to merge into a circle, fighting outwards as a living landslide engulfed them. But hard-nosed and resilient, they did not relent; in fact they became only more enlivened.

Unfordive continued his epic struggle, striking down his foes as though he were a god of war, until his vigilant ears picked up the distressed scream of his brother within the bloodbath. Any sense of morality escaped him as he pounced toward the shriek like a feral tigress, bobbing and weaving through slashing swords and axes, carving his path through chests and thighs as he charged. At the end of his rage his eyes perceived Seekoras, powerless on his back, with his sword out of reach and on the verge of being crushed by the falling hammer of a Sarnon. Unfordive hurled his body at the being and cleaved its throat, shredding through its trachea. The hulking Sarnon fell onto his back in a pool of blood as Unfordive landed on its stomach growling, with crimson fluid dripping from his skin and armor. He grasped his brother's hand and pulled him to his feet while panting, "Desara Norrath." Seekoras nodded passionately, wheezing as he clasped his sword to continue in the fight. A Human leapt toward them, but the rekindled Seekoras spilled his entrails onto the ravaged earth with a swift slash across the stomach. Unfordive gashed another's skull as the brothers moved back-to-back and fought outward.

The sun persisted on its magnificent course across the sky as the Deimor continued to be dissolved inwards. They fought on like the mighty warriors they were, unflinching to an army that seemed unassailable. They were ferocious and barbaric, fighting down to their nails and teeth. The alliance force was thinning, but it seemed inconceivable to them that the Deimor could achieve victory. These odds, however, seemed favorable to all the Deimor as the continued to kill mercilessly.

The Twin Blades battled in the center of the confrontation, the vigor in their eyes swelling beyond belief. Blades cut them and ripped at their flesh, but they felt no pain. Their fury was insurmountable and their skills unmatchable. They slayed and parried their enemies masterfully, leaving a wake of the dead bulging from the cruel earth. However, in this smog of dirt and cadavers, they knew not how many men still fought beside them, or if their cause was already lost.

The Deadlands were blanketed by a bloody haze and upturned soil. The Deimor army was scraped to the bone, with men falling continually. Those who retained breath, though, battled on with unbelievable resolve and fervor. The alliance, without realizing, lost soldiers at a rapid pace as their force was reduced to a size not differing much from the Deimor's.

Still in the center of the battle, the Twin Blades fought with incredible vehemence, until—suddenly—not another man came forth to face them. Their weary eyes scanned the murky field only to see ghastly eyes staring blankly back at them. They were void of life and had those eyes retained life, all they would envision would be the marvelous Twin Blades crumpled onto their knees with their swords holding them upright.

Air struggled in and out of their lungs as they wheezed. Their armor did not show, and neither did their skin; all that remained visible was a sheet of blood and entrails, their own and their enemies. Fallen upon their knees in exasperation, they faced each other, gazing in disbelief upon the mangled bodies they envisioned—their own bodies—bodies that were once recognizable and faces that they had once known so well, now butchered to a grotesque extent.

Their wet ears, protruding from soggy hair, picked up the

clamor of shouts and clanking iron far off in the distance as the battle weakly aged on. Unwilling to surrender to death, Unfordive attempted to rise but quickly collapsed to his knees in agony. His and his brother's bodies were too overcome with exhaustion to move even the slightest inch. They were too shattered to continue yet the putrid air continued to fill them with life. Any other men would have crumbled to their doom before withstanding the suffering they did that day and, despite his imminent death, Seekoras smiled feebly toward his beloved brother, finally with a glint of reason in his eyes. Words struggled to escape his lips; they only quivered without a sound. Tears filled the fading eyes of the brothers, dampening the once radiant orbs and trickling down their cheeks, absorbing blood and revealing leathery, rouge skin. Unfordive's marred lips began to curl listlessly into a slender smile and he used every bit of his remaining energy to mouth, "Desara Norrath."

"Desara … Norrath!" Seekoras cried out, emptying his lungs, and the two brothers lifted their swords one last time. Water burst from their eyes and red saliva dripped from their mouths as they placed their blades gently on each others' throats and paused.

Lives of discipline and honor, of servitude and glory, flashed before them as if in only an instant they had transpired. Time seemed to cease as they glared into despondent eyes with love and devotion—the wild jungle and intense fire meeting for one last momentous occasion. Then, with a final explosion of vigor, the swords passed through their throats, severing veins and muscles. Blood spouted from their ravaged necks as though they were sanctified fountains, while their bodies fell limp and collapsed dramatically onto the cold, dead earth. For the first time since their birth, the eyes of the Twin Blades were stripped of their animation and vibrancy as death finally caught up with them.

The fog of war that obscured the Deadlands gradually lifted, revealing the gruesome scene below. More than one million bodies were lifelessly strewn upon the dirt, dipped into a shallow bath of blood and with weaponry bulging from their torsos. Corpses littered the bitter earth as far as the eye could see and the once chaotic space became void of all sound but for the ravenous caws of scavenger birds circling high above in anticipation of a ceaseless meal.

The Deadlands was a fitting name for the horror that beset one's eyes in that desolate place. A vision imprinted into the ninety-seven minds still grasping life. For standing, scattered and exhausted across the field, were ninety-seven exasperated men who still welcomed air into their lungs; ninety-seven men of varied race—all but the Deimor—who survived the bloody onslaught that claimed the lives of an unprecedented number of valiant warriors. Words failed to birth from their parched mouths as they stood in a state of trauma, with skin, scales, and fur as crimson as that of their enemies. Hundreds of thousands of men had stepped onto that field, young and zealous men, and now fewer than one hundred remained. Only ninety-seven were to be left with the vision of their brothers and sisters dismembered and mutilated in a vermilion sea after Oblikaron's bidding had been wrought.

Thus is the history of Isinda, a history written in blood. How could man survive in such a barbaric world? How, in a world that was throughout all of its existence devoid of any moment without hatred or death, could life go on? Was peace so unattainable to the scattered races of Isinda? Or had the time come for a new chapter to be woven into the annals of history? A new age—an age of peace.

A Little Girl's Dream

"So blood shall run forth like a
river from my foes. Their sacrifice
for my god, for his enemies are
my own."

Divara Cantarus

Engulfed by everlasting turmoil and drowned in a sea of
blood, even the gods would wonder how a land such as
Isinda had yet to crumble. Into an abyss of swarming
death and destruction it plummeted, yet still it prevailed. For all
of the millions who seek no change, who live on with their daily
lives unwilling to make a difference, there are those who seek
to ignite the flames of revolution. Not a revolution against an
unjust rule or ruler, but a revolution such as the transition from
a nomadic life to a civilized one. There are those who would
seek a grand conversion from a way of war to a way of peace.

The story that will be inscribed onto the white pages of this
book is not that of Unfordive or Seekoras. It is a story of a man
whose greatness transcends that of the Twin Blades. What this

man meant to Isinda, I cannot force into the mind of any other, but I ask of you to read the words of his story and understand.

In the days following the Battle of the Deadlands, Isinda regressed to its old self. After the decimation of their last great army, the Deimor fell into disarray. With their princes slain and their king no longer to be found, the widely-spreadout Deimor lost the ability to maintain their dominion over the other races. Gradually, from west to east, they were forced out of their conquered lands and viciously pushed back to their unforgiving homeland. Surrounded by rugged mountains, they were driven into a corner by the coalition who wanted nothing but to eradicate the race that had once subjugated them.

By that time, the Sarnon and Suvrarian had already forsaken the failing alliance and returned to the seclusion of their own lands. The Humans, Scaldor, and Arikarnon were all that was left. They encircled the remaining force of Deimor and crushed them in the village of Deatorus. With nearly all remaining vigor sapped from them, the Deimor defended their homeland in the badlands called Undaro. Most of the remaining were women and elderly who were hardly able to put up a fight and, in turn, a massacre ensued—one that would be the final battle in which the struggling coalition would ever engage.

After the battle, the Arikarnon and Scaldor turned on the Humans, unexpectedly slaughtering them and leaving none alive to tell. They jointly held ill views of a western civilization containing an army in the east and decided that the best course of action was to swiftly cut the throat of the Humans.

Arrogant from their victory, the Arikarnon pitched camp a small way from the battlefield in order to rest before a long journey home. Seeing this as an opportune time to eliminate more potential enemies, the Scaldor ambushed their former allies during their slumber and butchered them in cold blood. They were ready to forsake any allegiances they had once held to others and even among themselves. The disjoined Scaldor fell back to their scattered customs and never looked back, along with the Humans and every other race that had once been a part of the alliance. The Deimor were mercilessly hunted to near-extinction. As all knew was inevitable, the coalition crumbled like stiff bread to a strong hand, and Isinda reverted back to the way it always was—chaos.

Nine thousand, one hundred and eleven days after the Battle of the Deadlands, the chill of Frigusa had just begun to grasp the eastern lands of Isinda. Flakes of frozen water continually landed atop the amber grass. Nature had tucked her children in for a long slumber beneath a colorless blanket. Gray stones grew cold under slick layers of ice, and the forests grew dark under powdered canopies. In the northern lands of the Scaldor, where the vast Desolura Forest lay, animals scarcely stirred. They slumbered under the conifers that shadowed the forest bed, eagerly awaiting the return of warmth.

On the western borders of the woodland, through a misty fog, a track of footprints approached from the north, making its way closer and closer to the towering trees. At the root of a thick evergreen tree, the prints, which were not that of boots, halted. Scaly, red, bare feet sunk into the deep snow until they reached the hard, shrouded earth beneath. From those feet rose lean, sharply-cut legs, which were scaly and red as well. The bottom of a white robe eclipsed the legs vertically from their upper thighs and extended upwards, curling over the broad shoulders of what appeared to be a man. Short sleeves revealed arms without a hint of fat, arms which appeared to have been carved by an artist and that were crimson and scaly as a fish. The waistline of the robe was pulled tightly inward toward his body by a black leather belt no thicker than the bark of a tree. Dangling from the left side of the belt was an ebony sheath dipped in gold, with lines down the sides of glistening silver. His sheath, however, was empty, for in the steady hands of the man rested a gorgeous sword. The shimmering iron, curved blade was tipped with pure diamond, which had been chiseled into a razor-sharp point. The hilt was sculpted out of solid jade and embedded into it were dozens of tiny diamonds, no larger than pebbles. The bottom was in the shape of an eagle's head soaring through a great sky, and on the base of the blade a dragon, as large as the hand of an average man, was etched with gold, a nail-sized gap where its eye should be.

Atop those legs, those shoulders, and that sword was the head of man no older than his early twenties. Crimson, thick, scaly skin enveloped his youthful visage, from his narrow chin to his ample jaw and upward still to his hairline. A slender nose protruded from his face just above his chapped indigo lips, parting into two slim, black eyebrows. Under the canopy of these eyebrows and over his hardy cheekbones rested two eyes firmly entrenched in his skull. His left eye was as blue as a wrathful sea, and his right burnt with the passionate flames that the eyes of the Deimor once held. Scraggly, jet-black hair fell in an unkempt mess down to his shoulders, highlighted by sapphire strips.

This was the stalwart face of a man who had become a hero. It belonged to the Blood Scaldor known as Zano, who, after roughly five years of wandering with his master and harnessing wisdom, arrived in the Desolura to return to the home that had birthed him. His face did not hold the bliss that a face would usually hold upon the return to a beloved home. Instead, it emanated a feeling of brooding hatred toward memories of that profane place.

His lips quivered in acrimony as his foot stepped forward into the deep snow. His free hand brought itself to rest upon the coarse, brown bark of a lofty pine tree with tawny needles. Chilled air flowed into his mucus-dripping nostrils and then departed from his tepid mouth. His infuriated eyes shut gently as he began to recall the agony that had befallen him in this home. All of the suffering began to stream uncontrollably through his thoughts.

...

Stygian darkness engulfed the world beneath the Desolura canopy. Skinny rays of emerald luminescence pierced through the pine needles, giving thin strands of illumination to an otherwise veiled place.

Deep in the woods, on the western side, all that could be heard were diabolic chants advocating death. Bulky stone hovels shrouded by lofty trees surrounded a tremendous structure. The triangular-shaped edifice projecting from the prickle-covered dirt was chiseled with steps all the way up to the flat top. The tan-colored stone was stained in varied sections with a brownish-red color—clearly blood that had been dried by the nippy weather. Two rectangular stone blocks rested, equally spaced, atop the flat surface. In the center of them appeared to be the High Priest of a tribe who lived among the huts encircling the great pyramid. A robe of gray animal fur was slung over his azure, scaled body, and a crest of vibrant feathers jutted from his dark, graying hair. His eyes gazed toward the green moon with a maniacal pleasure as he held a crude stone dagger toward the star-speckled sky. Wicked, cobalt eyes glittered around him, glaring upward from the base of the pyramid with a merciless bloodlust. Behind them were dull pairs of red and blue eyes, which watched the thirsty priest with empty, docile stares. Slowly, trickles of rain began to permeate the forest's canopy.

The Priest broodingly turned toward the stone block on his left to admire the scarlet-skinned little girl who lay upon it. Ropes tied tightly around her wrists and ankles were fastened to rusty iron loops with her arms pinned above her head. She was stripped bare, her body set out to freeze under the chilly air. Not even where her scaly coat lapsed to smooth cherry skin on her petite breasts and crotch did a cloth cover her. Saliva dripped from her trembling lips, and water gushed from her multihued eyes as she lay in inconceivable fear.

"To sustain our lives, Brazdor requires a sacrifice of young blood! And who here will take that sacrifice upon themselves?" the High Priest fanatically yelled, his eyes flickering as if he were being pleasured.

"The Blood Scaldor!" the possessors of the sapphire eyes responded with a ravenous hunger, as the passive eyes behind them quickly winced.

Rain began to bombard the area, splattering off the red-stained peak of the pyramid. The tree branches rustled and pine needles whipped through the air like tiny knives.

The High Priest brought the dagger swiftly to his side and knelt beside the exposed little girl, to the crowd's delight. Her throat ached from bawling to such an extent that she no longer had the capacity to speak. Soggy hair wisped across her face, sticky from the saliva and mucus that flooded from her mouth and nose. The onlookers cheered as the Priest tenderly rubbed the girl's stomach with his dagger and twirled the tip inside her belly button. She twisted and thrashed, yet she could not break the ties that bound her to the block and her imminent demise. The Priest chuckled maliciously as he rubbed the dagger near her crotch and with his free hand stroked her slender inner thigh. Shrieks of horror were discharged from her mouth; shrieks that implied her desire for help, to which none heeded any attention.

The aroused Scaldor rose to his feet and pumped his arms in the air as if to have conquered something. He placed his rough hand over the mouth of the girl, who wept relentlessly, her teeth clamping at his hand just out of reach. While this spectacle occurred, many eyes glared at the event with undying attention, like nothing else could fulfill their wretched satisfaction. The girl screamed and howled, but the Priest's hand held all sounds within her mouth. Her body convulsed and she screamed until she was sapped of any vigor.

Devoid of hope, the little girl turned her head to the side and was surprised to observe compassionate eyes gazing into her own. A youthful boy named Zano, who was bound to the stone block beside hers, sympathetically watched her. Rivers of tears dripped from her cheeks onto the stone, only to be washed away by the rainfall.

The wind began to pick up, gusting across the trembling forest and battering Zano's sodden face with needles. The stone dagger began to cut into her chest, just between her two tiny breasts, and saw a circular pattern around her heart. Blood leaked from her torso and chips of bone fragmented onto the Priest's wrinkled face. Her mouth quivered in unbelievable pain, but the caring eyes of the boy across from her held her stare. Blood replaced the saliva that dripped from her mouth as the dagger continued to hack into her ribs, yet Zano refused to blink in face of the atrocity. They stared into one another's eyes, as though he were ridding her of the pain she should be feeling.

The bloody circle around her heart wrapped around to where it had begun, and the Priest placed the dagger by the girl's side. The crowd roared in support as he forcefully dug his hand into the gash and ruffled through her insides, in pursuit of her pulsing heart. Though in unthinkable agony, the girl's mouth curled into the slightest bloody smile that her body would allow and Zano's curved just the same while tears distorted his vision. The Priest tore the still-beating sphere of red from the girl's chest, blood spurting out like an arched fountain along with her shredded bones and veins.

The High Priest held his prize over his head, letting the red liquid drip onto his face and lips as his lustful tongue shoveled it into his mouth. Now only a lifeless face stared ghastly back at Zano, her eyelids drooping over inanimate eyes. The crowd erupted and celebrated as they observed the Priest's bloody shower. His eyes rolled back into his head and with a sadistic squeeze he crushed the thumping heart and dropped it, sending blood flowing down the smooth stone steps, and streaming down his lumpy arm.

Raindrops pelted Zano's stripped body as the sound of demonic cheers filled his ears. The sight of the little girl, mangled and frozen, staring upon him with blank eyes, chilled his heart. As if she were his people's trophy, the Priest cut the bonds on the lifeless girl's arms and legs. He then spitefully tossed her limp body down the steps toward his followers. The demeaning of her body filled Zano's heart with immeasurable rage, and he violently tossed his body from side to side in an attempt to get free. The High Priest turned toward the futile efforts with a snicker and slowly licked the blood from his indigo lips.

The girl's carcass became unrecognizable, torn apart by biting and scratching in the Scaldor's wicked orgy. Veins throughout Zano's body pushed up trails beneath his scales and his eyes seared with a fury that his masters had never witnessed. The ropes dug into his wrists like razors and tore at the scales on his ankles, but the Priest simply laughed. His slave's anguish amused him, until through his clenched teeth, Zano chided, "Your time will come, demon. Sooner than you know you will be the man lying on this block with your heart torn asunder!"

The Priest's mouth gaped in disbelief that his slave had just spoken such harsh words, and in sentences as complete as his own. He knew that he could let such an intelligent slave survive no longer, so he clenched the crude dagger with all of his might. However, with a sudden zip of air the bonds on Zano's limbs shred in half and he sprang up like a wolf hunting his prey. Caught off guard, the heavy fist of the Blood Scaldor's brawny arms came crashing across the jaw of the High Priest. The bone snapped as he flew backward from the tremendous force and was sent tumbling down the steps, sloshing through the rain and the blood. Zano rose to his feet with his muscles flexing and grasped the stone dagger that lay at his feet. His nostrils flared with seething disgust as the Priest ordered from the soppy earth, "Kill him!"

From the shadows of the surrounding crowd, over one hundred Scaldor warriors emerged, wearing loincloths and animal skins over their heads. Their bodies were painted with twisting black spikes and they wielded crude, stone short swords and square planks of flattened wood for shields. Leaving their sinful festival behind they charged bestially up the steps toward the slave who opposed them, with animal-like hisses and growls.

Zano twirled the dagger in his soaked palm and roared ferociously, ready to take on whatever enemy came before him. His sense transformed into blind rage. He was indifferent to the fact that he was so outnumbered; to the fact that not another of his people had the ability or desire to assist him in his forlorn rebellion. His naked body was lined with near-bursting veins, and his teeth gritted with such a force that his gums dripped red as he snarled. Then, from the corner of his eye, he realized that four arrows were rolling around the block where he had lain, in the vicinity of where his limbs had rested. Black shadows appeared seemingly from nowhere at his side. He felt a forceful blow to his temple, just before his bloodstained vision went black.

When the Scaldor warriors reached the top of the pyramid, only rain plummeted upon the stone where the rogue slave had just stood. Their perplexed eyes scanned the darkness that enshrouded them, only to see several fiery pairs of eyes hastily disappear.

• • •

Zano's coarse fingers dug into the tree bark, chipping his frozen nails and tearing out pieces of the rigid covering. Tiny drops of water fell steadily from his moist eyes, melting small holes into the snow. His nose twitched and his forehead wrinkled as the rage of his past amplified inside his mind. One foot fell forward and he began to make his way through the shady woods, in which not an animal stirred. The location of the town of Fatradak had been imprinted into his memory and though he had never walked the route before, it was as if an innate compass had always pointed there.

Flickers of light and shadow passed over his face from the sunlight that softly permeated the pines. The foul stench of raw

Diarii meat and burning torches greeted his nostrils, causing him to clench the handle of his blade so hard that blood was obstructed from his fingers.

Zano concealed himself behind a thick tree and peeked out to see the town he had once called home. Through the light fog, he saw the geometrical stone hovels. Smoke leaked through small holes on their roofs. Scaldor and Blood Scaldor traipsed around the town, without any idea of his presence. They were not on equal terms however. The Blood Scaldor had chains around their hands if they were not working and those who were had crude blades at their back. There were about half a thousand of them, and just a few more of their masters. Women, children, men—it did not matter; any crimson person who dwelled in this town was a slave. They chopped wood for fire, they hunted, and they built anything their masters wanted. Any desire a Scaldor held was forced upon his slaves, whether it was to retrieve something or simply to please their oppressor. If a slave did anything his master disliked, he was beaten brutally until scarred. The cruelest mandate of them all was that Blood Scaldor were forced to breed whenever it was deemed necessary, and any child too weak to work was disposed of without remorse.

Zano knew these scars well, as even the children had scales ripped from their bodies. As the Scaldor nourished themselves and lived luxurious lifestyles, their slaves lived lives of fear and suffering, too oppressed to take any action. He remembered the anguish of his days there very well. The scars on his back recalled the constant beating by branches and whips, but mostly, he recollected the biannual festival where two randomly-chosen slaves were sacrificed gruesomely in order to please the god to which these Scaldor prayed.

Zano snarled brutishly as it all came back to him, as he glimpsed those same people who turned his early life into hell. He saw the settlement of stone houses and the ominous pyramid, which was no different than when he left it. As all of

Fatradak came into view he witnessed two Scaldor with their swords at a slave's back begin to walk out of the town.

The Blood Scaldor slave was a young male, lean from mal-nourishment, but strong from the work he performed each day. He was being taken out into the woods for punishment, though for what reason Zano knew not. Though chained across his wrists, his face held not a hint of emotion. Any feelings he once had had been sapped from him by an existence that no longer held meaning beyond catering to the whims of a people who owned him.

The three of them made their way closer to him, but in Zano's mind, the young Blood Scaldor became an apparition of the little girl who was sacrificed. She was alive, walking toward him in divine glory.

The two Scaldor men stepped past the tree, and a blade thrust swiftly forward, slitting both of their throats simultaneously. The slave collapsed in fear into the puff of red-splattered snow beside the bodies of his owners. Zano's hand trembled with rage as he stared at the boy sternly, his blade dripping with fresh blood and remembered that this was not the little girl he so fondly recalled.

The diamond tip of his sword cut through the rusty iron chains of the freed slave like an arrow through air and the boy's eyes gaped in befuddlement. Zano hoisted him to his feet and gazed into his identical eyes, which had grown moist in renewed sensation. Prudently, the boy pried a crude sword from his prior master's cold hand and bowed to his liberator. Though uneducated he quickly understood why this stoic Blood Scaldor had come home. He knew that this was the man who had disappeared when he was merely a child, and that he had now returned heroically, as the boy had always dreamed.

Like prowling wolves they crept through the dusty snow, taking cover behind trees and stripped bushes on their way toward Fatradak. They eventually found themselves unnoticed behind a stone house at the edge of the settlement.

"Do you have a name, boy?" Zano questioned firmly, knowing full well the chances of this Blood Scaldor meeting his doom.

"Car … Carthago," the boy whimpered quietly, beginning to grasp what he was about to undertake.

Zano nodded, then plunged through a gap in the wall of the hovel into a crudely-decorated room with little more than a bed of animal fur. His blade plunged into the chest of an elderly Scaldor man who sat upright in a rickety wooden chair, reading a scroll. His legs had been resting on the back of a young slave woman who had her hands chained like Carthago's. The elderly Scaldor's wife leaped toward her deceased husband in distress, but she was stabbed through the skull by the crude blade of Carthago, who had followed Zano through the gap.

The diamond tip tore through the chains of the slave woman, giving her a freedom she had never known. Carthago panted like an animal as he looked down in fury upon those who had once owned him. Blood was splattered on the gray floor as the two warriors left the home through a leather flap door, leaving behind two slaughtered corpses and a freed slave.

Militiamen armed with stone weapons and wooden shields charged at them with demonic chants, but Zano's ferocity could not be matched. Before his young companion could even lift his blade, the charging men had already been cut down.

The sound of a gong rang through the town, signaling to all that there was a rebellion in progress. Together, Zano and Carthago charged with smoldering eyes toward a crowd of Scaldor standing by a stack of wood their slaves had chopped.

It is amazing that even when slaves outnumber their masters, they will on most occasions remain docile and subservient, yet, when the slightest opportunity to rebel may arise for them, they will seek liberty without relent and without concern of the cost.

As Zano's and Carthago's actions became clear to the town, chaos broke loose. Any slave without chains turned on his dumbfounded master and began to fight back. Chained slaves—men, women, and children alike,—all saw freedom within their

grasp, choosing to pounce on their controllers like crimson pan-
thers. Blood Scaldor exploded from houses, covered in a liquid that matched their rough skin. Screams of death echoed in
the air as Zano massacred a force of about two hundred Scaldor with the aid of his young friend. Cries of rage and horror
could be heard beneath the canopy, both of the Scaldor and
their slaves. Torches fell onto the snowy ground, catching fire
to nearby wood and melting the snow that surrounded them.
The inside of many of the hovels spewed black smoke and in
minutes the Scaldor were forced to flee from the slaves into the
mansion of the High Priest.

When all of the freed Blood Scaldor gathered around the
growling Zano and Carthago, they saw the rotting corpses of
hundreds of Scaldor. They were the dead bodies of not only
men but also children, no matter how young, and the women
whom had birthed them. The slaves without chains picked keys
off of the carcasses and unlocked their brethren as Zano freed
the others with his spectacular sword. Once-white snow had
turned deep scarlet and the clean air was filled with smoke and
the foul odor of death. The mob of Blood Scaldor followed
Zano around the great pyramid, through the heat of the newly
sparked fires and the smog of gray.

They stood before the luxurious stone mansion of the High
Priest, in which there were at least one hundred able Scaldors,
not counting the wounded. Carthago pointed with a trembling
hand toward the hefty wooden doors of the stone manor. Zano
shook his head slowly and malevolently, signaling all behind
him to stand their ground. His fingers wrapped tightly around
his sword's hilt until his fingernails dug into it. His hair dripped
blood and reeked of death as he stepped before the doors,
which were a bit taller than the top of his head. With a ferocious scream he kicked them in, flinging the Scaldor who stood
directly behind them. Their chants no longer subsisted as terror gripped them. His blade swung and chopped as he ripped
through the Scaldor in the entrance. He was vastly outnum-

bered, but with the training he had the barbarians could not match him.

Fury overcame him while visions of his childhood passed through his mind, only serving to increase his incredible wrath. So swiftly his sword moved that it could not even be seen, and not a Scaldor in the room could attempt to parry it. He thrashed through waves of blood and flesh. Through cracking bones and entrails he plunged, unrivaled amongst the dwindling crowd. Women, children, and warriors with crude swords fell before his might, each feeling the weight of the slavery they had exploited each day prior.

Eyes closed and nose snarling, Zano stood with his blade in both hands amidst the bodies of nearly one hundred of the blue-scaled. Not a cut scathed his strapping body as gallons of his enemies' life fluids drenched his cloak. Two wooden staircases led to a second level at his left and right, but he knew that the rest of the Scaldor cowered through the leather flap in front of him. His hawk like ears picked up their whimpers and the scraping of swords against the stone floor.

With a torrential wrath his eyes glared at the flap and he held his palm up perpendicular to the ground. By the chant of a mystical phrase, a sphere of intense flame burst from his bloody hand, dissipating the leather and exploding on the other side. Screams of horror preceded Zano's leap into the clustered room, his blade tearing through the sizzling cloth of those within. Helplessly, they fell before his strength, just as the others had, until through the flickering flames and dense smoke Zano envisioned the one person other than himself who remained alive in the fray.

Ash and blood coated the man's fur robe and the illustrious feather crown which once rested on his gray hair lay torched at his side. The High Priest sobbed as Zano grabbed him by the hair and tossed him out of the room. Then, grasping the back of his robe, he hauled him across the wet floor and out of the mansion. Awestruck eyes met him as he left the building and heaved his prey across the snow, leaving a trail of scarlet in his wake.

"Kill the wounded," Zano whispered to Carthago as he passed him with a cold stare on his callous face. Carthago nodded and led a group of armed Blood Scaldor into the corpse-filled manor. The High Priest kicked and shrieked like an infant, tears spewing out of his sapphire eyes. Zano hauled him over his shoulder and with bitter tears rolling down his scaly cheeks, carried him up to the plateau atop the pyramid.

"Please ... spare me," the priest sniveled, begging for the life he had taken from countless others. It was at this moment the Priest realized who the man who carried him was. He knew now that this was the sacrifice that had so inexplicably escaped him and had vanished for nearly five years.

Like the children he murdered, the Priest pleaded for the life which Zano would not grant. The warrior slammed him on the stone block that had once been below the little girl and the High Priest flailed wildly as she once did, but in vain. Zano's strong arm was too much for him to shove away. He reached into the folds of his crimson robe and pulled out the same stone dagger that the Priest once used. Dread filled the wrinkles of the old man's face as Zano held him down by his skinny neck.

The wondrous sword dropped to the stone from Zano's left hand, and he wielded the stone dagger in his trembling right. Beside him, the little girl was walking, crying in his ears and sapping any measure of reason from him. He was consumed by hatred while he clenched the dagger with a bloody fist and with an inhumane roar he plunged it with all of his might into the bony chest of the spineless Priest. His victim gasped for air as Zano ripped the blade from his ribs and jabbed it in again, his sanguine tunic billowing as blood splattered onto his face and hair. Continually he sunk the dagger into the body until even the screams of the aged Priest could no longer be heard.

Even when the Priest's eyes grew dull and lifeless, Zano did not stop. He only grunted as he continued to maim the body.

For over a minute the dagger ravaged its prey, until it slipped from the grasp of Zano's drenched hand and tumbled onto the snow-covered pyramid. His knees buckled and he sobbed with his face buried in the entrails of the disfigured carcass, his hands digging into the unflinching stone. Only the sounds of his and the little girl's crying reached his ears.

Carthago brought his feet softly onto the top of the pyramid and gazed speechlessly at the dismal hero slumped over the mangled body of his former master. Zano's head slowly turned out of the muddled torso to see, through his misty eyes, the Blood Scaldor to whom he had brought freedom. The ghastly spirit of the little girl stood in ragged clothes at the boy's side with a smile on her face as Zano's mind brought him back to that day of his freedom.

· · ·

Through the darkness, the younger Zano could hear the conversation of two men but was unable to see who they were. His naked body lay limp against the coarse bark of a lofty pine tree, beneath the faint, emerald illumination of the moon. His blinking eyes creaked open, attempting to peer through the black smog of the night.

As he lurched forward on all fours, a mysterious character sitting against a tree at his front glared at him through two searing red eyes. Zano stumbled back in panic and his scrambling hand came across the stone dagger which was entangled in grass. The shady figure rose to its feet, laughing.

Zano jumped up and lunged at the figure, whose face was indiscernible under the hood of a black robe. Effortlessly, the figure dodged the attack and ripped the dagger from the Blood Scaldor's hand, sending the inexperienced boy staggering to the ground.

"Why do you attack the man who set you free?" the man laughed in a deep, shrewd voice, amused by the boy's antics.

54

Breathing heavily, Zano rolled onto his back and muttered, "Who ... who are you?"

"Ha! It speaks! You likely would not know boy."

"Are you a ... A Deimor?"

"There is more to you than meets the eye, isn't there?"

"You left them there!" Zano yelled as he leapt at the shady man, who merely tossed him to the grass.

"Their time for freedom has yet to come. There is much you do not understand; however you must know that I am not your enemy. You have your freedom now, but what would you do with it?" the man asked in a comforting tone.

"Why me? Why should I be free when they are not?"

"There are things you do not yet understand. You now have freedom, yet you know not what to do with it. Everything in this great world begins with choice and I offer you one now. Either I can leave you lying here in the forest, alone and naked, but with a freedom I know you have always desired, or you can come with me. You can travel this land of Isinda at my side and learn. I will open your eyes to a world that you know nothing about, but it is a world that is your own. Please ... I beg of you, take my hand."

Zano gazed at the dark figure before him as it reached a leathery red hand out toward his quivering body. Unknowing of what else to do and seemingly without another choice, he gently grasped the hand of the black-robed man with ruby eyes.

"Good. Now come, boy, the woods are perilous in this darkness," the man implored, urging him into the shadow.

"Yes ... Master," Zano whispered after gathering his dagger. This was a phrase he had become accustomed to saying and even with freedom it was a phrase that did not escape him.

• • •

The hundreds of Blood Scaldor congregated around their slouching hero. Zano's cloudy eyes scanned them all as he remembered the words of his master.

"You will return there," he had said during their travels, "but will you go back with vengeance? Or will you return to do what you know is right? That choice, like all others, will be yours."

Zano gravely observed the mutilated body of the priest and realized that, though he had returned with vengeance for those who had made him a slave, he did love his people just as Tarak had professed. Tears flowed down his scaly face, absorbing the crusting blood on his cheeks as he realized he had failed his master. Through his misty vision he saw the red and blue eyes of the people he had freed, gawking. Men, women, and children all stared at him, believing him to be their leader. What would people who had never known freedom do with it? Just as he had, they sought a new master.

The drained hero raised his drenched face out of the sloppy cavity of the carcass's chest and gazed through the canopy at the gleaming sun. It took him all of this time to truly attain freedom—not until the tormentors of his childhood and his people were deceased. For once in his life, the little girl's innocent and hopeful face did not linger in his thoughts. Listlessly, he knelt on the top of the snowy pyramid, finally free of his perennial chains.

A Masked General and a Kingdom of Bronze

*"I shall build a tower that stands like a gleaming
pinnacle on the horizon, a tower that shall bring me
closer to the heavens than any has ever come."*

Lord Brazdor of Water

Destiny. It is a peculiar idea. People live their lives day
by day, but is all of it preordained? Is there a certain
fate that clings to each person; a fate that cannot be
escaped? Are we bound to it? Are all of our choices made before
our lives have even begun? I would like to think not. I would
like to hope that every choice is our own and that the story we
live is written as we live it, not before.

Zano somberly trudged through the sticky snow to the
southern edge of the Desolura Forest. His white tunic was
stained crimson, and in his hair were tangled pieces of Scaldor
entrails. Blood crusted over his scales and his usually fiery eyes

were mourning and dull. His sword now rested in its sheath and the stone dagger was left atop the pyramid. No Blood Scaldor followed him; he was apparently alone in the darkening woods, for when the liberated had knelt in praise around him, Zano chose to abandon them. He left without so much as a glance toward his old home. They would have crowned him their king, but he simply walked away, with no desire to rule those who had forever been unjustly ruled.

He emerged from the last pine tree at the southern border of the Desolura and peered unto the beauty that awaited him. The sun had begun to set sluggishly behind the horizon of the elevated land before him, with the clouds surrounding it in different shades of violet and magenta against a sky of mild scarlet. The snow was tinted with a light pink hue and the amber of the pine needles was glazed over with burgundy. Snowflakes no longer fell and the powder was swept across the ground by a light breeze. Icy rocks reflected the cherry sky, which to Zano signified the blood he had spilled.

His bare feet began to take him across the taiga. The sun slowly descended and with it the sky transitioned into different shades. Frosty tears rolled down his lumpy cheeks as his steady posture became staggered. His legs were weak; his mind and body were drained. With a soft thud his knees buckled and he collapsed in exhaustion onto the cushioned ground, white particles frothing around his submerged body as his eyes gently shut.

When his vision cleared, Zano saw a cluster of puzzled male Scaldor clad in thin bronze breastplates and bronze greaves. He gasped, reaching for the sword at his side, but finding his belt empty, he began to scamper backward on his rear. When they saw that the Blood Scaldor had awoken, the cluster motioned curiously into the distance.

The glorious sunset had faded, and the scarlet sky had transformed into the dark veil of night. Dots of light shimmered along as formations of celestial luminosity trailed across the black void. The viridian moon shone like an emerald encrusted into the sky, giving the bronze armor of the Scaldor a sage glow. Zano quickly scanned from left to right in befuddlement and saw what appeared to be a camp. Cloth tents were pitched in every direction and campfires stood out against the darkness.

"Do not worry, Blood Scaldor. You are not our prisoner," a deep, ominous voice proclaimed. The radiance of a nearby campfire illuminated the man who pronounced his accord.

He was no shorter than six feet and appeared menacing, clad in a long, billowing black robe that draped down to the contrasting snow. Spiky, iron gauntlets enclosed his hands, and pointed iron boots jutted from the bottom of his garb. The hood of the robe was slung loosely over his head, shadowing his face, but Zano realized that this face was not the man's, but actually a mask fashioned of a dark metal. Two small spikes extended from the chin, which obscured his neck. It was without ornamentation, and the only protrusion was a rigged elevation for a nose. Six horizontal slits were carved where his mouth should have been and large holes shaped like snake eyes revealed demonic spheres of a deep, shadowy purple that gleamed through a grayish smoke. Their smoldering glare stunned Zano as he sat in awe of the figure whose shady mask caught the flicker of firelight with each oncoming step.

"Who are you?" Zano hastily questioned, as the portentous man of an unknown race drew nearer.

"My name is Merasu, the Grand General of the Bronze Empire, and I question how a Blood Scaldor appears before me without chains," he replied in a deep voice filled with great wisdom, much as Zano's mentor once spoke.

"I have not been shackled for many years. My name is Zano Cynery. It is an honor to make the acquaintance of such a distinguished man."

Merasu paused for a long moment upon hearing the name of the Blood Scaldor before saying, "Cynery? The name sounds familiar."

"Doesn't every name?" Zano countered.

"Perhaps. Your history is your own, but may I propose to you an offer?"

Zano rose to his feet, frozen sheets of blood crumpling off of his face along with the powder on his discolored robe. "An offer?"

"Yes. I know of your people's sad history and I ask you, do you know why I have brought this army here?"

Zano remained silent, but tilted his head slightly, intrigued by Merasu's query.

"We are here to conquer the peoples of this forest in the name of the Divine Emperor Sila. I know that your people dwell as slaves within the Desolura, and with victory here, it would be within my authority to unshackle them. You are coated in blood and I will not inquire as to why, but you strike me as a warrior who would only benefit my lord's army," Merasu praised.

Zano stood in utter silence. His mind brought him back to the bloody carcass of the High Priest. The rebellion of the Blood Scaldor flew past his eyes and the thought of bringing the rest of his kind to freedom warmed his heart. Without any time to think over his choice, Zano rashly bowed his head and answered the general, "Yes."

"Excellent. I have matters to attend to. Farewell, Zano Cynery, and may Oblikaron guide you in battle." Merasu bowed honorably and with unexpected grace.

Zano lifted his head as the dark figure departed into the shadows. He subsided into the snow blanket from which he was disturbed. The grunts of Scaldor soldiers preceded Zano's sword and sheath flying through the air and slamming into his stomach. They chuckled spitefully as he gasped for air and fell into a splash of green-tinted powder.

With heavy breaths to refill his lungs, Zano rolled onto his back and gazed into the clear night sky. He was well used to prejudice and was no longer bothered by it. His travels across Isinda had him well-tuned for the harshness of the world. He merely smiled and surveyed the celestial designs of the sky. The violet and white marks splashed erratically across a black canvas, which was speckled with twinkling stars. His blade found itself reattached to his belt, and Zano comfortably folded his arms behind his head. With the diversion concluded, fatigue took over and his eyes shut again, quickly lulling him into slumber.

The brilliant sun rose above the trees of Desolura, and rested gloriously within a sea of blue. A slew of clouds slowly made their way past, obscuring its radiance. The snow laid the same as it had, the weather still too brisk to melt it.

Atop a small elevation stood an army of Scaldor in which Zano now resided. There were nearly five thousand of them, all clad in bronze armor and wielding the same double-sided *naginata* the Scaldor had used in the Battle of the Deadlands. Their bronze breastplates were smooth and shining, with skirts of flapping, brown leather strips hanging from the bottom. Their bronze greaves were reinforced on the knees and shins, and tucked under lightweight bronze boots. In the front center stood a dark wraith wearing a black robe who stared venomously toward the forest.

The army was silent and erect, their eyes fixed toward the same position as Merasu's. Their armor gleamed like golden tears of the sun and their weapons dug into the snow. The only man without bronze was the red-scaled warrior who wore only a sullied robe.

The trees rustled as chirping birds flocked toward the clouds and away from the oncoming battle. It seemed so quickly that Zano was thrown into this affair, but he greeted the challenge without a bit of fear. As strong as his morals had become throughout his travels, he always remembered that before all else he was a warrior and that the blade was his creed.

From the shadows of the trees a barbaric horde of warriors emerged—warriors no different than those Zano had once served. They wore suits of tough animal skins and wielded stone swords and axes, along with crude wooden shields. With pugnacious screams, they burst wildly through the woods, forming messy lines and thrashing their arms through the air. Surprisingly there were no Blood Scaldor at their sides being forced to fight against the conquerors. Upon seeing the enslavers once more, the scales on the back of Zano's neck folded up with invigoration.

"I'll see you dead on the battlefield Blood," a soldier behind Zano taunted.

"I've seen more battles than you ever will, Scaldor. Let your blade speak, not your discerning tongue!" Zano replied indignantly, not even bothering to face his antagonist. The soldier grunted, but mocked the Blood Scaldor no more.

The savages went into an uproar, losing any sense of organization and falling into a chaotic charge. Snow dusted off of their bodies, floating in their wake and puffing up like tiny explosions from their feet. They were enraged by Zano's massacre of one of their tribes and, thinking it to be the Bronze Kingdom's doing, they foolishly decided to relinquish the advantage the forest provided.

"Let the bastards come to us. Oblikaron guide you!" Merasu roared as he pulled his sword from its black leather sheath. It was a claymore as long as half an Arikarnon, with jagged spikes fixed into the base. The iron was nearly black and fixed on a hilt that had streaks of lava red searing through ebony wood. The piece just under where the blade was fixed was carved into a malicious claw. At the very bottom of the weapon, under the handle, was the shape of a sharp-toothed dragon head, the teeth and claws of it all made from sharpened, glittering rubies.

Merasu's force hoisted their dual *naginata's* from the dirt and wielded them with both hands. As the savages hastily approached the army of the Bronze Empire, Zano disobeyed Merasu's present order to hold. He pounced forward, flinging himself with unparalleled might at the barbaric charge. His blade met the wave with unrelenting thirst, tearing through the front lines of the Desolura Scaldor. Twisting and twirling through the veiling snow, Zano sliced through chests and slit legs, causing the men at his rear to rush to his aid. Through this, the right flank of the savages was successfully repelled.

The rest of the Desolura Scaldor crashed into the coiling blades of Merasu's army, splattering blood onto the once-white snow. Zano's past coursed through him once more, releasing a fury that none could penetrate. His blade moved masterfully as he cut further into his enemies, spilling guts onto the tainted earth as the rest of the Bronze Empire's force steadily paced forward, driving the savages back with relative ease.

Suddenly, when victory seemed certain, a small army of Blood Scaldor burst out of the woods. All were appareled in tattered cloth shirts down to their knees, so torn that some appeared to be wearing nothing. The stone weapons, which once belonged to their masters, were now in their hands and some still had broken shackles bound around their wrists. Even women and children were among them, charging with boundless abhorrence. At their front sprinted Carthago with youthful ferocity, the High Priest's dagger in his clenched fist.

"Reinforcements come! Slay them all!" Merasu bawled over the turmoil, seeing these oncoming Blood Scaldor as another enemy.

"They're with me! Desara Norrath!" Zano screamed out in a hysteric exhilaration as he saw the people he had freed emerging from the darkness. The Desolura Scaldor were caught within a pincer attack and, after only a short while of bloodshed, were slaughtered. Zano's blade tore free from a blue-scaled chest, sending a final carcass plummeting to the shallow white powder where hundreds of corpses already laid entrenched by ice and snow, bathed in their own blood. His nostrils flared as he stood towering above his victims, examining the death that enclosed him. The sight of these slave owners frozen in demise brought a heartless smirk to his lips.

Carthago left his speechless brethren and cleared the valley of death, making his way toward his hero. "We, freedom ... Choose you," he struggled to say with quivering lips, as he held the dagger out with both hands. Zano indolently reached over to grasp the handle of the stained dagger as his eyes gave way to tears.

"I see. Perhaps the Blood Scaldor's future in Isinda lies with me," Zano softly cried with malcontent, holding the dagger before his smoldering eyes. He thought of the little girl's ravaged body, along with the mangled corpse of her murderer. With a potent gulp, he placed the dagger in his belt and rested his bloody hand compassionately on Carthago's shoulder.

The rest of the Blood Scaldor did not approach the unreceptive men of the Bronze Empire and stood fearfully, in silence. Merasu gazed intently amidst the horror at the two red-scaled men and placed his sword back into its sheath.

The battle concluded with utterly lopsided results. Fewer than one hundred of the Bronze Empire's soldiers were lost. Before the masked general departed the majority of his force was left under the supervision of a lesser officer with orders to enter the forest, subjugate the inhabitants, and to lay to rest the corpses of their fallen comrades. The rest packed up their encampment and joined with Merasu en route to the Bronze City. Zano was among this group of nearly one thousand, with the Blood Scaldor following closely at the rear of the people who apparently detested them. All of them walked except for Merasu, who rode atop a burly Diarii with short black fur.

The Diarii were lean, four-legged, stallion-like creatures, with hooves and teeth meant only for the consumption of plants. Two antlers rose from their heads in varying patterns, and they held diverse colorations of fur and spots. A long tail swooshed from their rears, just grazing the ground, which was a good distance from their backs.

Merasu sat comfortably on his mount's hide, his black robe draped over its torso and his hands clenching the antlers. "Your efforts on the battlefield were commendable. My lord could use a man of your ... *talents* ... under his command," Merasu said to the blood-drenched warrior beside his trotting mount.

"Thank you, but those that follow us are my people and I will not abandon them again. Your offer is appreciated, but I cannot accept," Zano answered with a somber tone as he finally began to take responsibility for the people he chose to free.

"They share my lord's blood Zano. When he hears of their actions, and of yours, they will not be shunned from his grace. You have an aura of greatness about you and I will not let such a capable warrior escape. In the Bronze Empire you will find a home for yourself and perhaps you may rebuild one for your people. The horrors they have endured can only improve and so I implore you. Rethink my request."

"I must convene with this king of yours before my mind can be made. Though I must warn you now that I will only forever, truly serve one master," Zano uttered, his mind wandering back to memories of Tarak.

"You are a peculiar man Zano … Cynery. Very well, travel with me to the Tower of Bronze and no longer will you have to wander."

"I will come. Though I must ask, what are you?"

"Ha!" Merasu chortled, "I am both a shadow and a wraith, a shade of what I once was. Questions must come later; for now, return to your people. The trip to the Bronze City is a lengthy one and my men will not be as accepting as I."

Zano nodded to the horned figure obediently and slowed down in order to be amongst the Blood Scaldor. Carthago hurried to his side.

"What. Happen. Us," he said with wretched enunciation and a concerned expression on his crimson face.

"I shall not leave you. Come, walk with me towards a new life," Zano grinned and waved for his people to follow as the open fields cleared his mind. Carthago smiled witlessly and jumped onto Zano like a child

The crowd made their way across the vast landscape of the Scaldor lands. Skyscraping mountains jabbed the sky at their rear, the mauve outlines just visible through the snowy haze.

Clouds deposited layers of white steadily on the earth's surface, thickening the blanket that had already been laid. They passed by small villages of Scaldor, whose residents lived as farmers or as breeders of cattle to be slaughtered. The villages of this region all supplied the Bronze Empire and received any needed goods from the illustrious capital.

The traveling army was hardly fed. The snow provided adequate nourishment. They had no need to rest. Through two cycles of the moon and sun, they traipsed through the deep snow, only stopping for an occasional respite.

The Blood Scaldor were not strangers to such extraneous labor, finding the journey far from difficult. Zano remained at their lead and found himself mostly beside Carthago. He told him tales of adventures across the land and stories that, for the most part, the young man could not comprehend. Unlike when he was freed, these Blood Scaldor were far from intellectual and hardly any of them could speak correctly, if at all. The Scaldor in front ignored their crimson brethren. If any came too close, they were shoved back.

After countless hours of walking, as the legs of every person grew weary, the sun began to rise on the third cycle. Light peered curiously over the horizon, and a spectacular view emerged from the twilight. Shimmering in the sky stood a pinnacle of bronze, which, like the spear of a giant, pierced a blue torso. The snow had subsided and in the clarity of light this Tower of Bronze scraped across Isinda's ceiling, just below the low-floating clouds. It was built of circular plateaus, each decreasing in size up to the tip, which could fit no more than one hundred people in its circumference. Every jutting plateau was covered in snow and a frozen waterfall cascaded from three sides of the circular shell.

The flat summit of each plateau was hollowed out and filled with crystal water, which was now frozen over and topped with white powder. The three waterfalls were unmoving in time, reflecting the golden glare of the sun and fusing to the stone bricks at the tower's base. A quadratic incision was cut into the west side of the structure, with bronze steps leading as high as the second level. Elaborate golden sculptures of every renowned Scaldor in known history were placed across the outer edges of the bottom level, gloriously overlooking the Bronze City. These sculptures continued up to the next levels and more were supplemented with the passing of every king or Scaldor of worth in the Bronze Kingdom. The arched wooden gates of the tower's entrance soared to the height of at least twenty men and down the sides of the steps water streamed into a moat.

The army halted in their tracks and the Scaldor breathed in the crisp air of their home. The Blood Scaldor gaped in amazement at the stupendous structure that punctured an endless cerulean curtain.

"That. Tower..." Carthago stuttered to Zano, almost unable to bring words to his dry lips.

"Yes, the wondrous Bronze Tower of Brazdor," Zano replied with gaping eyelids and a flicker of light in his pupils. Unlike his people, however, this was not the first time that his eyes had beheld the magnificent structure.

As the group stepped closer toward the Bronze City Zano's mind brought him back to when he and his master first came upon the radiant spire.

• • •

Zano and his liberator made their way across the twilight, emerging from the Desolura into an unending, indiscernible landscape. They ran south at a steady rate, unknowing of all else around them. Zano followed his new master in silence as a cloudy sky obscured the emerald moon. The air was a tad chilly, nipping at their faces as they cut through it.

Drained from the earth-shattering day's events, Zano could no longer continue after what seemed to be hours of running, and he sprawled out across the long grass.

"Good idea. This should be far enough," the Deimor said as he gasped for air and collapsed onto the ground next to the Blood Scaldor.

"I have never left the canopy of the forest," Zano said mournfully, glancing down at the drooping grass.

"Yet you feel no fear—no amount of sorrow?" the Deimor inquired, taking great interest in the boy.

"Should I grieve departing Pregarus? Why should I fear what I have sought since I was old enough to think clearly?"

"Your feelings are your own, boy. Do you have a name?"

"Most slaves do not," Zano paused for a moment, " … Zano."

"Zano? A name of Deimor origin. It means *flame* in Desthoroth. Strange how one may come about a name. For you its origin was most likely unknown. I am known by the name Tarak, of the Cynery family," the Deimor responded with a bow of his head.

"Desthoroth?"

"Ah yes, it is the ancient language of the Deimor. Most other races do not know it, but it lives on with what few Deimor there are left in existence," Tarak explained.

"The Deimor still exist?"

"To an extent. The races failed to exterminate us, eh?" Tarak laughed, but he was not joined by the Blood Scaldor, who wasn't quite sure how to take the musing.

"I have read of the Battle of the Deadlands. I didn't know such death could exist," Zano said, his voice filled with dread at the thought.

"Neither did any, and neither should they have. It surprises me that you have read of this battle and even more that you can read," Tarak noticed, realizing just how educated this slave truly was.

"No other slave could. I suppose I just found ways to teach myself against their will," Zano elucidated, as though his accomplishment was of no importance.

"I would like to hear your story, but the night grows old, and we should sleep before it withers."

"Wait! Who are you?" Zano shouted, not realizing his heightened pitch.

"I understand that you have questions, but this day has been hard on your mind. No man should have to endure what you have, so please get some rest. So little time in this world there is for resting, and it should be taken at any opportunity," Tarak advised, quickly ending the Blood Scaldor's onslaught of questions.

"Yes, Master Tarak. Thank you," Zano responded weakly.

"Thank no one Zano. Life will take more twists and turns, and then you will have time to give thanks if you still wish to do so. For now, sleep," Tarak demanded.

Master and apprentice shut their eyes in the damp grass as streaks of moonlight penetrated the clouds and fell onto their faces. Zano's fatigue quickly caught him, and he placed the dagger by his side, falling asleep within moments. His master followed soon after, with his hand resting protectively on the hilt of his sword.

Zano's eyes opened to witness a sight that he had never beheld. For the first time in his life, there was no shadow of trees obscuring his view, and the vibrant blue sky was no longer obstructed by thousands of tiny needles. Vast fields of shin-high amber grass stretched for miles in every direction. The unforgettable forest was behind him and merely a blur, allowing him to gaze across unending fields, littered with an occasional gray rock. As far as his eyes could see, there were no villages or towns. Only soaring birds and grazing Diarii were visible on the horizon. The blazing sun lit the landscape on the clear day and shone directly into Zano's adjusting eyes. To his rear, far off in the distance, jagged, majestic mountain ranges tore into the blue, capped with snow and cracking upward with brownish rock.

Zano's mouth gaped as a sight that most would take for

granted met his vision. He had never seen anything so vibrant, so bright.

"Stunning, isn't it—this world in which we live?" Tarak asked warmly, as he sat beside his apprentice. He had clearly been awake since the sun began its glorious ascent. Zano was finally able to see his master bathed in light. Scraggly, withering hair fell over his broad shoulders, and a beard of messy white flowed down from his bony jaw. His face was lean and his skin wrinkled, yet his visage emitted a hint of life that a young man would have. His eyes continued to burn with red intensity under the shade of his hood, and his creased, leathery skin had a rust-colored hue. Bushy white eyebrows shadowed his eyelids, and short strands of gray hair protruded from his wide nostrils.

"I have never..." Zano struggled to finish his sentence, in sheer astonishment at the beautiful landscape.

"The darkness of the Desolura may have obscured your view of Isinda, but you must always remember that, despite the war, this land is majestic," Tarak explained through his chapped, maroon lips as he reached into the folds of his baggy black robe. He pulled out a stale piece of wheat bread, tossed the modest slab onto Zano's naked lap and stated, "Eat."

Realizing that he hadn't eaten for well over a day, Zano tore into the bread. Crumbs spewed onto his lap and sprinkled his wet lips as he devoured the thin slice. Tarak laughed gingerly at his voracious pupil, whose expression still displayed a desire for more.

"We'll eat again in time," Tarak said. He glanced down at the Blood Scaldor and saw streaks of thrashed scales across his upper back, "Here, put this on. You can't run through the land in naught but your scales."

A frayed tan cloth landed in a messy bundle on Zano's thighs. He held it up so it would unfold and then placed it around his lean frame. The tunic fell only to his knees, and the sleeves had been torn off. With no belt to draw it tight to his waist, it draped loosely and fluttered in the light breeze.

After dressing, Zano glanced down to see the stone dagger of his former ruler entangled in the amber grass. Blood still tainted its crude blade and was splattered down the handle. Visions of the bloody little girl struck Zano as he shuddered, but his freed mind quickly attempted to suppress those haunting reminiscences.

"Your memories will never leave you Zano. They will survive in you like a sickness for all of your life. You must not dwell on forgetting them, but instead you must let your past drive you. Do not hate what has happened; instead try to understand it. All things occur for a reason, and not everything can be solved with sullenness. One day, your mind will be free of your hatred and suffering, and your past will simply be another part of your life," Tarak expressed wisely, with a soothing tone. A tear dripped from Zano's glossy eyes.

"I will always see her face. How can I rid myself of these feelings? Uncloud my mind of these lingering memories?"

"All questions are answered with time. Only you can liberate yourself, not I. All I can do is show you the way toward what you desire in the deepest recesses of your heart. True freedom."

"Show me the way Master," Zano pleaded, surrendering all that he was to his new teacher.

"I will, and so now we must move on."

"To where?"

"Wherever our naked feet may take us," Tarak replied. "Now pick up the dagger; it is a symbol of a past that you must not yet forget, only embrace."

Zano seized the dagger with his shivering right hand and wiped his tears away with his left. Tarak rose to his feet, fixing the sheath on his leather belt to hang sturdily from his left hip. Zano obediently nodded at his master and followed him as he began to make way at a quick pace across the infinite plains.

Endless fields of grass rolled past them, and only a few scattered villages obscured the horizon. The sun soared lethargically across the sky, passing through gentle puffs of white. The aged

Deimor's legs carried him with surprising success, the youthful Blood Scaldor just at his rear. They jogged at a quick pace with hardly a break, keeping a hefty distance from any signs of civilization. Then, as it never failed to do, the sun began its plummet into oblivion, painting a red shade across the countryside.

As they rounded a hill they saw, glimmering like a blood-pointed spear well off into the fog of Zano's abilities to see, the Bronze Tower. His feet came to a halt, to his master's displeasure, as his eyes widened at the view of the spectacular tower. He could see trails of gleaming water cascading from its lofty tip.

"How can mortals make such things?" he asked, hardly able to utter the words. Tarak turned and began to step slowly toward his astounded apprentice.

"They say that in the time of the walking gods, the water god Brazdor constructed this tower. These lands have always been blessed with a seemingly unnatural surplus of bronze, and with it, he forged a tower that he believed would be a walkway to the heavens. Now, the lords of the Bronze Kingdom, the most powerful of the Scaldor kingdoms, reside in this magnificent structure," Tarak replied, sharing his wealth of knowledge.

"Shall we go there master?"

"Sit Zano. It is time that we talk." Tarak plopped onto the soft earth. The sun had almost completed its descent into the unknown. "The Scaldor are in harsh times and would not be … hospitable … to men of our appearance. There will be a time for you to come here, but not yet."

"Then where do we go?" Zano questioned, now seeking reason to his master's aimless trek as he placed the dagger by his side.

"It is time for you to leave the Scaldor behind. I have been through much in my long life, yet always I have traveled with a blade in my hand. I seek to give you what neither I, nor any other man, has ever possessed. A chance to live within Isinda and witness all that it has to offer, instead of viewing it blindly.

What better way to make a difference in this chaotic world than to understand all that it is?"

"So where are we going?" Zano persisted in pursuit of an answer.

"I will bring you to the homes of every race. From the mountains of the north to the jungles and desert, the people of these lands will not accept you. They might even hate you—"

"Then why go?"

"To make them love you Zano. To be great, you must be loved greatly. To make a difference—"

"I am a slave! How could I make a difference?" Zano's eyes ignited with raging flame, and his nostrils flared as the memories of his grim past coursed through him.

"We are all slaves Zano!" Tarak yelled with a fury that caused the young Blood Scaldor to wince in evident fear. "Slaves to fate, slaves to hate, slaves to fear! I seek for you to learn to conquer these things. The only way is to learn all that you can; to experience every nook that this land possesses. For centuries, Isinda has been in chaos. Blood has spilled so much so that it could turn a sea red. There have been those who have attempted to end this turmoil, but never has any man been successful.

"We are all stars against a boundless curtain of darkness, waiting for one gleaming sun to peek through and bring forth the light. Listen to me when I say that I have hated and I have feared. I have brought death to countless souls and so will you before the end. These undeniable truths exist in all men, but instead of conquering them, they so effortlessly conquer us. So then millions will die in the Deadlands and millions more over the course of time. The Deimor tried and now there are not enough of us left to fill a castle. What race will be next to attempt to surmount this unconquerable land and fail? I hope I'm dead long before, because this land cannot be united alone. Peace must be brought forth by all the races, not just one. They need to be shown how senseless their hate is; to see that fear drives them to unspeakable ends."

Tarak paused with a tear in his eye and leaned backward to lie out on the curling grass. His lips shivered and his breathing was dramatic, as though he were at a loss for air. Zano stared at him through twinkling eyes as wide as could be, a membrane of water glazing them.

"You want me to bring peace?" Zano stuttered, shocked by his master's words. By being bred from hatred and secluded in a forest all of his life, he knew well the dark history of this land, but he never had looked upon it in this manner.

"No man can bring peace alone. I want you to see the beauty of this land as I only now realize it exists. I'm too old to make a difference. My skin too red for any to pay heed," Tarak slumped, short of breath, and calmed his nerves, shrinking his pulsing veins to norm.

"My skin is red also, Master."

"Yet you are not Deimor. You are a production of rape and war, a race not natural. You are a slave who doesn't fit his mind. As much as people may hate you for how you appear, they will pity you for what has created you. You hold neither land nor title. No history of illustrious kin. In fact, your family is unknown to you. All you hold is a craving for knowledge. I can see it in your eyes!" Tarak's voice swelled with hope. "You sought it as a slave and now so with freedom. You are young and have time to live, time to see all that Isinda is. I will bring you to all of the races. I will let you see how they live, how they breathe, and how they sleep. I will allow you to understand the wondrous mysteries that envelop Isinda and see the magnificence that it took me so long to realize."

"Where then do we go?" Zano reverted back to his old question, still with gawking eyes.

"To the lands of the Arikarnon." Tarak's gaze met the blackened horizon dotted with glimmering specks of golden white to the south. "I suppose this area is suitable. Let us retire for the night."

Zano lay down beside his master and stared up into the

darkened sky. The sun no longer rested and the glowing, emerald moon peered through the shade. "How can I make a difference?" He thought again of his master's words, wondering how a man as insignificant as he could bring any change.

"That is a question that you must answer for yourself with each choice that you make. I can only guide you toward knowledge; you must understand it. Now tell me, how is that you came to be so intelligent living a slave's life?"

Zano's eyes shut. His teeth gnashed as the deep-rooted pain resurfaced.

"With every chance I had I listened to my masters speak. I eyed any tome or scroll my hands could ever grasp. Eventually the letters began to make sense to me and stories were formed. The suffering I withstood didn't matter, only the hunger for knowledge—for a reason I existed in the way that I did. My masters thought me a fool. They assumed none of their knowledge could ever pass on to me," Zano explained. His slight triumph brought a glint to his pupils as he said this with a bold smirk.

"Their doubt indeed was foolish. Did you ever find your answer?"

"I was different. My people were different. Difference built hatred and for that we were enslaved. To them we were of no real importance, so they sacrificed us in the name of whatever god they prayed to. We were savages who needed to be tamed." His grin flipped, and his nose wrinkled as hatred resurfaced.

"You will come to learn, boy, that all men are savages," Tarak reverted to his incisive demeanor. "Do you hate the people who tortured you?"

"More than anything in this world," Zano growled, his eyes shining like flawless jewels.

"That is why I believe you can make a difference."

"I don't understand," Zano murmured, shrinking backward into the grass.

"You hate with reason. Do you hate, say, the Arikarnon, or any other Scaldor in this land?" Tarak inquired.

"No."

"Exactly," Tarak continued, believing that he made his point, though it remained above Zano's plane of understanding.

"What?"

"You will learn in time what I mean. Zano, I beg of you, when you meet those who hate you for naught, do not return the favor. Diminish their loathing into love. There is greatness within you—I see it, and I feel it as I sit in your presence. Yet you cannot win over all men without this," Tarak ripped his sword from its gold-tipped ebony sheath and held it in his gaze. The blade was sharp, glistening iron and curved like a *katana* up to the tip, which was fashioned of pure diamond. The hilt was solid jade and littered with tiny gems, and the bottom was carved into an eagle head. On the base of the blade, there was an etching of a dragon, with a hole where its eye should be. "Do you know how to use a blade?"

Zano's eyes popped from his head like a child's, gaping over the blade's extraordinary splendor.

"The most I've ever swung is a stick...Wait!" Zano's head tilted, and his hair flapped across his shoulders. "I thought you wanted me to bring peace?"

"To do this," Tarak laughed, "you must learn to speak with wisdom *and* with blood."

"You will teach me?" Zano asked.

"Yes. At sunrise, your lessons will commence. For now, the sky has grown dark. Sleep, and regain your energy. We will begin our trek toward the Akai Desert at sunrise."

Tarak rolled onto his side in silence and Zano stared intently upward, trying to remain quiet but unable to do so.

"I read that the Deimor had horns. Where are yours?" he queried, finally relieving himself of a lingering question.

"They were once here, but the world has grown less accepting of such a trait. My living required me to relinquish them," Tarak reflected.

"What happened to you?"

"As your story unfolds, so too will mine. Now sleep," Tarak answered wearily.

"Yes Master," Zano sighed, dissatisfied with his master's response.

The youthful Blood Scaldor rolled onto his side with his fingers curled around the blood-coated dagger and closed his lambent eyes. Tarak switched onto his back and rested his sword on his chest. His glossy blade reflected the brilliant stars and radiant moon, and he stared into the black sky until fatigue caught him off guard.

"He will be the sun," Tarak whispered to himself and turned to see his sleeping apprentice, who shivered and whimpered in apparent fright.

Nightmares of his past cluttered Zano's mind, and the old Deimor sighed. With a slight smile, he hummed a soft melody and closed his eyes. Once again, beneath the luminous emerald moon, master and apprentice slept, just at the beginning of their vast journey.

· · ·

Now, for the first time in his short life, Zano made his way toward the alluring tower. His people followed him with the same wonder that once took hold of him, close behind the pleased army of Scaldor and their dark leader Merasu. Zano took in a full breath of air and smiled at the remembrance of his deceased master.

"Does peace begin here?" Zano murmured to himself, placing his actions in the forest behind him. Carthago raced to his side and warmly he placed his arm around the boy's neck.

By the Grace of an Emperor Divine

*"As long as this crown resides atop my head,
you are my servant, along with all of my other
subjects. For with it, I am a living god."*

King Shorn of the Bronze Empire

Zano and the army began their descent toward the tower and as they crossed a white hill the entire city came into view. A towering wall of rigidly-cut stone blocks encircled it, a few miles in diameter. Guard towers with curved roofs, swooping downward from a crest, divided the wall. These roofs were fashioned with bronze tiles and dotted the wall at equal intervals. Four gateways facing east, north, south, and west were entrenched into the fortification, with crosshatched iron gates that could only be raised from the inside.

Around the perimeter of these walls were thousands of farms which lay dormant under a glittering cover. They mostly produced rice, but some grew wheat, and others still raised cattle or sheep for meat or for cloth. Tiny, wooden farmhouses drenched in white dotted the acres of farmland, and only the unfortunate Scaldor who dwelled in these huts still walked the land outside of the city walls.

As the army approached these outlying farms, Merasu halted and trotted back toward Zano and the Blood Scaldor. "Your people must stay here while we enter," he ordered of Zano, whose expression revealed his detest of the order.

"They helped us fight. Are they not worthy of entering?" Zano snapped.

"It is not that. I just do not believe they will be received cordially until we speak with my lord. Let them wait here for you to return while we decide their fate."

"Very well," Zano sighed with displeasure. Merasu nodded with a grunt and rode his Diarii back to the head of the cluster.

"We must stay?" Carthago asked softly as he came up to Zano's side. He was clearly confused by the situation and overwhelmed by all that had happened to him in so short a time.

"Only for a while. I'll be back before sunset," Zano responded in an attempt to comfort him.

Zano motioned his people to stop and turned to follow Merasu and the Scaldor. Carthago stayed behind and explained to the rest of the Blood Scaldor that they had to wait for their leader to return.

The army entered a dirt pathway through the inactive fields that was carved into the deep snow. They followed the cleared trail leading to the massive iron gate on the north side of the Bronze City.

A black bird whizzed past Zano's ear and perched atop the snow-covered ramparts that rose up from the earth before him. Sunlight shimmered off the tower roofs, and the tip of the Bronze Tower gleamed over the wall top. Zano wondered, as the tower disappeared behind the thick wall, how such small creatures could construct a wonder so colossal.

Merasu and the army came to a stop before the great iron

gate, and he shouted up to the gate guard, "His highness's army returns."

The guard, who stood atop the parapets and between two towers, picked up a flag and waved it. The flag had a white background and outlines of scales were painted in red across its entirety. By this signal the rolling and clanking of chains initiated, pulling the iron gate from the dirt and hiding it within a slit in the stone.

Merasu began to trot forward. As he passed through the entrance a crowd broke into cheer and petals of cerulean flowers floated down from the hands of civilians. Two lines of nearly one hundred Scaldor guards, each dressed in the same bronze armor as the others, formed around the entering army as a throng of rugged Scaldor mobbed them in joy. Mostly there were women who desired to see their husbands home alive. They wore clothes that were tattered and wet. Their faces were covered in dirt, canopied by unkempt hair of black or gray.

Cries of "Praise Brazdor!" and "Thank the heavens!" rang out through the clamor. Priests bowed in prayer before the entering soldiers, but the civilians were kept back by blades. The bloodied army made its way down the ornate, stone, processional street, which was cleared of snow, toward the tower which could be seen from any spot within the city.

Zano's eyes shifted back and forth. It was the first time that he ever had the opportunity to enter this brilliant capital. Thousands of buildings lined the streets, all of which eventually led to the tower. The structures they passed were shoddy, made of weathered wood rather than stone. Each roof was curved the same as the wall towers and covered with identical, untarnished bronze tiles.

All of the houses were similar, with arched entrances that were wider than they were high, constructed in a post and beam method. Square openings served as windows and each had more than one rectangular cavity covered with geometrically-designed wood doors. Most were two stories, with curved, bronze awnings separating the stories from the outside point of view.

The streets were bustling with activity. Merchants sold pottery and food—mostly rice or bread—from roadside stands. Traders transported goods on the hides of Diarii throughout the city. Guards patrolled the roads vigilantly and at no time was there a shining soldier out of sight. As the army passed by more wives flocked toward them, cheering and praying blissfully over their warriors' return.

As they neared the soaring Bronze Tower the applauding mob started to diminish in mass. The remaining crowd began to transform, and the Scaldor's cheering was soon equally of men and women. No longer did they wear crude clothes, but instead were appareled in silk or velvet outfits. From their draping robes to feathered shirts, all were dyed with an assortment of bright colors. These wealthy Scaldor were also festooned in an assortment of fine jewelry.

The houses were no longer shoddy or made of wood, and each had only a single entrance. They reached higher into the sky but housed less, and the glossy, white stone walls were far from rudimentary. Each had a small garden at the front of their arched entrances and bronze doors, with bare branches that would only flourish in the warmth of Forunhor. A low fence separated each yard, while iron gates with assortments of seals stood before the path to every gate. Each opening on the buildings was lined with a bronze coat and the doors were carved with ornate designs. Here, the merchants sold meats and poultry, as well as fruits and vegetables that looked to be well out of the reach of those who were not wealthy.

Zano realized how segregated the rich were from the poor when he saw that guards stood, trustingly, at large distances from each other in this section. He passed under a barrier of beautiful cloth drapes of colors as vivid as those in a rainbow and then, just before him, stood the round base of the Bronze Tower in all of its vaingloriousness.

The eyes of the army, as well as Merasu's, did not even acknowledge the structure. They were no longer impacted by its sheer splendor. Golden statues shimmered in the sunlight, popping through dazzling snow on the first elevation. Bronze steps led to a massive gate, starting wide, and then thinning out at the base. Three glistening waterfalls of ice poured down the structure on either side, reflecting the city through unblemished curves. The ice reached down into a thin crevasse, no more than three feet wide, which encompassed the enormous base of the tower. A plaza of elaborately-painted stone surrounded this rift, with dormant gardens distributed across it. The trees and bushes were bare and covered in snow, and the plaza was patrolled by a constant flow of soldiers.

The sheen of the building was flawless, with no corroding effect from constant water flow. They say that the shine of the bronze was the same then as it was on the day of the tower's completion. Zano gazed up to its peak, which rested just below the clouds, and he realized just how intricate the tower was. All the way up to the tip the bronze was engraved with thousands of pictures—beautiful moldings, which told long-lost stories and depicted scenes of its creator. The statues on the edges seemed to be forged by masters of the craft, without a detail omitted. Toward the top, where high nobles dwelled, large, arched punctures allowed light to enter.

Two guards came and took Merasu's Diarii just as he dismounted. He began to climb the steps. The stone stairs were engraved with what seemed to be scales, and down the sides ran two streams of frozen water. Zano walked by Merasu's side without a word and the blood-crusted army followed them. The wooden gate was a deep mahogany and on it a dragon with men shadowed by its grandeur was painted in gold.

They came before the entrance, and at that instant, the giant doors creaked open. They entered into a long hallway, wide enough to fit nearly ten men side by side. The floor was of swirling black and white marble, and the walls solid white marble, adorned with gorgeous gold-framed paintings. Ornate crystal candleholders hung from the white ceiling, small flickers of flame lighting the hall. Many arched doors of bronze rested on either side of the corridor with hooked handles of gold.

The group made their way down the lengthy hall toward a dark opening at the end. On either side of the cavity, there were marble staircases that curved around the circular room into which the opening led.

At the foot of the shadow, Merasu turned to his men and stated, "You may take your leave. Oblikaron bless you."

"Yes sir!" they replied in drone-like harmony and in two organized lines they made their way up the twisting stairs. Zano parroted Merasu and stepped into the room, which was shrouded by darkness. It was a circle, with a floor of wooden planks held together by iron strips. Chains ran up the side of the stone inner wall in which there were exits at what seemed to be each level of the tower. No lighting existed in the endless tube except for the candlelight permeating through each opening.

Chains and pulleys began to rattle, until suddenly the floor jerked upward as it began to slowly rise.

"What is this?" Zano shouted above the loud racket of grinding iron, alertly scanning the dark tunnel.

"It is a way to rise up the tower without the burdensome task of climbing stairs. Fascinating that its chains run so high," Merasu replied curiously, his violet eyes glaring like amethysts through the holes in his foreboding mask.

"Where did your men go?"

"The tower is not used by the common man. It is here where my lord's army sleeps, trains, and arms. The levels of this tower are packed with his armies' rooms, and only high-ranking officials, or royal family, are permitted to live on the top floors. You should be honored that you have the privilege to visit his throne, for few ever do," he said, his voice emanating pomposity.

"Should a king not live amongst his people?"

"My lord is a living ... god."

"I see," Zano groaned.

"You are not so easily caught in the illusion, I see?"

"Do you believe it?"

"He bleeds like any other man, but to his people he is the reincarnation of the Water God Brazdor. It is difficult to grasp, I understand. Just know that when you come before him, you must bow. And never stare into his eyes," Merasu explained, skeptical of his own words.

"I'll take note," Zano grumbled sarcastically.

"Will you? We near the throne floor."

The crackling of the chains began to slow, and the lift stopped where it had no more room to go upward. Torches were sufficiently spaced out along the circular, white marble walls. The ceiling rounded up into a dome of gold mosaics. A bronze gate, with etchings of two waterfalls on each door, stood before their eyes as the only exit out of this area. Merasu nodded and Zano returned the gesture. The doors slowly unfastened, and bright light shined into his unprepared eyes before he took his first step in.

He had traveled to the far reaches of this land and suddenly, all of it paled in comparison to the magnificence of this room. The shape was a semicircle, starting wide at the doors, and with every inch lavishly decorated. The shimmering bronze walls were engraved with complicated patterns and chiseled with sculptures that appeared almost lifelike. Hundreds of stately paintings dotted the walls, all with vibrant and luxurious colors. Thousands of candles in crystal cylinders lined the outer walls, and round columns of swirling white and gold marble rose in two rows to a ceiling that struck even Zano's hardened heart. The smooth, vaulted ceiling gradually dwindled in height from the gate to the throne, and it was expertly painted with an elaborate depiction of the Bronze Tower and its city along the gently arched center. At the far end of the room, within the artwork, there were clouds, and from them emerged the hand of a god which reached out with a blue-scaled arm to dip a single finger into the pool at the tower's peak. The cascading waterfalls spilled from this, and on either side of the bronze pinnacle were two fiery azure eyes, just visible within a light blue sky.

Between the outside of the pillars and the candles at the room's edge lay two crystalline pools of tranquil water. On the front of the pillars, facing Zano, white cloths were draped, flowing with the outlines of scarlet scales painted down to the gold-trimmed bottom. Between the rows of pillars, a violet carpet of velvet was unfurled over the glossy, white marble floor, fringes of gold sewn onto the edges. At the end of this carpet sat the flawless throne of the proclaimed god, the target of every perspective. Light showered down upon it from a shaft cut at an angle through the wall behind. The seat was made purely of bronze, with a rounded back that extended upward at least eight feet. There was not a rigid edge on the masterpiece, and the metal was etched with tiny anecdotes and pictures. It rested on a square dais of solid gold and on either side of the seat protruded bronze dragonheads that spewed water into the docile pools.

Behind the illustrious seat was an intricate mural of a dragon, its scales as white as snow. It was coiled and faced to the side, with wings curling against its torso and concealing its limbs. The creature was placed against a solid cerulean background and its eyes were shut. Water leaked like a waterfall from its fanged mouth and nose, while its spiky tail pointed toward a scaly throat.

Zano scanned the room, overwhelmed by its opulence as he stepped forward onto the violet carpet. Bronze clad guards unfastened his sheath and grabbed his dagger. He snapped toward them, but was stopped by Merasu uttering, "Hold…" under his breath. Zano was unaccustomed to his weapons being confiscated and never did he part with his blade easily.

Gradually Merasu began to step down the carpet without being deprived of his sword. At each column, nine on either side, a fully-armored guard stood with a double-sided *naginata* in hand. Each footstep reverberated off the walls as untrusting eyes stared down the unwelcome Blood Scaldor.

"I have been awaiting your return," said the man in the throne with a deep, resonant voice. A gorgeous robe of lavender silk draped down past his feet, with swirling patterns of embroidered gold. Gold pads curved over his shoulders, fastened to a white cape that was curled under his body and hanging slightly off of the edge. His bony, blue-scaled fingers popped from the robe's drooping sleeves and rested on the rounded end of the chair's sides. Long, charcoal, blue-streaked hair ran down behind his back, and atop his head was a crown. The circlet was fashioned of pure sapphire, bending around his skull with spikes, like the tips arrows, lining the top of an azure halo. From its bottom fell strands of gold string beaded with flawless rubies.

His face was that of a man who had experienced much in his life. It was long and lean, but seemingly frail unlike Zano's. It was hard to tell the age of a Scaldor whose hair doesn't gray, but the scales under his eyelids had begun to droop. His facial expression seemed like that of a man of wisdom, yet his eyes still burnt with a blue as vibrant as his crown.

Merasu knelt on one knee before the golden dais, bowing his head so that his black hood eclipsed his dark mask, and replied confidently, "Much of your force remains in the Desolura to subdue its savage inhabitants my Lord Sila."

"And the losses?"

"Close to none. It was a grand victory in your name!" The voice beneath iron swelled with fervor.

"Praise Brazdor! And who is this blood soaked—" he paused with detest as he glanced at Zano "—*man* you bring before me?"

Zano stood defiantly, his eyes fixed directly on Sila's brow.

"This is—" Merasu began to answer, but he was cut off by Sila.

"He may speak for himself."

Merasu submissively apologized as Zano responded in a dignified tone, "I am Zano Cynery of the Blood Scaldor."

"Why do you not kneel before your emperor and god?" Sila questioned lividly, taken aback that this insolent man of a lesser race stood in disobedience.

"I have knelt before many men, Lord of Bronze, and I plan never to kneel again. God or peasant, my feet stand firmly where they are. You wouldn't want my robe to bloody your hall would you?"

"Merasu, who is this insolent savage you dare bring into my hall?" Sila yelled, furiously seeking an explanation for this folly.

The masked general touched his metal forehead helplessly to the gold dais and explained the presence of a Blood Scaldor. "This man was free long before we arrived my lord. He has agreed to aid us in your name. His efforts on the battlefield and influence with the Blood Scaldor turned our effort into a massacre. Without his presence, you would not see so many of your worthy followers returning today."

Sila stroked his chin curiously and replied, "Yet he walks into my hall with such inexcusable behavior?"

"My lord—"

"Silence Merasu! Please, everybody leave. I will speak with him alone."

The divine emperor gracefully waved his hand, indicating for all of the guards to bow and hurry out of the room. Merasu grunted and hesitantly followed them, closing the massive doors behind him.

The emperor raised his frame from the throne, his robe unfurling down over his feet, and walked past Zano in a fashion more intrigued than angry. The hot-tempered Blood Scaldor's eyes kept steady on the robed man as he awaited his next move. He was impressed that Sila was brave enough to send his guards away. The emperor's confidence was, ~~to an extent,~~ somewhat inspiring to him.

"What is your quarrel with me, Blood Scaldor? I am not the same man as those who enslaved you," Sila questioned as he slowly paced down the ornate hall, his garment trailing along the majestic carpet.

"I have been free for more days than I can count. The blood of my enslavers has already been spilled. Do not discern me as a savage without any means of reason!" Zano roared back, seething with irritation.

"Not a savage? You come before my throne in this discourteous manner and you ask me to see you as civil?"

"Am I savage for refusing to bow before lies?" Zano shouted wrathfully.

"Yes, for I have not lied," Sila reputed arrogantly.

"Then I suppose I am a savage, but at least a savage does not deceive his people! At least I do not proclaim myself a god reborn and dress as lavishly as one at that. I do not shield myself behind a curtain of spectacles and deceit!"

"Only those who have served as lords understand the position, Blood! Do you see me not as a god?"

"I see you merely as a Scaldor with a crown on his head. Even the barbarous Scaldor from whence I came did not claim to be divine!"

"Yet my people do. These are harsh times and a man cannot simply unite all of the Scaldor, as I hope to do, without having the ardent support of his people. They serve me as their emperor and god. It is this support that has allowed me to come so far. I see you are not so easily fooled as most of my followers are, but they accept the power that I claim runs through my veins," the emperor explained, his countenance revealing that he truly believed his actions to be just.

"So you rule your people through a ruse?" Zano's voice cooled down, but his inner rage had yet to subside.

"All lords have some way of keeping their subjects' hearts on their side. Merasu was foolish to bring you here if all you came for was to bicker over the way I rule my kingdom!"

"I found quarrel when I arrived in this throne, but I did not come for this."

"What then Zano brings you before my grand throne? Do you come to slay me? For then, you have already succeeded ..." The emperor knelt beside one of the smooth pools and ran his fingers through the tepid liquid, which placidly rippled away.

"If I came to kill you, you would have been dead many moments ago." Zano took a deep breath and continued, "No. I have come here to fight for what you fight for."

"And what is that?" Sila took a sip of water from his scaly palm.

"You say that you wish to unite all of the Scaldor; to bring the scattered kingdoms together as one?" This was it - the desire for something worthwhile, which Zano was hoping to discover in this encounter.

"So the savages' intents are made clear. I am not far from achieving this. In fact, it is only a matter of months before the scattered *do* become one. It is keeping them under my rule that is a predicament," Sila laughed, "but why stop there? Perhaps one day I can have even more success than the Deimor had years ago." He stood up and looked to the tower painted onto the ceiling, as if gazing forth into the future.

"I may not agree with all your means of ruling, but I do see promise in you. You are brave Sila, enough so to dismiss your guards and I respect you for that strength; a strength that may see a difference in this land," Zano's words resonated with his undying aspiration for peace.

"Perhaps it is stupidity, but Merasu believes you to be worthy of my praise. I honor you with my trust and, despite your discourtesy, I wonder if you are a warrior fitting of my army?" Sila inquired, though he appeared to already know the answer.

"Had I been an enemy of the Bronze Empire at Desolura you would never have seen your men return."

"Ha! Really? So the savage will serve me and call me a god? You will become my crimson warrior?"

"As I said, I will never kneel before you, but I will serve your cause. Though there is one request that I must make," Zano said.

"Are you so irrational as to make a request after I discounted your insults and deemed you worthy?" Sila queried, astounded at the warrior's perseverance.

"The rest of the Blood Scaldor are to be freed."

"So the savage has honor. Very well. They will be liberated and all of the Blood Scaldor who follow you will be under your jurisdiction," Sila said, pondering as his hand stroked his protracted chin. "There is a small village to the northeast where you are to bring your people and settle."

"You would entrust me with this task?" Zano lit up in astonishment.

"You have made a mockery of my hall and you have scorned my ways, but you did it because your beliefs are stern. You do not hide behind a curtain of lies and the sparkle in your untamable eyes shows me you can be trusted," Sila explained. He had an unsteady faith in the blood-stained man who stood, seemingly out of place, before his ostentatious throne.

"You have my word and I would die before I break it," Zano vowed without a hint of deception on his countenance.

"I knew that many moments ago, but my people will not be as tolerable as I of those not like them. Their minds must be won over through actions. If the Blood Scaldor wish to be a part of my empire, then they must contribute as my own race does. Your village must provide food and also a legion of soldiers, which I may call upon at any time. Only one with red scales can rule the red-scaled, and so I leave that to you," Sila ordered as he stepped directly before the crimson warrior, meeting his gaze.

"It will be an honor." Zano bowed his head.

"Good. Now take your leave. Merasu will guide you to the village, as I see that he is a man you have come to trust," the emperor said as he surprisingly returned Zano's gesture. "Farewell."

Zano spun around with a glance back at the blue eyes of

Sila and, with echoing steps, made his way to the door. Sila elegantly wheeled around and fell into his bronze throne, still trying to emit an impression of divinity.

"One day," Sila chuckled from his seat, "I will tame your savage nature."

"All men are savage," Zano replied calmly and defiantly, with his face still turned away from the throne. The emperor's mouth gaped at the harshness of those words as the foreigner swung open the great doors of the throne room. The guards glared at him with hateful eyes as they reentered the throne room, shoving his weapons into his stomach. The great doors slammed shut and Merasu nodded. Zano stood unaccompanied in the marble, domed room, atop the creaky wood of the lift.

He made his way out of the exquisite halls of the Bronze Tower and into the wealthy section of the city. The streets and houses were coated in a thin film of white dust, for tiny snow-flakes had begun to flutter down. Frosty eyes watched him as he traversed the city streets, but none dared approach a man who had just left the emperor's tower alive. Still, guards readied their weapons and mothers tucked their children away out of the sight of his bloody attire.

As he came upon the poor section the glances became more welcoming, as though those unfortunate people did not care that a foreigner was on their streets. Most didn't even realize he was there, for they were too worried over filling their stomachs and scrounging for any bit of coin. A dirt-covered man in rags, huddled against a shoddy wood wall, strummed a pleasant melody on a cracked lute. His ceramic mug for donations was completely empty, for the poor had nothing to give and the rich had rejected him.

Nearing the immense gate, Zano heard the screams of a child in a tiny alley to his right and quickly turned the corner. An older Scaldor with graying hair was beating a young boy, begging for money or food. The boy yelped in pain, screaming that he had nothing and Zano feverishly bounded toward the burglar who continued his unpardonable actions.

"Someone else wants to play," the robber laughed in a gritty voice and swung at Zano with bare fists. The dexterous Blood Scaldor quickly dodged the blow and came upward with a fist to the man's stomach. His left hand grabbed the Scaldor by his flabby throat.

"You heard the boy! Now leave him be!" Zano shouted. The burglar gurgled from the pressure of a strong hand.

"Thank you," the boy whispered, then ran away coughing in torn, powder-covered clothes.

"Unhand him, Blood!" said a youthful man behind Zano. The wolf-like warrior turned to see two guards in shimmering bronze armor, double-sided blades in hand, facing him. He tossed the burglar aside, who yelled with a mouth full of spit, "He's trying to mug me!"

"This man was robbing a child," Zano explained and was unnerved by guards' response.

"Likely story," they grunted.

Always ready for battle, Zano wasted no time and grabbed the jade hilt of his blade, ripping it from its sheath. He grasped it tightly with two hands as one of the guards chuckled, "Huge mistake."

Simultaneously, they swung at Zano, who parried their strokes with ease and, sprawling between them, he twirled up with a swift slice across each of their backs. They fell forward with gasps, spewing blood, but just before Zano could place his finishing strike, a deep voice behind him bellowed, "Stop!"

The ragged burglar hurried out of the alley, and Zano turned heatedly to see Merasu atop his black Diarii with blazing violet eyes.

"I leave you alone for minutes and already you've found trouble." The dark figure laughed, releasing the tension. His mount began to trot with heavy hooves into the thin alley as the soldiers moaned in pain, holding their backs while writhing through crimson snow.

"You!" Merasu screamed at a middle-aged female Scaldor who was passing the alley. "Take these men and mend their wounds."

"Of course, my lord," she replied obediently, quickly sprinting and grabbing the hand of each of the soldiers. She dragged their wounded bodies out of the alley, leaving behind a bloody trail.

"I know they probably deserved it Zano, but I do not believe my lord would enjoy hearing of an assault on his men," Merasu explained, showing that he held no ill will toward Zano's actions.

"I did what I had to," Zano replied coldly, with drops of blood trickling down his face.

"Forget it…Come let us meet your people outside the walls. I will guide you to their new home." The masked general beckoned and received an approving nod.

Side by side they made their way out through the huge wooden gates and into the endless fields of unworkable farmland. Glares continued to rain upon the foreigner, and though their lord had welcomed him, Sila's people were not especially fond of his presence.

The black -hooded figure and the crimson warrior at his side made their way down the treacherous path, now slippery from snowfall. They came over the hill to see the crowd of Blood Scaldor lounging in the soft blanket, some even beginning to sleep. Carthago ran toward his hero and asked plainly, "Enter city?"

"No," Zano responded with a smile on his face.

"Where go?"

"Lord Sila has granted us a village to the northeast. Now you will have a home of your own."

Carthago cheered and ran back into the crowd to spread the good news.

The sky was spotted with light gray, the blue hardly peeking through. Sun rays struggled to penetrate, yet they did not fail to bless the landscape with abundant light. Zano smiled toward Merasu and then looked out onto the rolling hills that sparkled toward the horizon, with icy rocks jutting out like tiny boats across a white sea.

A Village Over
Two Ponds

*"The flames roar, and the iron sparks amidst the
screams of the dying, as the demise
of Isinda's greatest warrior comes not by blade,
but by arrow. Oh gods, I beseech you, take me
home to my equals."*

Kuldaro, Eldest son of Shorn

S eeping through the airy puff of clouds, snowflakes fluttered to Isinda's surface—each flake frozen, one not identical to another. Varied projections of ice ejected from the
centers, with diverse patterns and formations. If one examined
each flake as closely as the eye could see, he would realize how
fascinating snowflakes truly are. Ornate pieces of art sculpted
by nature, the hand of man unneeded. It is inevitable, though,
that each flake will end its course of wondrous floating, eventually reaching the hard ground, where it will mold and no longer
be discernable from others. They lose their individuality and
fall into a sea of sameness. This process applies to men no dif-

ferently. All beings are different, either by looks or personality, yet place them together in a crowd, and when this crowd is analyzed, all of the uniqueness utterly disappears.

These snowflakes gently showered Zano's skull like arrows from creatures too miniscule to see. The downfall was not heavy and would have been no more than a drizzle were it rain, but it landed on him and all around. His people did not see it, and Merasu cared not to appreciate it, but the crimson warrior realized the beauty within each speck of white suspended before his fiery eyes. He began to wonder when the sea of colorlessness would disappear and, though he looked forward to the return of warmth, he could not escape how gorgeous the landscape was to him. Endless stretching of white plains, soft to the body's touch, yet frigid to its nerves. Instead of irritating rain pounding on his head with soppy splashes, gentle flakes descended on his skin with no more force than that of a butterfly. The celestial silence soothed him, and the sparkling snow was serene.

Zano's navy-streaked, jet-black hair waved behind him in the brisk breeze and Merasu's draping black robe billowed. Carthago walked beside the crimson warrior as a son walks by his father, his eyes quickly scanning the horizon, as much amazed as he was nervous. It is difficult stepping out from a darkness that has shaded an entire life. Zano knew well this lessen. It was not solely Carthago, however, for the same look existed on all of the Blood Scaldor, even more so on the faces of the older Blood Scaldor who were so attuned to the seclusion of the dark forest.

Suddenly, Merasu jerked on the reins of his Diarii and it gave off a shrieking grunt. Zano's feet halted as well and his eyes followed the dark masked general's pointing finger down a rock precipice no more than two feet before him. The bluff led down to a valley of flat, snow-covered land and far off into the fog another crag of rough-faced rock rose to the same height as the one Zano stood atop. The valley stretched out into two terraced slopes on either side that rose up to the same level as the bluff's peaks. Two small ponds rested in the rift, one lying in the very center and the other along the rock wall, diagonal from Zano's position. The ponds were frosted over with sheets of ice and a thin caking of powdery snow. Barren trees, with no more than twigs and bark, rose in no apparent pattern. Here there were no evergreens, only foliage stripped of its vibrance.

The gorge was mostly vacant except for six houses, which were relatively well built, constructed from wood in a post and tie beam fashion, with open patios across the front ledges and sliding doors of textile with wood strips for support. The roofs were of the same curved-out pattern as the houses in the Bronze City, and these, too, were matted with bronze tiles. Dark gray wisps of smoke puffed from tiny holes in the upper sides of each structure.

The group began to make its way along the fall and around to the hills that led into the tranquil village. The Blood Scaldor were silent, holding a constant gaze toward the quiet town, which they presumed would become their home.

As Zano began to descend down the incline, he could make out the details of the community through the veil of fog. The houses were arranged in a circle around the pond in the center of the valley, each facing the ice-covered water. Thin trails were carved into the powder that led to the steps at the front of each abode, with one track breaking off from the circle and leading to a bridge that crossed the pond against the precipice. This arched wooden bridge was assembled very simply, unlike the many ornate structures in the great Bronze City. Across this bridge, on a small island within the pond, stood a bronze altar to Brazdor, the Water God and patron deity of the Scaldor. The statue was unremarkable and crude but served its purpose as a place of worship for the residents of this village. The bronze was greenish and rusted as was the bronze on the roofs, for this metal was not enchanted like that of the capital city.

The Diarii snarled as Merasu lifted his hand, signaling the group to stop where they were. They stood at the base of the incline with puzzled expressions, Zano's gaze intently watching the six houses as a figure emerged with a slow limp. The Scaldor coming into view wore a long cloth robe of a rough brown material, with a tan sash around his waste. A turban of the same material was wrapped around his head, and beneath it was an aged face. His scales were worn and warped with wrinkles and clefts; his long hair and bushy eyebrows were gray. His lavender lips were chapped and chipped; his dull blue eyes laying deep into his droopy eye sockets.

The old Scaldor's leather boots traipsed through the deep snow toward the crowd, and his face hinted at great confusion. As he approached them, he seemed to realize that the dark shade before him was the renowned general Merasu. Even in this remote village, which was roughly a day's walk from the Bronze City, Merasu was quite well-known. For how could so unique a figure be forgotten?

"What brings you to Sotto my lord?" the man inquired as he knelt on the wet ground, bowing his head in a demonstration of inferiority. His voice was weak and worn, and the last letter of each word he pronounced came softly.

"I come on behalf of Lord Sila. He requires your assistance elder," Merasu answered politely, but in a strong voice. He dismounted and stepped toward the kneeling man. By his motion to rise, the Scaldor vaulted up onto his feet, sending bits of snow flying from his flapping tunic.

"What does his highness require?" The man's face was stern. He was honored by a request from a man he thought divine.

"Recently, the north has been conquered. As you may know these people held the Blood Scaldor in captivity—" Merasu explained before being cut off.

"Serves them right! Those abominations of our race should never be allowed to walk free!" the old Scaldor protested. His manner was ignorant and likely of a man accustomed to the norm. Zano slammed his foot forward with a glare but was halted by Merasu's outstretched arm. The aged man squinted and realized that the crowd at the general's rear was not blue, but a deep crimson. His face was flushed with shock while he stumbled back in fear, seeing the imposing look of the crimson warrior.

"These *abominations* are exactly the reason why I am here," Merasu replied sarcastically.

"What do you"—the old man gasped for air—"require of my humble village?" His eyes were wide and his nostrils flared in apparent fright as Zano held his gaze with a dreadful stare that would infuse fear into the heart of any man.

"His highness desires to make peace with these long-oppressed people. He has requested for me personally to give to you his ordinance."

"And what is that my lord?" the old fool stuttered.

"He has requested that you allow these troubled people to settle this village and live amongst you," Merasu replied calmly.

"You are asking me to allow these ... *people* ... to stay in my village?" The old man's remark drew an even nastier glare from Zano, who clearly desired to cleave his impudent head from its shoulders.

"This is not a request knave! This is an order. Either you take these people into your village, or you and your followers will be taken by me to the Bronze City. I do not see his highness receiving resistance well," Merasu snarled, revealing a less benevolent side of him than the one Zano had at most times seen. His smoldering, purple eyes began to smoke like blazing amethysts and his daunting mask gave the old man no alternative but to obey.

"For ... forgive me great Merasu. It would be my honor to house them in his highness's name," whimpered the elderly Scaldor as he bowed obediently.

"Good, then I shall take my leave. I expect no trouble when I return." He paused and glanced at Zano, then back at the Scaldor. "Farewell, elder of Sotto." His eyes dulled, and his voice grew calmer, like the voice Zano had come to know.

"May Brazdor bless you my lord," the elder said as he bowed so far that his nose nearly scraped against the snow.

Merasu turned, sending his robe whirling around his body and as he lifted his leg over the torso of his Diarii, Zano grasped a fold on his clothes and gave him a tense look.

"Worry not Zano. There are few of them and they would be wise not to attempt anything less than courteous," Merasu said comfortingly while pulling the rest of his frame over the animal's hefty back.

"Well," Zano sighed, "my people have not eaten in many days, and I don't suppose this village has much to offer besides snow." He released the black cloth.

"I will send a carriage. It will arrive in a few days. For now, you and your people must live on what can be spared."

"It would be greatly appreciated," Zano said with a slight bow of his head.

"I will return when I can. Do not fear his highness's city; you are welcome there. May Oblikaron guide you, Zano of the Blood Scaldor."

The masked general bowed and cracked the reins of his mount, sending it bursting from stillness and sprinting away from the crowd in an explosion of white dust. Zano turned, expecting to see the elder but saw that he already begun to slowly limp toward his house. Now, without Merasu to protect him, the ignorant Scaldor fled in fear of the warrior whose raging expression sent a chill up his spine.

Zano stepped forward in a huff and heard the rumble of many feet shuffling behind him. He looked back to see his people with childish expressions. He signaled them to wait before rushing through the sea of white into the circle of houses.

The old man was limping sluggishly across the pond, making his way down the trail that led to the shrine. Infuriated, Zano hurried after him with his right hand groping his blade's hilt until there, past the dilapidated bridge, the man knelt on both knees, gazing at the feet of the statue with his hands pressed to his chest. Slowly, Zano placed his bare foot on the creaking wood and strode along each plank. With cautious steps, he came up behind the man, who was deep in prayer and utterly still. A gust of wind swirled snow in a haze about them, as if to illustrate the god's anger with the foreigner's presence. Rather than leaving, he listened intently to the whispering prayers of the terrified elder. "Please Lord Brazdor, protect us from these godless wretches. Let my people come to no harm," the elder rambled.

"We wish you no harm," Zano said, attempting to speak to the man with Brazdor's heavenly voice.

"P ... p ... please don't hurt me," the witless old man cowered, grasping the foot of bronze with all of his might. It was at this moment that Zano realized how ignorant this man truly was, how long he had lived by his ways, which were too long-standing to mend with ease. He quickly disregarded the resentful words that had been said and turned to a soothing approach.

"You have nothing to fear. My people simply require a home, and the decree of your emperor has told us to live under you," Zano explained tenderly, trying to rid the anxious Scaldor of his fear. Gradually, the elder calmed, though his trembling did not subsist. With strained vision, he scanned the crimson hero, but knew not what to say, so Zano continued on instead.

"Do you see my scales?" he questioned, still with a warm tone.

"They are red ... like blood," the elder stuttered.

"That is the only difference between us. We didn't choose this fate, and though we may appear to you as abominations, you are no different than us. From your eyes, I can tell that you have lived for many years longer than I, so I beg of you not to live under a shade of ignorance."

"You people are godless!" he replied spitefully, reciting differences that he felt defined his perceived superiority.

"Faith in a god delivered us into slavery!" Zano responded, hiding the fury the old man's comment ilicited. "Should we pray to that which has devastated our lives?"

"You are descendents of the Deimor! Those demons conquered us once before, and you are no different!" the elder yelled, holding no regard for the fact that the Blood Scaldor were half his own kind.

"The Deimor," Zano winced, his eyes shutting for a short moment, "are long since deceased. Their blood may run in our veins, but we are not them. Believe me when I say that you may trust us."

"Demons are untrustworthy," the old man contested, still unwilling to believe Zano's promise.

"Demons are the spawn of the abyss. We are the spawn of flesh and blood. Your emperor trusts us. Can you not?"

The elder rose to his feet, no longer trembling. Because of his undying adoration for his lord, he had no alternative but to have faith that the Blood Scaldor meant him no harm. "I do not suppose I have a choice," he sighed hopelessly.

"There is always a choice. But thank you," Zano said, nodding approvingly, his cold face finally breaking into a smile.

"If I have no wiser option but to let you live among us, then I must tell you that your people will have no option but to work. Sotto hasn't the resources to sustain you all," the elder explained as he walked past and crossed the bridge, with Zano following briskly.

"We will work as hard as we must. I promise you this."

The elder did not respond and instead trudged through the snow, then off of the trail and toward a black spot on the wall of the rock face. Zano followed through a vapor of white flakes and stopped as the elder did, at the mouth of a gloomy cave just higher than his head. Flickers of orange light were all that was visible through the murky darkness.

"You and your followers will stay in this cave. It shouldn't be too unusual for people of your stature," the elder spoke bitterly and without waiting for a response turned to limp away to the entrance of one of the bronze-roofed houses.

Ignoring the foul comment, Zano went to retrieve his eager

followers and brought them to their new dwelling. Carthago followed in juvenile excitement but appeared to be disheartened when the dismal fissure came into view. With a gasp, Zano braved the cavern and traversed through a dark, damp tunnel at a slight downward incline which led to flickering light. His bumpy, bare feet slid vigilantly over the slippery, unseen rock as Carthago followed with his hand on his back, the rest not far behind.

After a sluggish hike through rigid rock, Zano emerged into a room lit by nearly a dozen torches. The space was not man-made. It was a creation of nature, a gap beneath tons of cold earth, large enough to comfortably fit half a thousand people. There were no furnishings, only spiky stalagmites and other speleothems jutting from the darkness, as well as other razor-sharp formations of solid rock. The hanging spikes dripped plump water droplets and a hot spring bubbled at the far end of the elliptical grotto. Zano entered inquisitively as flaming light dithered over his crimson face and the bright eyes of the crowd glowed with alarming radiance. He moved all the way to the bubbling spring and waited to speak until all of his followers were present.

One at a time, the Blood Scaldor filed in, their eyes scanning the fantastic formations of rock and squinting to see the thorny ceiling that hovered far above. Once the entirety of the Blood Scaldor entered the dimly-lit area, Zano began to speak as their undisputed leader.

"My people," he said hesitantly, "finally our travel has ended. Here we may find a new home. You have suffered and so have I, but now that suffering can end." His voice emanated deep passion and echoed off the craggy walls. "Now you have freedom."

His people stared at him, yet they seemed not to fully comprehend the meaning of his words.

"Freedom?" Carthago whispered quizzically.

"Freedom." Zano paused to gather his breath. "It is living a life without chains. I cannot say that you no longer will have to work, but merely that it is in your power to leave here whenever you may desire." His gleaming eyes grew soggy, and he began to hesitate between each sentence, overwhelmed by emotion. "It is no longer feeling the whip for breaking an unjust law. It is no longer living in the darkness of naivety and under a shadow of torture and death. It is the choice you have to follow me now, for I intend to keep none from departing if it is their will. I received my freedom long ago, but now all of you may live the life that I have led."

"We follow you," a man lost in the crowd of glowing red and blue orbs declared with a bow. The kneeling of every Blood Scaldor followed his statement, as they were ready to unquestionably follow Zano's lead. Unaccustomed to the world and with no means of guidance, these freed slaves had no option in their dull minds but to follow a man with a familiar life broken of chains.

"Stand," Zano requested. "What reasons have you to bow before me? All of you have spent your years kneeling, some longer then others, but that era of life is now over. I will lead you, but I stand above none of you." The crowd rose to their feet, though it appeared to be more from his orders than from understanding. "Here is a chance for all of you to start anew. It may not be much, but this is our home and what we do with it is not up to me—it is up to you. I can order and explain, but the choice to act upon these judgments is yours. In the morning we may begin a new life, not as slaves, but as a free race. Now my people, you have been through much. Rest, and soon our future will grow clear."

Zano's insightful words took hold of the crowd and he took initiative by lying beside the warm spring, ceasing to speak. Following his lead, not another word was said by the Blood Scaldor. They joined him in lying upon the rugged, hard rock that now served as their bed.

Blissfully, Zano closed his eyes and faced upward. Carthago gazed upon him for a time before falling fast asleep. The others joined them silently. Clearly, they were inundated with changes that they could neither explain nor understand.

Unlike the outdoors, the cave was warm and humid, with heat radiating from the torches and from the steam of the spring. Shadows wavered over quiet faces while the dimness made sleep easy to come by. Women, men, and children all slept side by side peacefully, in a place that, for the first time, they could call home. Though most wouldn't consider a bleak cave such, for these unenlightened people it was more than the shadows of the Desolura ever yielded.

Zano's placid slumber was disrupted when he was awakened by Carthago's whimpering. The boy slept uneasily at the base of his outstretched feet, trembling and sweating profusely, obviously suffering from nightmares not unknown to the memory of the hardened warrior who observed him. Zano looked around the room and realized that not just Carthago was in torment from the unrelenting nightmares of his past. Well over half of the Blood Scaldor were shaking, the worst in the youngest. Memories of horrid days chipped at their minds and even in the stillness of repose they were not safe from the agony.

A tear swelled in Zano's ruby eye as he recalled his own past, which was no different than theirs. It took him a lengthy time with Tarak to completely obliterate nightmares from his sleep, though he never was able to rid his conscious thoughts of the haunting memories. It was only when his master taught him to clear his slumber of dreams that the nightmares ceased and left him with tranquil sleep, purged of all but a blank void.

Gently he fingered the smooth hilt of his sword, as if caressing the head of a newborn baby. He wished more than anything to purge his people of their woe. Even though their hands were red with the blood of those who had enslaved them, he believed with all of his heart that there was no true revenge for what was done to them. To be forced to live as animals is a fate that no man should have to endure—to live each day knowing that you may be chosen for sacrifice to a higher power, in which you do not believe, is an unforgivable wrong. More than that, to strip people of their will for life—that is the most heartless injustice of all.

These thoughts troubled Zano's mind as quietly he rose and tiptoed his way around his shuddering people, passing through the long, saturated tunnel of rock. He exited into a star-speckled black sky, with not a light to be found save for the natural gleam of the jade moon. The village was in silence and the snow had halted its descent. The cold air nipped at his scaly cheeks as he traipsed past the green, illuminated houses as quietly as he possibly could. Tears iced over on his cheeks as he strolled beneath the tranquil sky and made his way up the hill to the edge of the rugged crag.

The crimson warrior stared off in deep thought across the gorge. The radiance of the moon was at his back, making him appear no more than a silhouette before its glow. Sparkling particles of snow drifted past him and the expanse of white reflected a dull, moss color. His hair flapped and wisped over his face. With a steady hand, he reached down to grasp the grooves of his sword's jade hilt, slowly unsheathing it from its ebony case. The moon's color glimmered off of its shiny surface and the diamonds appeared to be emeralds. He held it firmly, vertically between the intense concentration of his smoldering eyes, and saw his own reflection painted onto the swift blade.

Zano stepped forward and sliced his sword through the air with a low whiz, like a falcon through the sky. Under the twinkling stars of the heavens, his weapon twirled as he brandished it masterfully. His body flowed, as amorphous as water. His fingers changed position as though he were playing a flute, the hilt twisting agilely within tough hands. With low grunts, his imagination brought him into battle, where he whirled with unfeasible grace and elegance rivaling that of an eagle soaring majestically through a forest, lithely dodging each tree. His breaths were steady and quiet. The blade swung down, grazing against the infirm snow and sending it into the air with a wisp.

He raised the unblemished blade to the line of his eyesight, both of his hands firmly clutching the handle. Gradual drafts of steam emitted from his chapped lips, his eyes burning with spellbound passion.

"Zano is okay?" a young male voice asked from a figure shrouded in darkness.

The dazed warrior snapped his head toward the sound and sighed when he saw that it was of no danger. "Just clearing my mind," he muttered as he broke from his unfaltering stance and stabbed his sword into the frozen dirt. Fixing his rustled robe, he folded his legs and sat, sinking into the thick layer of snow. His robe was still stained with red and probably would never appear white again. Gently he rested his hands on his knees and gazed off across the shrouded valley, out into the star-speckled black horizon.

"What is there?" Carthago questioned as he took a seat on the natural blanket beside Zano.

"Exactly what you see. Endless black waiting to be absolved by day," Zano said. His unblinking stare was fixed in the distance.

The two grew silent, for Carthago followed Zano's actions and expected something to happen. When the boy's juvenile mind proceeded to get bored, he glanced around until Zano's sword captured his attention.

"How you fight?" Carthago asked with his eyes wide.

"This?" Zano smirked and placed his fingers on the hilt. "Years of practice and countless deaths. So you wish to learn the ways of the sword?"

"Yes," Carthago answered hastily.

"Learn to speak and read correctly, then I will teach you how to use this," Zano said. He pulled his blade from its icy holster and rested it across his stretched lap.

"You teach me?"

"I will teach you all. I hope that one day you all can see what I have," Zano's voice swelled and his fingers stroked the sleek blade.

"What have see?" Carthago continued to question, his calm, bright eyes staring inquisitively into Zano's.

"This land and more," Zano said, then paused pensively, "but now is not the time for me to tell you. For now, I need you to watch over the cave and rest."

"Yes master," Carthago replied without challenging Zano's response. The boy got up and began to jog away along the cliff's snowy edge.

"Carthago!" Zano shouted to the withdrawing figure. "Call me Zano." The young boy's black outline nodded and then dissolved into the darkness.

Unlike Tarak, Zano rejected the title of "Master," not desiring to see a free spirit bound. He loved his master with all of his being, but in his heart he knew that he had never desired that title—he merely hated his own name. Zano did not want to lose his name; it was who he was. This was the name passed on to him by a mother he had never known and a name he had no reason to avoid. Most who have dealt with death and that have done wrong run from their names, but to Zano it was his name that kept him as a snowflake unable to merge with the rest.

"There will be many Zanos before this world is dead, but there will never be another Zano like you," Tarak had said once during their journeys together. It was then that Zano began to realize how different each person really is. It was these words that bound him to his name. If you haven't a name, he thought, how could history possibly remember you?

Zano's gleaming eyes shut and he placed his elbows on his knees, his hands extending upward with open palms. He meditated with absolute awareness, long black strands of hair sweeping over his crimson face as he entered a trance of focus. Tiny orbs of flame sparked from the surface of his palms. They flickered like perfect rubies from the distance, standing out against the emerald glow of the moon. Orange light illuminated either side of his strapping face and reflected off of the glossy surface of his blade.

With his mind cleared of thoughts and his muscles loosened, it was as though he were no longer under the forces of this world. Streaks of white particles swarmed around him, twirling about his frame, seemingly attracted to his energy. The splashes of light in the sky sparkled above him as he rested in eldritch tranquility.

A BLIND BEAUTY

*"We are Windor tainted; corrupted by the foulness
of this land. Thus, our true magic deserts us, and we
are left, blind to all things."*

Visior, first lord of the Blindar

How does one determine the ever-malleable meaning
of home? What defines a place as such, even if it is
no more than a cave in a cliff or a box on the street
of a city overflowing with buildings? If such place is home to a
man, when it is within his sights, will his eyes light up like jewels beneath the sun's glare? It is more than just a sparkle in his
pupil; it is a feeling that runs deep into his heart and imprints
on the very folds of his brain. A home lost physically can never
be lost mentally; instead it will linger on forever in the recesses
of one's thoughts, only to be recalled if that memory is sparked.

What conveys the great significance onto the mind that
makes one place worth more than another, even if that place
is as shoddy as a bench? Is home just an area where you have
felt love and continue to receive it? Or, likewise, hate? Or is it

simply a place you may call your own? Perhaps the meaning of home molds differently within the intellects of all, and the only constant is the feeling one will experience when true home enters his grasp.

Frigusa had nearly finished running its frosty course, but it would not cease without a grand exodus. Outside of the cavern flakes of snow descended in heavy coats alongside threatening chunks of hail as tough as stone and large as eyeballs. The sky was inundated by gray, the sun unable to pierce the lofty clouds which unloaded upon the helpless terrain. Fog was so dense that vision was impaired, even if tiny bricks of ice did not pelt one's eyes. The Scaldor, in their warm houses, did not dare brave the outdoors and instead rested near toasty fires, with plenty of food to nourish them.

Zano sat, legs crossed, on a small, rigid pulpit, watching over his people with a steady eye. Most had already woken to find their stomachs growling fiercely and their bodies aching from writhing across jagged rock in troublesome rest. A constant pitter-patter reverberated through the grotto as steady streams of chilled water splattered on the unforgiving ground. The red-scaled folk roused only to realize that they were unable to venture out into the world. Secluded in an undersized cavern, they had to stay occupied with only each other. Their leader sat and watched quietly, his blade twirling gracefully, digging into the rock and twisting under his hand which rested on the jade hilt. Children whimpered because of the cramps in their famished stomachs and women fetched snow to be consumed from the dark maw's rim.

Zano observed his people at peace among each other, not knowing what else he should do. Hours of dark silence passed, and Carthago, for the entirety of this time, sat at the foot of his mentor, mimicking his stillness. At midday, a presence loomed in the cave's entrance. A steady, heavy step, followed by a scraping of rock reached Zano's ears and he sprang up to engage the intruder before any others could. However, all that he found was the elder from the day before, his hair powdered white and his cloth robe dripping wet.

"Blood. I need your aid," he ordered firmly and with a hiss, not expecting a denial to his request. Zano grunted as if to imply asking a question and the elder continued, "I need one of you to help me with a bucket of spring water."

In his wrinkled hands, he clasped two warped, wooden buckets by rusty iron handles, but before Zano had a chance to respond, Carthago answered elatedly, jumping out from the shadow and shouting, "I'll help!"

The elder shoved past and entered the grotto, handing both his buckets to Carthago, who grabbed them exuberantly. Unnerving glares swarmed the Scaldor as he passed through the crowd, an unwelcome feeling filling his heart, especially as Zano rested his hand gingerly on the handle of his menacing sword.

Carthago scooped water out of the steaming spring and filled each container to the brim. His youthful muscles carried them with ease as he followed the shuffling elder out into the blinding white. The haze was so thick that even the houses were indistinguishable, like silhouettes against an endless blankness. Frozen rain bombarded their heads, stinging with each impact, and Carthago could hardly keep his eyes open. His vision was reduced to a slit that could only see uncolored detail, so he trailed the sound of the old man who had braved this weather many times before. They trudged through the snow for so long that even the naïve mind of a former slave realized that they had gone too far to still be in the vicinity of the houses.

Suddenly, one of the buckets was kicked forcefully from Carthago's clenching hand, the impact sending him stumbling backward. Adrenaline forced his eyes open explosively and he quickly raised the bucket to block the blade of an impending dagger. The iron tip pierced the shoddy wood, and the Blood Scaldor pushed the bucket forward, sending the old man sprawling onto the ground. Newfound youth derived from hatred flowed throughout the elder, who tore out the iron dagger and sprang to his feet.

Ice showered down as he thrust forward at the beleaguered Blood Scaldor, who dove out of the way into a burst of snow and rolled back to his feet, attempting to find his bearings. A wood container crashed into the side of his skull, collapsing him and shrouding him with vertigo. He rolled onto his back, overcome with throbbing pain, and watched blurry spheres of azure nearing him. The shimmer of iron dashed toward his heart, but he grasped the dagger-wielding arm and with all of his remaining strength, struggled against the pressing blow of the elder, who snarled and gritted his teeth with unnatural fury.

"You will not harm my people!" the crazed man roared with bloodthirsty rage.

Carthago's muscles grew lax from the might of an old man who should have held one-third the strength he possessed. Just as the weary arms of the Blood Scaldor buckled, a diamond tip ripped through the enraged elder's chest and cleaved his ribs. Blood and bone rained on Carthago's terrified face, coating his eyes and flowing past his trembling lips.

Like a rag doll, the cleaved corpse of the elder was tossed into the deep white with a puff of snow and scarlet. Carthago gazed upward with red-stained vision to see the hulking figure of Zano menacingly towering over his sinking body. His chest heaved with iron lungs and his crimson-stained blade drooled voraciously. His eyes seethed with the fury of the heavens and his face showed no signs of fear or remorse. The plummeting ice evaporated before it could reach his rough scales and the snowflakes dissipated inches from his frame, unable to dampen the stained robe which billowed over the intense, dry heat he emanated. Fumes expelled from his mouth with each heavy breath, as thick as smoke from a flaming torch.

Carthago's stare appeared iced-over and his heart beat a mile a minute as blood seeped down his hair. A strong hand extended from the fog of red, ice, and snow, shivering above his chest. His hand of lesser stature reached up to clasp the out-stretched gesture as though it were the key of life.

Carthago's feet met the yielding ground and he wobbled, still in a drowsy state from the blow to his temple. Two dimming jewels of cerulean were visible through the gray haze. A mighty arm wrapped around his waist and pulled him along. The boy's rescuer was hushed and his nostrils flared wildly, a bloody sword in his clutch. They tramped together through an onslaught of arctic conditions. Ice dug mercilessly under the flaps of their scales. Nature's assault tore holes in Zano's attire and penetrated the tatters that clothed Carthago.

Barraged by chilled pebbles, they made their way until the damp opening of the rigid cave enveloped them. Snow vanished, and Carthago began to limp weakly, his ankle twisted from the hard fall. The passageway widened into the torch-lit cave, and inquisitive globes of ruby and sapphire observed their entrance. Both remained hushed. Carthago's eyes stretched open in disbelief, blood splashing on the cold rock in frosted shards.

Zano placed the young boy's exhausted body against a pillar of stiff earth and swiftly dipped his sword into the steaming spring water. Carthago grunted, exhaling deeply while his eyes finally rested.

"Are you injured?" Zano questioned.

Carthago shook his head, a drip of water leaking through the lashes beneath his one red-hot eye. Zano sighed thankfully as his blade found home within a sheath of ebony. He watched intently as the waves rippled out from where his sword had plunged. Blood followed closely in their tracks, dissolving into the heat of the spring and evaporating invisibly with the unremitting steam.

"You okay?" the gentle voice of a young girl no older than Carthago asked, emerging into the orange torchlight. Her lips were chapped, but her face pretty, and her figure was slender and immature. Warm, inviting eyes glowed from her emaciated visage and long, straight, black hair draped down over her bony shoulders.

Carthago turned his bloody face toward the girl and gave off a faint smile, his crusted lips like the plains of an arid wasteland. She reached her lean hand into a puddle that formed in a nook and arose with a palm full of ice-cold liquid. With an angelic elegance she rubbed her smooth fingers against Carthago's blood-drenched face, wiping off the scarlet fluid and scraping off bits of translucent white. The young boy rested comfortably as the graceful touch of her hand continually stroked his face with waking water and cleansed it of the gruesome fluids of a crazed old man.

Zano smiled genially and rose to leave the two in peace. He found the spot in which he had rested earlier and folded his soaked robe under his legs. He then crossed them into a meditative position on the damp rock. Seeing him sit, many curious Blood Scaldor gathered around their leader to inquire what had happened in the harsh world outside of this cave. Deciding to entertain them, he told of how he followed Carthago out into the hazardous hailstones. Everyone in the gloomy cave gathered in a semicircle around the storytelling; all watched intently as Zano's mouth shifted and a story was eloquently woven. His words drove them to disregard their starving bellies and to relinquish the thoughts of troubled pasts. Seeing the dissatisfied faces of his people after his short story was finished, Zano continued on about a battle he had fought within the icy depths of the Narsano peaks.

Throughout these stories, Carthago and the young girl did not rouse; instead, they sat with affectionate gazes. The girl wiped her bloody hands and picked a scrap of bone out from the slit under a scale on Carthago's cheek. Then, as if they had known each other for countless hours before, their scarred lips locked and held for a seemingly eternal kiss. Zano paused in his tale, noticing this, and with adoration for the newfound lovers, quickly resumed.

Their lips parted with bridges of lustful saliva and their eyes gaped infinitely into each other. Two sets of thin hands grasped firmly, almost like they were near death—their hearts near bursting.

"Carthago," the boy whispered with a desire for her touch.

She responded delicately, "Verana."

Passionately they kissed once more and held each other tightly, their hearts mending. Across the obscurity of the cavern, they appeared as only one, the steam of their lust ascending to the stalactite-littered ceiling.

Within the annals of Zano's memory, he recalled love; he remembered the soothing touch of a woman, but instantly he shoved these recollections into the caverns of his brain and went on with his storytelling.

The day passed and was followed by another. Snow and ice pounded the earth outside of the murky rock, unyielding and growing worse with each hour. The cavern was neither departed nor entered, and the Blood Scaldor slumbered in a plague of nightmares. Their stomachs growled, only nourished with snow and spring water cooled by the cold rock. Always, Zano watched over them in blissful meditation, his blade always in hand, anticipating Scaldor retaliation for the elder's death.

Carthago no longer spent his hours by his mentor's side. Instead he spent them huddled against a wall with his new lover, their forms fused as one amidst the dim shadow and their gaze held constant toward one another.

The Blood Scaldor shivered and their rags grew wet. They cuddled for warmth, and many searched for insects to ingest. The youngest moaned and coughed, but they had learned resilience from their many days as slaves. They were enduring creatures, the Blood Scaldor, seemingly suited for both slavery and battle.

The sun rose and with it came a sky clear of snow. Clouds floated through the air and no longer obscured the sky, leaving the sun's brilliant gleam visible through the thin entrance of the cave. A thick layer of snow coated the land with a pallid sheen and the air grew but a few degrees warmer. The change was unmistakable.

Zano sat quietly in the gloomy cave until the loud snarl of a Diarii stirred him. Sword in hand, he made his way past his sleeping people to the brightly-lit exit of the jagged tunnel. As he stepped out his vision turned white and he flinched, the intense light meeting his eyes for the first time in over a day. After they adjusted he saw a wood caravan with a leather overhang, its wheels fashioned of bronze. Two bulky, brown Diarii stood at its front, with straps hoisted around their necks. Sitting, with the reins in hand, was a middle-aged Scaldor. He wore a black silk robe and a straw coolie atop his short hair. Zano bolted toward the merchant, his feet moving quickly so as to not submerge in the deep snow.

The caravan rested at the peak of the incline between the cliffs, and the man stepped down, sinking into the boundless white, ready to meet Zano.

"By the grace of our divine Emperor Sila and the will of Merasu, I bequeath you with this gift of food and clothes," the merchant announced. He bowed as Zano came directly before him. His eyes apprehensively met the sword that dangled loosely in the crimson warrior's right hand, and, upon the realization that his sword was still in hand, Zano foolishly slid it back into its sheath.

"All of this!" the crimson warrior exclaimed. He gasped as he realized that the space under the canvas of leather was packed with crates of goods.

"As well as the cart and one Diarii," the merchant replied.

"Give your lord my humble thanks," Zano said with a slight nod of his head.

"I will indeed. Farewell Blood," the merchant said, then took his leave and unlashed one of the Diarii. He mounted the other beast's stocky back and with a modest bow trotted away as quickly as he had arrived.

Zano stood beaming, a chilly breeze streaming across his cheeks. The leather cover flapped and the Diarii reared, every strand of its fur swaying simultaneously. He then glanced down the hill and glimpsed three Scaldor, each middle-aged and with long black hair, treading toward him with their cloth tunics fluttering. The Blood Scaldor's smile faded and swiftly he slid his hand down to finger the smooth hilt of his sword.

"Do not worry, Zano," the man in the middle assured him as he reached his hand out and then lowered it gracefully. The battle-ready warrior eased off his weapon and his intense glare grew welcoming. "We know of our elder's death. Not even his wife could sway him from his shameful actions. The snow does not hold the secret of what he did and neither did the knife-pierced wood. Huldra, his lady, is now our eldress and she claims to trust you, so we must."

"Confer my thanks to her," Zano said, expressing his gratitude, but clearly confused as to why the wife of the man he had slain would forgive such actions.

"If this is the will of the heavens, then we bow our heads in friendship," the man explained as the three Scaldor looked to the sky and then bowed deeply. "This is all for you?" He gestured to the cart with a puzzled glance.

"My people have not eaten in days and they sleep in rags. Whatever is unneeded I will grant to you, but it is my request for you not to see this as an act of superiority but an act of necessity," Zano pleaded, realizing that these Scaldor felt a sense of jealousy that the Blood Scaldor received goods from their divine emperor while they had not. He saw in their eyes that, though they displayed hospitality, they still perceived their red-scaled cousins as inferior.

"I see." The man sighed. "You may bring the cart down to your people. Farewell Zano, and when the ice thaws I will hope that our people may merge as one." The three men bowed graciously and with distrustful feelings, found themselves back in the warmth of their houses, which greatly eclipsed the warmth of the cave.

Zano placed his hand on the hide of the Diarii and leapt up with ease. The creature snarled, intimidated by the imposing warrior atop its back, but it was calmed by a gentle stroke through the long strands of its mane. He nudged the animal with his foot and it began to trot forward. Clumsily, the caravan followed, its immense wheels thudding over each lump in the terraced incline.

Zano transported the endowment just before the gloomy entrance of the cave and halted the fatigued Diarii. With a shrill neigh, the beast lowered its frame for its rider to dismount and the crimson warrior yelled into the cave, "Come my people!"

Then, with a yank, he tore the leather canvas off to display goods. Dozens of wooden crates formed a jagged hill on the flat, wooden bed, each tied down by thick strands of rope. They were packed with not only food, but also clothes and other items. Some were filled with wholesome bread, not the sort the Blood Scaldor were used to beneath the shadows of the Desolura. There was rice, a significant crop in these lands, the color of light tree bark.

The Blood Scaldor exited the dark of the cavern and their eyes were forced to adjust as Zano's had. When attuned they beamed ecstatically. Food filled their stomachs, though they had not yet eaten, and their tattered apparel was replaced with clothes more pleasing in thought. The icy air chilled their bony faces and the breeze blew dust and dirt from the creases under their scales as they steadily emerged.

Eventually all of the emaciated Blood Scaldor filed out excitedly and circled the great bronze wheels of the caravan. Carthago and Verana appeared last from the shadows, and the boy exchanged a nod of his head with Zano.

"The lord of these lands has presented us with this gift. No longer will you starve, my people," Zano said as he scanned the enthused faces of all of his followers. "Now let us get these goods into our home."

Zano's stern face broke into a smile, followed by a cheer from the rest of the Blood Scaldor. In small groups, they grabbed the cumbersome crates, hauling them into the cavern. These people were working together for a common cause. Men lifted beside women, child with elder, and lover with lover, until the crates found their way into the cave.

As the last of them found their way into the shadowy tunnel, Zano stared at the one crate left out by chance. He approached the vessel, which was well-made with no cracks or gaps in the wood. He lifted the loosely-fastened lid and his eyes beheld a work of art. It was an extravagant suit of armor—a piece fit for a lord, not a wayfaring warrior. His eyes gleamed as he examined the folded apparel, which was forged of leather-reinforced bronze plating and decorated with patterns of dark ebony. Lying atop the suit was a letter written with black ink on frayed tan paper. Zano lifted it and read the fine script.

Lord of the Blood Scaldor,

How fares your new home? I trust that my people offer you no resistance. It is my sincere desire for the Scaldor and the Blood Scaldor to live amongst each other in harmony. I hope that these goods will aid your followers in this endeavor; however, this suit of armor, which was forged by the finest of my blacksmiths, is for no other but you.

The word has been sent to free the rest of the slaves and you are to be their leader. Do not willingly surrender this duty, for your people know not how to lead. They require you and so do I. You must know that I am unfit to lead the red-scaled and, therefore, I have named you, under the eyes of my court, Zano, Lord of Blood. This armor is for you and my people will learn to respect you and your wishes. You are indeed an honorable man, so my trust lies with you. When you receive this letter, I humbly request that you visit me. We have matters to attend to.

The gracious Emperor of Bronze.

Zano smirked as he finished reading, focused on the word "gracious." The emperor's conceit amused him as he creased the letter and placed it back inside the crate. He then picked up the armor and placed it on the rough wooden platform.

The breastplate had a protruding section over the chest and, emerging from beneath the ridge at the ribs, a rounded segment curved over the stomach, with a concave over the abdomen. Two sharply-cut pauldrons fashioned for broad shoulders connected the front half of the breastplate to the back, along with loosely-tied straps of leather down each side toward the waist. Lavish designs of black swirled around the front and back of the plate, and the pauldrons were painted white with the same red scales as the Bronze Kingdom's flag.

Zano glanced again into the crate and saw, folded at the bottom, a robe produced of exquisite silk, with silver bracers lying on top. Reaching in he grabbed the black garment, watching as it majestically unfurled. Feeling the sleek material, he quickly unfastened his belt and placed it down along with his sheath and dagger. He then tore off his blood-stained robe and stood, the cold air chafing against his naked body. Holding the garb above his head he hoisted it down, letting it drape to just below his knees. The soft silk felt incredible against his scales and it wasn't doused with blood at that.

Pleased with his new attire, he picked up the bracers and fastened them onto his forearm with iron clips. They were engraved with the same depiction of a dragon that was on Sila's wall, the silver smooth as ice. Approvingly, the crimson warrior stroked his hand across the bronze breastplate and raised it before his gaze. It was fashioned so magnificently that the metal was pliant enough to bend along with his movements without cracking.

As if in ceremony, he placed the armor over his shoulders until his head protruded through the hole for his neck. The leather interior comfortably fit over the soft silk and the plate fell down to just above where he refastened his belt and armaments. His brawny chest fit snugly and his stomach was tight against the leather. The pauldrons ended just under his firm deltoids, curving sharply over his shoulders. The bottom of the silk robe, laced with dazzling gold trimmings, extended out from his belt, expanding to wrap around each leg.

The Lord of Blood fixed the apparel so it was just right and shook his sheath so that it hung perfectly diagonal to the ground. Sunlight gleamed off of the bronze, which shined no differently than the resplendent Bronze Tower. Just like that, Zano went from being a rugged warrior doused by the stench of death to a dignified man with a regal appearance. Armor, however, could not change the untamable beast that dwelled within his heart. No amount of gold or silver could sway the powerful, yet honorable, soul which constituted his very being.

Contentedly, Zano traversed the dark tunnel and entered the torch-dotted grotto. The eagerly awaiting Blood Scaldor were quickly overcome with admiration. Their leader, now adorned with extravagant attire, appeared as grandiose as anything they had ever seen. At the same time, the crimson warrior was astonished to find that his people had not yet begun to eat or change clothes; instead, they waited for their chief to join them.

They had stacked each crate with great collaboration along the rock wall to the left of the spring and now sat in an outward-fanning semicircle, patiently wanting. Zano's still-bare feet gave off a quiet clap with each step, and as he came to the edge of the half circle he stated, "My people. The emperor of these lands was gracious enough to supply us. This food must last until we can provide for ourselves."

The Blood Scaldor gazed ravenously at their leader, but even through their unrelenting desire, they still respected his words.

"I must journey to the City of Bronze," Zano said. He paused and pointed toward Carthago, who sat beside Verana, nearly hidden within the crowd. Surprised, the young boy left the clinging hand of his lover and came before the crowd with Zano's hand on his lean shoulder. "This boy, Carthago, will be in charge of rations while I'm absent. Anybody who disobeys him will have to deal with me." Every Blood Scaldor nodded in understanding.

"Be scarce with the food," he whispered through into the boy's ear.

"Little food?" Carthago asked innocently, unsure of the meaning of "scarce." Zano laughed and responded with a soft pat on the boy's shoulder. "How long be?"

"Not but a few days. You'll do fine," Zano comforted him and then began to walk through the crowd, which parted at his feet. He opened a crate, which was stuffed with tiny bags filled with cold rice. He attached one to his belt. His people's eyes lit up and the muscles on their legs implored them to rise and claim food, but Zano motioned them to stay with a swift wave of his hand and, like loyal dogs, they obeyed.

"Each of you will share one bag with another. The bread will be split evenly amongst you all as the sun sets," Zano decided, and to these people, his will had become law. Back through the crowd he plunged, and, save for a broad smile toward the fervent young boy, not another word left his lips.

The sun's warmth licked his face as he departed the gloomy cavern. As though it had always been his own, he hopped onto the husky back of the Diarii. He then detached the reins that held it secure to the caravan and with a snap of his heels the creature snarled and began to sprint forward. Zano had lived and ridden with the mighty tigress of the Suvan jungle and riding a Diarii, to him, was as simple as the swing of a blade.

Like a blur across the white landscape they dashed, Zano's armor shimmering like a firebolt. His coal hair streaked through the gushing of freezing air and the base of the silk robe fluttered splendidly. The Lord of Blood, adorned with glossy armor and atop a stalwart steed, appeared to have the opulence of a king.

White hills rolled past, as though the ground were shifting, and the beast's sturdy hooves pounded through the deep snow, an explosion with every step. The sun idled at full peak, its blazing radiance piercing the clouded sky. It was then, when the shadows attested it past midday, that the brilliant pike of glittering bronze materialized on the horizon. The Diarii grunted, seeing its one-time home and Zano patted its thick neck, informing the animal that it could slow its pace. The vision of the great tower still brought a tingle to the crimson warrior's nerves, its splendor growing with each movement forward.

•

As Zano neared the Bronze City, a tavern through the west gate and in the wealthy quarters, known as "Beauties' Hand," was sprawling with activity. Foaming ale dripped through the yellow teeth of drunkards as they muttered nonsense. Wooden tables with matching chairs were set around the room, packed by Scaldor of wealthy stature on one side and those ragged and soiled to the other. A sizable man in a white apron, his belly as round as a dome, manned the stone bar on which bronze tankards rested. He shouted, "Freshly-brewed ale, three Bronka!"

Bronka was the monetary system used uniformly throughout the Bronze Kingdom. A scale-textured bronze coin was worth the least, a silver coin more, and a gold coin exponentially more.

Those not of wealth came just for the ale—a momentary release from their daily troubles through intoxication. They foolishly spent their earnings on a drink that could never advance them through society. On their side the tables were tarnished and the chairs rotting, never refurbished for those deemed unimportant.

The rich, on the other hand, sat on polished furnishings and were treated by waiters who retrieved ale at the whim of their pretentious stomachs. Through this mob of affluence, where the unfortunate could not see, was the real show—women. Not wives or daughters, for these people were forbidden from entering taverns, but prostitutes and an exotic lead dancer. They danced on a sleek, white marble stage to the soothing melody of an aged Scaldor's harp and never lost the gaze of their intent viewers.

The four blue-scaled prostitutes wore nothing. Their exposed bodies were more the show than their rather graceless dance moves. Their hair was black and flowing, and their bodies were thin and attractive.

The main attraction at center stage was a woman not of her audience's race. A deep purple hood hung over the foreigner's eyes and shadowed her face, with gold strings at the rim. Her jaw was slender, and her lips sparkled with a pearly turquoise. Her hood fell into two strips of violet silk over each ample breast and wrapped down between her supple thighs and up to her back. Her frame curved superbly and as she danced not a fold formed on her downy, milk-white skin. Wavy hair of a vivid turquoise draped out of the hood and bounced on her shoulders with each movement. Her lithe, pallid legs moved into unbelievable positions and her arms waved elegantly, with fingers like dithering spirits. Her shapely stomach was garnished with a tattoo of a decorative sun around her belly button and was of the same color as her hair.

Though her skin was unscaled, she performed, gorgeous and untainted. Lambent sapphire eyes drooled over her as she moved with an unparalleled charm, her concealed features amplifying the lust of her fans, who dreamed that she too would provide them with pleasure for a price.

Unlike her partners, there was no price to pay for the gorgeous foreigner, who abolished these men's racism with goddess-like beauty. She never spoke or signaled, only danced in a way that, if intently studied, gave off a peculiar aura of depression.

Drunken men chortled heartily and pointed at her with shameless smiles, wishing that the dancer would reveal the rest of her pleasing figure. Tankards slammed and ale spewed onto the floor, missing the lips it was meant to touch. For hours the women performed, taking routine breaks during which the prostitutes would take the highest-paying customer past an opaque sliding door behind the bar. The foreign beauty never followed them. Instead she sat on the cold marble, hanging her head in apparent disgrace and awaiting another dance.

The sun was preparing to descend,\ and the foreigner sat in the same manner, ignoring the taunting from aroused men. A stream of ale splashed at her side from the frothing tankard of a middle-aged Scaldor man who had encroached on her stage. His clothes were scarlet and made of satin. His mouth foamed with cold ale, which bubbled on his indigo lips.

"Fancy a round?" he said crudely, in a drunken stupor, and grabbed the wrist of the gorgeous woman. Swiftly and without remorse, she shook his hand off and nudged him in the groin with her elbow, sending him to the marble floor cursing while she returned her hand back to her lap.

"You swine!" he screamed, brown liquid spewing through his teeth as he brutishly grabbed her by the shoulders. Eclipsing her strength, the wealthy Scaldor tossed her off of the stage and sent her crashing through the edge of a circular wooden table, which shattered under the force. Her back was splintered and the cloth over her bosom tore. She yelped, but none came to her aid. The others simply cheered the man on, consumed by their tainted state and neglecting her seductiveness.

The man of girth behind the bar, who acted as though he were the owner, waddled toward the fray, eager to rescue his most lucrative performer. The inebriated man jumped off of the stage in an uncontrollable rage and grabbed the girl by the cloth on her front; it tore from her body, leaving only her hood behind. The spectators roared in approval at the sight of her stripped form, the ale exterminating any bit of compassion within them.

With a whimper, the foreign dancer grasped a shard of wood and jammed it into the torso of her assailant. Blood squirted onto her exposed body and the mouths of the viewers gaped as they rushed toward her, instinct forcing them to defend one of their own race. The man in satin held his side in agony, the wood fragmenting in his innards as he fell to the floor, writhing with pain.

Roused by the disturbance, the poor lifted from their tables to observe. Feet smashed into the side of the thin girl, who cowered on the ground as the provoked crowd blocked the owner from her rescue. Her cries were squelched by inebriated madness and cursing. Strong arms lifted her bruised body and tossed her through the bronze entrance of the tavern, luckily already opened. She tumbled out onto the patterned street, not yet fully cleared of snow and slid into the armor-clad foot of a soldier. The irate patrons of the bar piled through the door but were stopped in their tracks. The crowd that had been walking the streets near the incident swarmed around the girl and gazed on intently.

The soldier halted and he, along with twenty others, fanned out to keep every citizen near the foreigner back. Their double-sided blades kept the mob in check, but upon realizing who these soldiers guarded, they knelt to the ground with subservient *kowtows*. With his eyes fixed on the disrobed beauty, sniveling at the base of his robe, stood Sila, light glistening off of his sapphire crown and his lips smirking.

"Who is it that disturbs the peace of my city?" he questioned agitatedly, his fuming eyes fixed on the foreigner beneath him. She did not answer. She only proceeded to weep, her milky skin blotched with purplish-black bruises.

"The witch stabbed me, my Lord!" shrieked the satin-clothed man who crawled through the door with the help of the oversized proprietor, a shard of wood sticking from his blood-drenched torso. The owner tried to plead his dancer's case, but before he could speak he was silenced into a sheepish bow by a haughty slice of Sila's hand through the air. The crowd did not utter a word, their noses pressed against the powdered street as curious faces popped from windows on the lofty stone residences.

"Rise girl!" Sila roared, causing even the surveying Scaldor to shudder. She lifted herself feebly to her knees, her hood still shrouding her eyes.

"A Blindar?" the emperor murmured to himself, then ripped the hood off of the dancers turquoise hair. Her eyes were tightly shut, with streaks of cobalt emanating like jewels in a spiky pattern around the lids. An emerald tattoo of a crescent moon was etched onto her forehead, appearing almost mystical.

Tears flooded from her eyes and dripped to the street, melting the snow as they landed. Sila's people peered at the outsider, making every effort not to lift their fallen heads. The watchers from windows quickly hid, so as not to anger their all-powerful lord. Even the soldiers loosened the grip on their weapons and gazed upon the girl. Nearly all of the Scaldor present hadn't the slightest clue that the Blindar even existed and knew nothing of this mysterious female.

Infused with terror, she said nothing, even as the emperor reached into the folds of his robes and pulled out a dagger with a sapphire blade. "The punishment for this crime, foreigner ..." He paused and scanned his people, his heart warming when his look alerted their peeking eyes. The whimpers of the Blindar filled his ears and he finished his decree, "... is death."

The bar patron with the pierced body smiled pitilessly and the owner sighed with dismay as he carried the wounded drunkard back into the tavern. The Blindar scraped her trembling fingers along the street, awaiting her death, until a commotion broke through the crowd. Sila's head jolted upwards as he saw a crimson-scaled warrior dodge the blows of his soldiers and then kneel over the Blindar's body like a shield. His armor was glossy and bronze, the red scales on his shoulders revealing to the emperor that this was Zano.

Two blades halted at the Lord of Blood's neck just before slicing it and the soldiers wielding them cowered back at the motioning of their emperor.

"What is the meaning of this?" Sila shouted, baffled and overflowing with aggravation. The crowd looked on, just as puzzled as their lord and overwhelmed with the presence of two foreigners on their streets. The dagger shimmered, thirsting for blood, but the emperor stayed his hand.

"This is my lady. Spare her. Has she not been punished enough?" Zano whispered, staring up at Sila with his eyes shelled by tears and lustrous with fervor. The emperor bit his lower lip, not desiring to appear merciful, but thoroughly aware of the worth of the Lord of Blood.

"How dare you intrude?" he shouted, to the delight of his people. Before the Blood Scaldor could respond, he continued, "The punishment for you both will be decided in my throne room!"

Zano grit his teeth with rage, but his quick wit recognized that the emperor was merely helping him through a cunning ruse. The crowd, with their heads to the stone, groaned and cleared away, still craving the spectacle of death.

"Grab them!" Sila snapped with a swift grin at Zano and the guards hesitantly grabbed the crimson warrior by his strapping arms. Fearful of his might, they refrained from putting any pressure on him, allowing him to essentially walk at his own free will.

"Return to your duties!" one of the soldiers ordered as he hurried to follow the exquisite robe of Sila. Two more guards lifted the unclothed Blindar, their fingers brushing up her smooth pale skin, purposely not avoiding her rear or her ample breasts. Tears continued to flow from her fastened eyelids and her sniveling did not cease.

Fearing the wrath of their lord, the mob rose from their *kowtows* and dispersed, quickly forgetting the incident and the radiant dancer whose beauty enthralled an empire.

Shadows of the Past

*"The heart of a man is so very weak.
So easily it is invigorated by love
and even easier still it may shatter."*

Scriptures of Cathalu

It is revealing to ponder the effect a woman can have on a man—an effect so drastic it can turn any life in a completely different direction than was ever intended. So drastic, in fact, that it may even change a man's dreams. Countries can be turned upside down, blood spilled, and walls reduced to ruin in search of love. Why is it that a man cannot be as the animal is: instinctual, seeking only a mate for what is natural? Does his heart bind him to follow its whim even if it allures him to the frosty ends of the world? Must he go to a place far off into the barren reaches of existence for the sole purpose of finding that woman who will love him emphatically for the entirety of his life? Is it so unfeasible for men to live without wives or mistresses—to exist in a world where the opposite sex is seen as no more than a means to reproduce?

No, it is this precisely that makes the many races of Isinda more than just simple animals. It is the warmth of a lady's touch, a woman who, even when you are drenched in blood, would receive you with a kiss. It is that person who would follow you into the daunting depths of the netherworld, their hand in yours, who makes him intelligent more than all other things.

Zano neared the Bronze Tower as a false prisoner and memories flooded his waking thoughts. The world swirled about, morphing and distorting as though he were instantaneously tracing through time and space.

• • •

Zano and Tarak neared the end of their journey together. They had ventured through the Akai Desert, west to the Suvan jungle, north through the rugged earth of Human lands and finally to the icy home of the Sarnon. Years after their first meeting in the Desalura they left the frosted Narsano Mountains at the beckoning of a woman who honored them with a trip to her place of inception.

Zano had greatly matured since his liberation. His face had grown stalwart, and his frame was now sculpted with muscle. He wore a white robe with his unkempt black hair drooping over it. A brown leather sheath encasing a rustic iron *katana* dangled from his belt, alongside his crude stone dagger.

His master did not cease to age. His face was thoroughly wrinkled under the shadow of his hood and he could not conceal the deep cough that now burdened him. Even his eyes had grown dull, their luster sapped by a strenuous journey and countless days of life. However the robe of black that attired the Deimor was no different and his belt still held the ebony sheath of a jade-hilted sword.

They walked side by side, at the rear of a mysterious, but beautiful girl no older or younger than Zano. Her body was concealed by a loose-fitting navy blue dress, as plain as the attire of her followers. The back of the garb extended upward into a baggy hood that drooped over her eyes and down to the tip of her nose. Her lips were a glittering turquoise and her downy skin sleek. She led with her head fixed forward, not bothering to examine the world around her. Her bare feet progressed with unexpected grace, for it was no secret to her followers that she was without natural sight.

To their left the formidable Narsano Mountains of the Sarnon lands towered, their craggy surfaces buried beneath sheets of lucent ice. Their peaks punctured the very clouds and the sun's gleam could not be seen behind their immensity. Ice ran down toward their bases and then, suddenly, as though there were an invisible barrier, ended where the mountain sloped into amber grass.

The grassy land on their right was unmistakably the realm of Humans. When the almighty gods sculpted Isinda they left more than one rift in climate. There, the long period of Forunhor was in motion; the days were marked by warmth and arid air. The fields of tawny grass were littered with thousands of rugged rocks and engraved with many precipices and canyons.

The sky above was a placid blue, blemished by a few off-white smudges. To their front, past the robed beauty, an outlandish forest of curvaceous trees with indigo leaves no less ominous jutted out from the landscape. Past the twined trunks of the fringes, not an object could be seen. It was as though light failed to cross the threshold of the woods, or was restricted.

As the unusual group approached it chills ran through Zano's nerves, and Tarak took each step vigilantly. His head swiveled with every movement of a bird or rodent catching his eye. The girl they followed paid no heed. She was unfazed by the brooding forest that loomed ahead, perhaps because she could not see it, or, more understandably, because it was her home.

The canopy of writhing trunks bent over them while they passed through a partition of darkness, much like that of the ice and warmth. The air grew chilly, not quite as brisk as in Frigusa, but noticeable nonetheless. Tarak anxiously grabbed the folds of Zano's robe, but the Blood Scaldor pulled him forward, attempting to ease his wariness. The girl halted, nearly cloaked with shadow, and whispered, "The Dresvario is a treacherous place. Age-old enchantments have morphed the woods into a labyrinth. Do not lose me, or you will be damned to an eternity shrouded in darkness as unnatural as I."

Her voice was lingering, almost heavenly, yet it was unbelievably comforting. She had a spiritual charm about her, which could either be luring the adventurers into a trap, or quite simply the opposite.

"Lead on Suvia," Zano answered graciously as his lustful hand grabbed the cloth that encased her supple back. With his free hand he attempted to spark a flame, but the darkness stifled his powers. He felt the fire being drained from his veins, but it did not bother him. He felt safe behind her.

"Are you sure we can trust this girl?" Tarak asked uneasily into Zano's ear, his eyes rapidly scanning, awaiting an assault from the unfathomable dark. The elderly Deimor had traveled to the many reaches of this land, but his adventures and wars had never brought him to this place. He feared the black magic of these people, who had needs more sinister than Zano yet knew. He had hoped never to venture to their home, but the heart of his pupil implored him to the enigmatic nightmare. Cautiously, he clenched the Blood Scaldor's shoulder and with his free hand on his sword's hilt they took careful steps through the unseen.

Suvia moved with steady curls and ducks, attentively copied by her followers on a trail she seemed to know well. Eerie creatures cawed and growled, causing the hairs on Tarak's neck to stand at full height. Zano, however, was unbothered. His mind was too enamored with the girl who held a clasp over his heart and gaze.

It seemed like they had trod miles through the unknown,

past snaking trees and oddly-shaped leaves that unexpectedly jabbed out. The forest was so obscure that even the glow of Zano's eyes was squelched, and the girl he held onto was no more than a sensation to his fingers. Tarak breathed heavily, his hands trembling, revealing a side of himself his student had rarely seen. After nearly half an hour Suvia stopped, her bare feet sliding across the gritty earth, and her followers nearly trampled over her.

"We are here," she said, her voice deep with pride as her mind probed the blackness with intangible sight. Zano looked around, yet saw nothing. The home that appeared to her was undetectable to his simple, unsound senses. Tarak sighed, clearly feeling that they were either near death or hoping fruitlessly, only to be forsaken. Suvia's heightened senses felt their stress and quickly she calmed them.

"The darkness shrouds my home as well," Suvia said. "It is before you, but you cannot feel it as I do. Follow me."

Her tone was enchanting and though even Zano began to feel his nerve, they followed in a trance, unheeding to the wraiths which crept about them. Suvia tenderly grasped the Blood Scaldor's hand and towed him, with Tarak at his back, through undetected stares that seemed to be piercing into their minds. They were glares that came not from eyes, but from thoughts and feelings that mended with their own and formed an impression of sight. Had the girl not been with them, they would be passing without a clue of existence in their proximity, ensnared by darkness and a flood of fearsome thoughts.

Suvia's calmness was pacifying, keeping the shifty emotions of those tagging along at bay as her movements brought the two crimson beings through what seemed to be an organic opening. She halted them and tugged Zano to her right and Tarak to her left. There, she told them to sit and hesitantly they obeyed, only to find that they landed upon rough benches fashioned of tree trunks. Their heads searched in hope to see, but still they were enveloped by a smog of inexorable nightfall. Utter silence pervaded until, finally, it was broken by Suvia's pleasant voice.

"They are my friends. They will bring us no harm!" she argued ardently in response to a voice that no other could hear. Then, again, there was the same haunting silence. As Zano explored it, it was as though there were nonexistent sound waves passing between the girl and another. Through some mystic arts, she spoke with somebody of the Blindar race, not with words or expression, but with her thoughts. A convection of sentences was occurring between them on a plane unknown to Zano or his master. Though he could not hear it, he felt the words transferring through a supernatural realm of shadow and blindness. They could hear all else in the frightful Dresvario, but the Blindar conversation was undisclosed to them. Suvia only spoke aloud in order to help them comprehend the enshrouded happenings.

"Must we be masked from this world around us? They don't view me as any more of a monster than you do!" Her voice was swelled with detest toward an unknown being of either miniscule or tremendous strength. Waves of passion flowed through Zano's mind, as he could feel an impalpable energy coursing about the pitch-black room.

"Why must this curse bind us? What have we done to deserve an eternity in shadow? Our ancestors sought to learn and to explore. So do they. Shall we punish them for a cause no different than was our own people's?" Suvia snapped, accentuating her last word and then plunging into the abyss of telepathic conversation. Then, after a few moments, there was quiet on both planes and Zano could no longer feel the waves of emotion, as even the dialect of minds ceased to subsist.

Tarak and his pupil twitched when an orb of illumination lit before them like a tiny sun. The luster blinded them for a moment, the sphere emanating a light bluish radiance, but with adjusted vision they realized that though the orb appeared bright, it was quickly consumed by murk, now emitting only a

138

luminance much like that of the moon, but at a radius of only a few feet. Within its dull glow was the figure of a man with a broad jaw. His face was littered with creases and the folds of a hood hung over his eyes just as Suvia's did. His skin appeared azure from the orb's glow, though in truth it was a pale white, and his lips were a deeper turquoise than hers, more fitting for a male.

"My daughter is quite taken with you, though my comfort is restless," the man said with a deep voice. It was far more daunting than Suvia's and the fact that his visage was consumed by mystical abnormalities did not make him appear any less alarming. The aberrant orb pulsed weakly, revealing the shady Blindar and then blending with the stygian darkness around him.

"We offer you no harm," Tarak affirmed, his voice shaky, clearly absorbed with his fright of these people and this place.

"So I am to believe. Yet here before me sits a Deimor and a man with only half of the same blood. Even outside of these woods, your company would scarcely be accepted, so why come here?" He was baffled over the odd companionship and the half-blood race he never knew to exist. Zano ceded the right of dialogue to his master and intently monitored their words.

"I don't suppose I can keep my thoughts concealed, however, we have our own motives and they are no different than what your daughter said. I have no quarrel with you or your people. I only ask for the safety of my apprentice," Tarak said. He appeared confident, attempting to show the Blindar the truth in his cause.

"I will not prod your mind Tarak of the Deimor, only for your name," the Blindar jested, "and your apprentice Zano will meet no harm. My daughter has brought you here to learn, so I will not inhibit you from any knowledge you seek. You are under her watch and this will be the last time we speak, but know that if you are to betray my generosity, I will not hesitate to send both of you plunging into the timeless chasm of swirling darkness that is my curse!" Suvia's father sent a chill down the outsiders' spines.

"You have my thanks, lord of the Blindar," the old Deimor said with a cordial bow. He received a modest nod from the shady lord. A conversation passed through the leader's mind to his daughter, who bowed in understanding. She then took the glowing orb from her father's hands and, as quickly as he had emerged, he was shrouded by darkness. It was as though he had never been present.

Suvia stepped toward her company, her clothed arm visible in the azure illumination, but the rest of her no more than a navy contour over black. Zano attempted to speak but was hushed when she spoke, "Come with me."

//////Her voice was calm again and implored the two to rise. Tarak masked his fear as he left through the primordial gap, his heart pumping with mistrust. They pursued the blush of the sphere with foreign minds penetrating their own. Like a book, the Blindar read the inscriptions on their brains, partly out of curiosity, but predominantly out of fear. Outsiders were far from welcome in the outlandish sections of Isinda, especially in the woods of this little-known race. Here, over the course of history, had been done horrid atrocities—unspeakable evils to those uninvited. Even the mighty Deimor, throughout their grand campaign, strayed from the Dresvario, feeling a distress no different than what Tarak felt.

Wicked noises echoed through the trees, and the eerie leaves rustled as Suvia traversed the unknown with her company. Vile thoughts seemed to pass through the unheard realm, thoughts of blood and of murder. Promptly, the two foreigners comprehended that had Suvia not been with them to quell those ideas, their lives would surely have come to an agonizing end.

A hand brushed disturbingly against Zano's arm, and he twittered with a soft yelp as Tarak pushed him forward hastily, eagerly seeking to arrive wherever Suvia was taking them. The opacity of the forest was overwhelming to him. Even the orb was not enough to make it appear natural here, where the sun's gleam was interminably forsaken.

Suddenly, the gorgeous Blindar halted and said, "Here you may rest, my friends."

Zano and his master observed the area but perceived only black. Suvia placed the orb on the ground, and its faint radiance revealed two shoddy cots fashioned of straw and laced together with leaves. This was no tawdrier than what the adventurers were accustomed to, and they were keen to get off of their weary feet. Hurriedly, Zano collapsed onto the makeshift bed, detaching his belt and sheath and placing them at his side.

"Are we safe here alone?" Tarak questioned before he would take comfort.

"You have my father's blessings. Therefore, you will come to no harm. Do not be frightened of stirring in the shadows. I will join you soon, but for now I take my leave."

Tarak sighed and unfastened his belt, then took his place on the straw adjacent to Zano. He did not lie down, but instead unsheathed his sword and sat upright with his hand grasping the handle. His obscured eyes shifted but failed to adjust to the smothering twilight. Zano lay with his stomach facing upward toward an endless void. They could vaguely make out each other's features, the orb making Zano appear more like a Scaldor than one of the Blood derivation.

"You are here, Zano. What next?" Tarak asked somewhat sarcastically, his voice soft but stern.

"I had to come. You know that," Zano responded, seeking to defend his cause and unwittingly implying the strong feelings he held for Suvia.

"Relax, my friend. This is your journey, not mine," Tarak reassured.

They broke into intimate silence, unfazed by the patter that crept toward them. Silent minds observed with interest, prodding their emotions and their history, forcing Tarak to stroke his sword's hilt acutely while he preached to Zano as he had done so many times before.

"For years, we have traversed this land called Isinda, to all the far-off reaches of its vast landscape. We have lived amongst its diverse peoples and learned beside them, you as well as me. A flame burns in your eyes and in your hand. You have grown immensely since we began. Your arms are stronger, your brain swifter, and your legs more agile. I have seen a man who could hardly wield a stick learn to flaunt his blade as expertly as the grand warriors of old. I have seen a man challenge the Windor, captivate a princess, and quell the blight of a necromancer. Yet, most of all, I have seen within you grow something else: an impassioned love for this land for which you would undoubtedly die," Tarak said, his tone overwhelmed with vehement emotion. He had spent years watching this man, who began as an ignorant slave, mature into a renowned hero.

"All indebted to you," Zano said with a bow, unwilling to take sole credit for these alterations.

"No," Tarak smiled, but the Blood Scaldor could only faintly make out the change in expression through the miasma. "It was solely the feat of you. I spoke, and I preached, but it was received graciously by open ears. Always, I offered you a choice. Perhaps you never realized, but at all times it was doubtlessly there. There was always that will within you to accomplish more, to exceed my expectations, and to surpass me in every way. You chose to fly when I asked you simply to walk. You have grown into a better man than I ever could be."

"Why do you speak like this?"

"Zano. I am withering away with each passing night. Your energy—your essence is all that keeps me from eroding into the dirt, to be devoured by the unseen. I ... " Tarak trailed off, knowing he was far from immortal. He coughed intensely as Zano retorted, and phlegm swelled in his dry throat.

"No, do not say these things!" he shouted, his love for his master engulfing his feelings, forsaking reality.

Tarak cleared his gullet with a grunt and continued. "Worry not. I have days left to live," he said. The crunch of a branch drew his glare, but when he identified it to be of no concern, he went on. "I speak like this because finally you have made a choice completely against my will. You risked death and darkness for your own resolve and have been proven correct. I have brought you to all of these places, and in each, I have attempted to further your learning. I have imparted to you lessons that you have always comprehended wholly. Never did I plan to come here with you, yet here we sit in this realm of obscurity. However, here there is no lesson for me to convey unto you—no lecture that I have the aptitude to teach. You know the lesson of which I speak, but that is not all you will come to find here. I have implored you to be selfless and accepting of the ways of each race, but you must know that there are horrors here, terrors that you have yet to witness. Yet, if you see past these dreads, past this dominion of twilight, then it is here that you will find something as unknown to me as peace." Tarak paused, his lips struggling to find the word he sought.

"What?" Zano begged to know. He could predict the word, but he couldn't rest until he heard it from the wise mouth of his mentor.

"Love. The gentle touch of a woman, no matter how blind her eyes." Tarak's voice trembled. He had grown too old for love, its splendor constantly eluding him, overshadowed by a life consumed by war.

The phantoms in the dark drew close, absorbed by the manifestation of emotion between two men closer than blood. Their supernatural senses were enthralled, watching the growth of Zano, as though on a screen, through his master's mind. It was uncanny how, though they were blind, they could see with more clarity than the seeing—a clarity not with color, but with feelings and emotions, the very inner machinations of life.

"Tarak," Zano uttered empathetically, "love must not always be vested within a woman."

"I know. Amorq al uldark," Tarak responded with the sacred-sounding words of Desthoroth.

"What does that mean?" Zano queried. He was always eager to learn a new phrase from the ancient language.

"'Love is blind.' Surely this is true," the Deimor answered ardently, truly believing in his words. "as it has been conveyed upon me here in the shadows darker than the underworld. Do you love this woman?"

Zano hesitated for a moment to gather his thoughts then responded, "I have traipsed through the unknown and challenged this onslaught of black just to hear her voice. I have trusted her, risking certain death just for the feeling of her company—the mysterious sensation of enchantment that cloaks me while in the presence of her aura. If this is not love, then I beg to know what is." Zano's heart overflowed with the fervor of his thoughts. In his mind, she stood before him, drenched in light, beautiful against a snow-white vista. Her milky skin glistened under the sun's radiance, her lithe, naked body awaited his touch. Even in thought, her magnificence raced his heart. Saliva accumulated within the confine of his wet lips, but quickly he returned back to reality.

Tarak waited for Zano to come back to him and depart his daydream, and then he replied, "That is something I cannot help you with, yet your voice tells me that this is the truth."

"I have not loved a woman since I could only watch Miara choose for me to remain and her to die in the Suvan. Or before, when I saw the heart of that little girl I adored be cut out!"

"Miara did what she thought was right, but you did not love the girl. You loved a face in the moment. Despite how you might screen it, you love your people. It was your malice toward the man that tore out her heart, the realization that such acts are utterly wrong, and your desire to end such atrocities in this land that drew your love." The wraiths veiled by shadow listened closely, intrigued to hear what the answer would be to

Tarak's statement. A tear rolled from Zano's sapphire eye and down his lumpy cheek as he brought himself to speak.

"Should I return?" Zano asked softly, his mouth aquiver.

"We have spoken too much in the proximity of eavesdroppers. Your answer for that comes later. For now, ease your mind, and get some rest," Tarak voiced calmly, not seeking to agitate his apprentice any further.

"Yes, Master. You're right," Zano ceded with disparagement to his master's abstinence, though not without understanding of his rationale. Tarak shuffled in the straw and held his sheath to his chest before closing his eyes to darkness no different than his surroundings. The orb hardly served as the luminosity the moon would emit, but it made the sleep a tad more natural. It allowed the men to rest securely at heart and coaxed Tarak through an attack of potent coughs until his old bones quickly fell fast asleep.

Zano lay on his back, staring into the forlorn night. His mind was restless with visions of the unearthly beauty piercing his heart with her nonexistent stare, visions of the Blood Scaldor shackled and whipped, and of the little girl's dreamy eyes immersed in his. Deep within his spirit, he craved these thoughts, for they engrossed his very existence. The talk with his master had roused the entirety of his life and will before his obscured eyes.

Hours passed before Zano fell into a conscious slumber. His eyes shut, and he rested, but his mind was wary of all around him. This was how he slept, for in the flurry of horrific nightmares, his astute master sought to rid him of these burdens. In an incomprehensible manner, Tarak eradicated his apprentice's dreams, both pleasant and dreadful, and brought his resting mind steady tranquility.

Suddenly, Zano's acute ears picked up a sound that was very close in proximity; he stirred to a kneeling stance. He glared into the endless shadow and saw nothing as Tarak continued to sleep peacefully on his side, wheezing with each breath. Slothfully, Zano cradled the orb of light in his sturdy hand and stood. Sphere out in front, he shuffled across the ground, only a tiny aura illuminated before him. He heard a slurping noise below him, and, with his palm outstretched, kneeled to investigate the disturbance.

His hand scampered up a stream of silky cloth, and, curiously, he proceeded. With gentle fingers the fabric came to an end, and the radiant orb exposed to him what lay below it. His free hand felt a hulk of fur, obviously surrounding the muscular frame of some forest animal. He held the light to it and then witnessed a spectacle he had no intention or desire ever to see. He saw the mouth of a woman fixed onto what must have been the creature's throat. Blood dripped, glimmering with an ominous bluish hue, and hellish fangs extended from her mouth, sucking out the animal's life fluid like water. She was in narcosis, unknowing that she was being fearfully observed during her vile feast. Zano's eyes gaped as he came to the realization of who owned this face. His heart froze as though chilled by the ice queen's kiss.

"Suvia!" he gasped in panic and stumbled backward onto his rump, the orb pulsing on his heaving chest. Suvia unclenched from the creature's throat with a splash of blood that splattered onto Zano's face. She wheeled around with a swirl of air, her telepathy tapping into the alarm of a man she thought to be in slumber. The Blood Scaldor's lips quaked as he lost his ability to speak. His eyes were aghast and fixed dreadfully on the silhouette before him, blood glinting on his cheek.

"Zano!" Suvia yelled, startled and at a loss, unsure what action she should undertake.

Zano scrambled back, his hands scurrying across the earth in search of his blade. In fear of a monster, he unsheathed a sword, his master's, and stuck it toward the looming figure, the radiant orb in his other hand. The glossy blade glistened, and the jade hilt morphed like a chameleon to an azure hue. It trembled in his grasp while his mouth grew silent, and his body backed up against the straw bed.

Suvia advanced in a foreboding hush. Her robe was gray with shade and billowing fantastically. Her lips grew shinier with every step as the light of the orb made her outline clear, but Zano held the blade at point, ready to pierce her upon an attack. He was overwrought with his inner savagery, tossing away all counts of his love at the horror of the vampiric woman he only thought he had come to know.

She drew ever closer to the diamond tip, which pierced the cloth just above her breast, and there she stopped, so near death. Zano was unable to deal the blow. His body shivered, his arm seeking desperately to slay the hellish woman, but his mind remembered their bond. His psyche clashed within as the blade was held unmoving at her rapidly-beating heart. Zano gazed at her while her thoughts charily surveyed him. Her mind read his desire and realized that it wished for her not to come to harm.

Eternity passed, it seemed, with Suvia's life hanging by the single thread of a frayed rope. She reached up and pushed the sword away with the back of her hand. Hastily, Zano returned it to its fatal position, but the Blindar only repeated her action. This time, the Blood Scaldor huffed, and the sword dropped from his sweaty palm, softly banging on the dirt floor. His hand remained outstretched, continuing to be curled as though the handle had not vacated it.

Suvia knelt and grasped the shaking hand with her own. Her hand was petite and frail compared to the red hand that could so effortlessly crush hers.

"I would never harm you," she whispered angelically, quelling his panic with the mere serenity of her voice. He stared at her with the same intensity with which he had stared upon the little girl in the shadows of the Desolura with. Though the look was for a different reason, in truth they were utterly the same. His heart was slowly unfurled by her beauty.

"This is the curse of my people. It is my blight, but it is

me," Suvia continued, her tone divine and unerring. Zano's lips moved, but not a sound came out. His facade told his feelings with one thousand silent words, and she felt it with the inner reaches of her mystic mind. Her mouth gradually approached his, and it took no more than seconds for Zano to realize his fault in judging her. He seized her, pulling her with a mighty tug toward his face. Their lips locked with unblemished passion, her lissome body smothered by his pulsing muscles, which squeezed with savage lust. The heat of his anxiety was released in a boundless kiss, blood seeping into his gums and down his throat. His body steamed in the fervor of the moment, evaporation from his own conjured flame that was not quite ignited enough to cause harm.

Suvia's thoughts were scrambled. Her only sensation was the burly frame of her man, clutching her with all of his love. She grew absolutely blind, unaware of all around her. Her thoughts traced out into the empty realm where love conquers all.

Their lips severed with a hanging bridge of blood. The man's eyes gawked endlessly upon the lady's dazzling lips, just visible through the radiance of the orb.

Her feelings recovered, and she knew that the fear was vanquished from her lover's mind, that his adoration of her was untarnished.

"Forgive me. I know not what I do," Zano pleaded, near tears and unforgiving of himself.

"My love for you is eternal," Suvia pardoned him, no less enchanting than she had ever been. Zano's hand rose and tenderly stroked her soft cheek.

"We all have our curses. We all have our blessings," he expressed, his fingers gingerly rubbing the palm of her flawless hands.

"What is your blessing?" she inquired, her mind still too diluted to penetrate the barrier around his.

"You," Zano whispered with a smile, and in the heat of the words, she pressed her lips against his once more. They collapsed as one onto the straw, their mouths interlocked and their legs entangled. Zano's thighs, which were as hard as the trunk of a tree, squeezed hers gently as they wriggled off the straw and across the dirt with shameless actions.

They paused, Zano kneeling above her and staring down amatively into a sea of black where Suvia disappeared. He reached over and placed the glowing orb by her head so he could see her crescent lips, which were still shadowed by the hood of her robe. Delicately, he stretched out his arm and grabbed the frills of the covering. She flinched, pulling her head back to escape from the hand that would reveal her mysterious visage. Unwilling to submit, Zano gripped the hood again and slowly pulled it off of her face.

His eyes scanned what was exposed. Long, wavy, flowing hair draped down over her shoulders, taking on the color of the orb. Cobalt tattoos, as brilliant as her lips, spiked out from her closed eyes, and a crescent moon of dazzling emerald glimmered on her forehead. Her eyebrows were thin and no different than her hair, and, to Zano, she was the most stunning being he had ever beheld. Her mouth was crooked in uncertainty, her telepathic abilities impaired in this moment of myriad emotions.

"Beautiful," Zano intimated, overcome with the magnificence that could conquer a kingdom with its charm. The back of his finger amorously stroked her forehead for a moment, and then their lips came together once more. His scales bent against her supple white skin as their forms fused into one being of infinite affinity.

The black room overflowed with the vapor of their intimacy, which rose in a frenzied craze from beneath Zano's scaly skin. His powerful arms encased her so protectively that they eased her as she became nervous at the loss of her abilities. Her mind had gone astray in a sea of adoration from which she could not escape.

Time passed by, but for them, the world was still. They were lost in the nothingness that absorbs those who abscond all else for love. For hours they tumbled, her mouth moaning from their instinctual act, and his grunting like the barbarian he was deep within. The darkness, however, ceased to lift as they finally fell into slumber, their bodies weary from an explosion of vigor. Locked mutually by extremities they slept—Zano with the tranquility of nothingness and Suvia dreaming of the face of her lover. Dust swirled about them within the reaches of the orb's rays, rising with the steam that simmered off of Zano's boiling frame.

Shadow refused to lift even as the morning drew near. Here, in the aphotic forest of the Blindar, the nightfall was as consistent as the cycle of the sun and moon. Tarak slept soundly, his hair entwined with strips of straw. Zano lay bare on the cold dirt, his lover nowhere to be found. The orb illuminated the side of his face but failed to serve as a device for his awakening.

The darkness would have retained their slumber for hours more had Suvia not brought a hearty meal of some strange meat, which she placed at the feet of both master and apprentice, the heavenly aroma quite enough to rouse them. Their eyes saw nothing different upon opening, and with blind reaches they followed the scent to plates topped with bloody meat. Ravenously, like starved, homeless men, they grabbed the meat, which was fresh off of the bone. Their teeth tore through the skin, rending the tough meat down their throats. Suvia, who was now no more than a shadow creeping about the room in a convivial manner, handed a tankard of water to the elderly Deimor. Next, she walked over to Zano, who was absorbed in a feast as bloody as her own. His teeth were young and sharp, easily tearing through the meat. She knelt by his side and affectionately ran her slender fingers through his tousled hair.

"We are not so different," she whispered with a warm smile as she placed another tankard of water into her lover's firm hand. Not wasting a moment, he guzzled the refreshment before continuing in his repast of a meat that was unknown to him, but as delicious as anything he had ever had. He placed the plate down for a moment, but promptly found Suvia dressing him in his robe, which he did not oppose.

"So what next?" Tarak asked, lost in the endless miasma.

Zano looked intently at the beauty in search for an answer. He desired with all of his heart to remain with her, to spend his life in love and abandon the spiraling path of blood and death that lay before him. Still, though he wished this, he knew it to be unfeasible. Over his grand journey he came to learn that the hilt of a blade was all that was fit for his hands. He could not exist in the peace that he yearned for. His sword thirsted in the same way that the Blindar do. This was his curse—the blight that plagued his very existence and manifested on every fold of his brain. Without his sword plunged into the gory depths of an enemy, his heart was met by a chilling bareness.

"There is nothing for you in this place. I promised my father you would depart upon awakening," Suvia explained, discouraged over the fact that her lover had to leave so immediately after his arrival.

"But it has been only a day!" Zano exclaimed, his detest of the forest absconded by his adoration for the woman it detained.

"Silence, my love. I cannot disobey my father's will. Quickly finish eating, then we must head off," Suvia clarified, though she was clearly distraught.

Tarak expended no time consuming his breakfast. It was obvious that he had no longing to remain. Zano however, felt quite oppositely. He moved sluggishly, each chew elongated in order to extend his time beside the woman who had spellbound his soul.

As Zano fruitlessly procrastinated, his master gripped the lambent orb. Tarak searched for his belt, only to find his ebony sheath vacant. He chose not to question the detail when he saw the diamond of his sword glinting only a few feet away. He wrapped the leather around his robed waste and fastened it, then slid the blade into its sleeve. Suvia giggled, no longer affected by the happenings of the prior night. Zano couldn't help but smirk, even as he viciously gnawed on the meat, blood streaming down his scaly chin.

Finally, Zano finished his prolonged meal and solemnly prepared to depart for the light. He fastened his belt just as Tarak did, but his blade was already at home in its encasement. The old Deimor patted him on the shoulder, and then, with orb in hand, stood ready to follow Suvia's contour.

"This way," she beckoned and was followed directly by Zano, who took hold of her robe, and then by Tarak, who held his palm at the Blood Scaldor's back.

Suvia began to make way on a trip slightly less ominous than before. The unfriendly thoughts of the mind wraiths who encircled them were not filled with notions of murder, but instead curiosity over the bizarre relationship that bound the three. The orb faintly illuminated them, making the walk a tad more pleasant, but the feel of this place was far from mitigating. Howls sounded in the distance, and the wood's otherworldly ambience struck trepidation into even the bravest of souls.

There was no goodbye when they left the home of Blindar. Even the foreigners could sense bliss in the minds of the inhabitants, as once more, they followed Suvia exactly. Her every duck was mimicked, and each turn was copied with the utmost precision.

As distance was gained through the coagulated haze of shadow, words entered Zano's brain that instilled a feeling of dismay.

Return here, and you shall be received by the perpetual abyss. Release my daughter from your young mind, outlander, or may the gods shield you from my wrath.

The voice was deep and recognized by the Blood Scaldor, who clenched his free hand with resentment. It was not in his nature to submit. He would slay any foe to retain his woman's love. His heart was set, and he knew that he would never release her existence from his psyche. Suvia detected her love's consternation but made nothing of it. Zano realized that she had heard her father's decree as well but chose not to pay heed. She knew that if it came down to it, she too would contravene her father's will and pursue her heart's most crucial desire. Tarak continued to pace, ignorant of the cold-blooded pronouncement, only wishing to acquit himself of hellish twilight.

Finally, as though breaking through a fog of black smoke, the three emerged into the sun's brilliance. Zano and Tarak shielded their unaccustomed eyes, which were afflicted by a stinging sensation. The rays at first felt blistering across their bodies, even Suvia's, until their diverse coverings adapted.

It took nearly a half minute for them to fully adjust to this new atmosphere, and then Zano turned toward his love. He lost himself in the sight of her, picturing her face unconcealed by the hood that was now there. The glittering beams of the golden sun wavered over her milky cheeks. Her turquoise lips sparkled, and her robe fluttered in a morning breeze, absorbing heat with each passing moment. Once again, he was taken aback by her magnificence, his eyes immersed in the limber curves of her peerless frame.

Suvia's senses read each vibration that emanated from his skin. Her thoughts reached out with an unseen hand and formed his image on her brain, comprehending where the balmy light touched his scales and where it was lost to shadow. All else was indiscernible to her, but she could distinguish him as though she were not blind. Their hands came together. She could feel the heat radiating from within his scales. The achromatic visualization of her love embraced her with strong arms and became no more than a figure of intense radiance. His eyes smoldered with passion, and in her mind, they were as dazzling as two colorless suns.

His strapping limbs squeezed her, and she subsided into his heaving chest. She could hear the rapid throbbing of his tough heart as she pressed against it. His hands glided around her silky back, weaving in and out of each curve. She was tiny against his body, but he was vulnerable in her arms.

"I will see you again," he promised, with tears flooding his eyelids, his nose sniffling. His hand pulled back her head, and his lips pushed up against hers. She was lost in his kiss, her intellect blind, and her heart near ready to burst. The scales on the rear of Zano's thick neck prickled upward as his hands squeezed her supple skin, longing never to let go.

"I love you," she uttered softly as their lips released, still overwhelmed with raging emotion. Zano's hand fingered her cheek tenderly as the leathery hand of his master fell on his broad shoulder. The hand grasped with the adoration of a father, and Zano knew that it was time to be off. A tear dripped from his chin and splashed on Suvia's lips. There, at the edge of the Dresvario, their souls were intertwined their hearts were merged as one, and they were eternally engrossed in each other's love.

• • •

The memory was tangible to Zano as he entered the elaborate tower. He was overwhelmed with ecstasy that he and Suvia were reunited. His heart, which rested beneath a hardened chest, was finally filled, its missing half now returned.

Underworld's Swell

*"My hands blister. My back stiffens.
My heart aches. Yet here I sit. Here on the prison
stone. Was I not in the right to rebel?"*

Isitir the Dissenter

Nobility—it is the scourge of all great kingdoms. Thought to be their potency, it is this artificial belief that forces collapse to ensue. What mortal was born with the right to decide which man is noble, to decide which family embodies blood exceedingly pure? That these men may sit on their haughty rumps, engulfed by coin, is the bane of all majestic sovereignties. While the peasants grow weary and bearded from rain and from dirt, the nobility holds a whip at their backs. Engaged in backbreaking labor for hardly a portion of salt, these unfortunate men cultivate the land to produce all of the nourishment the nobles require to endure.

As the wealthy nobles grow portly, those less blessed are required to kiss their feet. It is this system of inequity that springs all rebellions. It is when the uneducated gain support from those who realize they could have victory, that revolution occurs. Never, over the course of history, have the allegedly dignified revolted. They have instead been the origin of it. It is their greed and corruption that force the deprived to the very edge of a cliff—a precipice where staying means to exist under oppression and grueling labor until set free by death, or where leaping and hoping for victory means, for a moment, that the peasants may become the nobles.

Thus, the cycle will continue, and the voracious will ascend. Once more, the few will hold dominion over the mob, for this appears to be the unalterable nature of intelligent life. So, perhaps, nobility does not spring from blood or the will of the heavens. Maybe, instead, it stems from simply being able to hold that status, to defend it along with wealth, against inevitable change. The succession of nobility is as universal as the shifting of kings.

Emperor Sila sat arrogantly in his exalted throne, the white dragon at his rear as majestic as it had ever been. Flickering candles imitated the sluggish ripples of the water below them, and bronze-clad guards lined the violet carpet, at attention. Their heads aimed forward toward the warrior across the way, and their backs were against the garlanded columns. Zano stood in all of his grandeur before the emperor, his armor suggesting his significance and superiority in rank to the guards. Suvia knelt at the base of the dais, not out of respect, but out of the bruising pain that scorched her exposed body.

"You have made a fool of me!" Sila roared, causing Suvia to flinch in fear of being struck once more.

"Is mercy impossible? Even you must know that this woman broke no law," Zano replied with the composure of a master strategist.

"Perhaps. Still, she lives, so why quarrel?" Sila groaned, clearly agitated that this Blood Scaldor had persuaded him, but eager to move past the tumultuous happenings.

"I thank you for your compassion," Zano said with a bow more gracious than he had ever offered before.

"Do not defy my authority again. My people hold an image of me, and compassion toward an outsider, let alone two, will not bode well," the emperor ordered nervously.

"We will cause no more trouble. You invited me here. What need you?" Zano asked, quickly attempting to change the subject.

"Well," Sila sighed, "how suits your armor?"

"Perfect fit," Zano smiled, easing the emperor away from irritation.

"Good. And Sotto?"

"No problems to speak of. However, with more Blood Scaldor en route, our dwelling is a bit undersized."

"I will see to a shipment of wood, cloth, armor, and weapons."

"Armor and weapons?"

"As I said earlier, if you and your people are permitted to reside within my kingdom, then you must aid it. You will train and lead a regiment of Blood Scaldor, as well as assist the natives of Sotto in putting together a more lucrative settlement," Sila demanded.

"My people have only recently been freed. They tremble in their dreams. We dwell within a sodden cave. With thousands more on the way, the cave will grow obsolete, and we will be forced to build our own abodes. Still, you want an army?"

"The nobles will take umbrage with me if you cannot provide. I will attempt to aid in any way that I can. Hopefully, your people hold the same vigor as you. You may depart; I have asked of you what I intended. Do not betray my generosity, Lord of Blood," Sila warned, seeking not to supply Zano with too much influence in his lands. He then slouched into his throne, resting his head on the smooth bronze.

"My eyes will wait on the horizon, Sila," Zano said, then hardly bowed. He was disgruntled with his task, but realized that this was the only option.

The Lord of Blood wrapped his mighty arm around Suvia's

waist and aided in her steps. Her senses failed, as overcoming pain was all that she felt. Her sniffles saddened Zano, who realized that she knew not who clutched her so tenderly. The guards stared at them with swiveling heads, impressed with the opulent appearance of the crimson-scaled warrior before them. Their eyes unfolded over the unparalleled beauty of the bare woman who was so minuscule in his grasp.

The massive gates of embellished bronze swung open to the lift, where in the center stood a familiar figure. His black robe felt no breeze, and his purple eyes blazed beneath an iron mask. His demeanor was as imposing as the shadows that wavered over his frame, empowering him with dread.

"The Lord of Blood," Merasu greeted with an unusually alluring tone and appreciation for the title. Astonishingly, he paid no heed to the stripped Blindar, whose succulent body was a feast for the eyes of most men. The doors slammed shut, and the room grew dark, illuminated only by torches along the walls of the domed ceiling.

"Merasu," Zano struck his own chest in salute.

Chains began to rattle and scrape, and a violent tremor set the lift in motion. Steadily, it made its way down the stone-walled tube with a deafening clamor.

"You look unusually ... stately," Merasu mused.

"And you deathly," Zano said, feigning sincerity, then broke out into a laugh. He was joined by the black figure, who chortled heartily.

"Nice to see you again."

"And you. Where do we go?" Zano queried as he squeezed Suvia due to a shudder of the wood floor.

"Deep into the earth," Merasu answered.

"Is it your home?" Zano asked with a smile.

The lift continued deeper into the earth than the crimson warrior had ever braved. Suvia collapsed onto her rear, baffled over the occurrences. It grew utterly dark, almost fitting for her homeland. The stone walls morphed to solid rock, carved only for the platform to be able to fit. Suddenly, the floor jerked, and the crackle of iron ceased. The motion subsided, and Zano grasped his love to raise her.

"This way," Merasu beckoned.

He took a few steps forward, then stopped to unfasten a barely visible gate of corroding wood. The doors swung open, the sound of rushing water and the clank of pickaxe against rock meeting Zano's ears as they walked out into an almost surreal world. Thousands of torches lit the caverns below, revealing a place fit only for demons. The ceiling was littered with stalactites and other formations, atop which the Bronze Tower rested. Water cascaded through slits above, tearing a path through the craggy walls, then down into a gash in the terrain—a gargantuan pit of endless black that extended into the very depths of the underworld. Endless water flooded down this cavity, so unfathomably deep that after years of filling, no amount of liquid was visible.

Wooden pathways lined the cavernous walls, each leading up to the lift, which was a vast distance from the farthest plank. Many thousands of male Scaldor lined the walkways, each with shovel and pickaxe. Zano then realized that the reason why flame glittered off the walls was because they were not made of rock. No, they were made of glossy bronze, which to him was nonsensical, because bronze did not naturally exist. Still, there it was, millions of tons of the metal without any need to be fashioned of alloys.

The Scaldor workers smashed the metal, attempting to extract each inch of bronze for the kingdom. They were soiled, nearly unrecognizable under the layer of black soot. Many were naked, while others wore rags that could hardly be classified as clothing. The walkways were patrolled by a constant flow of guards, who brandished whips and batons of bronze.

"Welcome to the Water God's Forge. They say that one day Brazdor spilled blood onto gold and fell in love with the chestnut gleam, that with divine hands he morphed the rock beneath his city into solid bronze. There was no need to mix metals, for they were mystically blended into this vast sea of shimmering crimson-gold. It shines fantastically, more pure of luster and color than properly-formed bronze. Brazdor called his metal Braz, in honor of himself, but over the ages, people have eradicated the name in exchange for a more familiar term. Other kingdoms covet this one for its unending surplus, and calling it bronze alleviated our ability to hold leverage. Centuries of mining have twisted this cavern into another world entirely," Merasu explained, amazed by his own words.

Zano stepped out to the edge of a cliff, his arms clasping Suvia tighter than before. He glared out into the distance and then down the endless pit, which piqued his curiosity.

"They unearthed this pit, into which I have seen men fall. It is boundless, like an abyss that sucks you in with no means of escape," Merasu continued his lesson.

Zano observed these laborers with utmost pity. They appeared to be emaciated, their muscles burning from the constant swing of their tools. Any who took an unauthorized break was whipped or beaten back into work. Their scales were torn and scarred, and their expressions seemed to relinquish life.

"Are they slaves or criminals?" Zano asked restlessly, his heart reaching out for their anguish. He knew well the torment of slave labor, and it sickened him to see it done to another.

"They are the men who have nothing else, who do not garb themselves in armor and who do not have the aptitude to forge or to farm," Merasu expressed somberly.

"They work for nothing!" Zano shouted, his words reverberating off of the empty vastness.

"They live in this hell for sometimes days at a time. Their pay is food and what little bronze they can salvage, which is scarce enough to feed any man, let alone his family. Since Sila took the crown, thousands more of these "miners" have been added. They are pushed to the brink of death, and some even choose to brave the black pit rather than to subsist."

"And he calls himself a god. All that's left is a sacrifice in his name!"

"All for the greater good," the black general said sarcastically.

"Are weapons and armor worth this? Such a wealth is unnatural," Zano said, and his lower lip quivered.

"All this is necessary for the unification of the Scaldor. Only this kingdom is blessed with such an abundance of material. Our troops never wear worn armor to battle. Their weapons are at all times kept unsullied. Sila has taken this kingdom from being weak at its knees to being all-powerful. We are mere months away from the unification of the kingdoms."

"Yes," Zano sighed weakly, "that is commendable. His cause is dignified, but his means are ruthless."

"The world is ruthless, Zano. Surely you know this," Merasu preached, much like Zano's old master once did.

"Why, then, have you brought me to this ghastly place?" Zano asked dispiritedly.

"To show you this. Realize that you may see my lord do horrid things. You will see him be cold-blooded. They are all necessary evils for him to bring his dream to fruition. Do not lose heart in your service, for kings die, but dreams do not," Merasu said, and his wise tone comforted Zano. The masked general knew that this sight disheartened the Lord of Blood but wanted to be there when Zano first witnessed it. It is said that the right words at a single instance can change the course of history.

"Let us depart. I cannot bear to linger here any longer."

"Go on. I will have the lift take you up," Merasu gave his farewell.

"What of you?" Zano questioned with worry.

"It is beautiful here. Is it not?" Merasu admired the place of malady and shadow.

"No." Zano gave off a nervous smirk. "Farewell," he said and bowed genially.

Merasu returned the gesture, and Zano turned with his woman in hand. He wondered who the masked man could be.

He knew not of any race that contained eyes of violet and had never seen any of the general's other features. He speculated over what kind of person could wish to loiter in this murky subterranean world that smelled of rotting flesh. With no answers coming to mind, he simply shirked the thought and entered the dim lift.

Suvia had yet to come to the realization that the man who shielded her was a heart she had once touched. Zano stroked her smooth back, running his fingers gently down the groove of her spine. The lift halted, and they entered the long, lustrous marble hallway. Soldiers entered and exited bronze doors, almost completely ignoring the foreigners, except for an occasional glance at Suvia's bosom. They reached the gated exit and were greeted by two guards with the usual gritty appearance.

"My lord wishes us to escort you to the city walls," one guard said snobbishly.

"As you wish," Zano answered with a respectful bow, unaffected by the soldiers' disapproving manor.

The gates opened up to a pleasant day of late Frigusa. The sky was vast and blue. The sun beamed with concentration, unblemished by clouds, and the city streets were lively once more with silk-garbed men and women strolling the streets without a care in the world. Their eyes met the convoy rejectingly, but they were unwilling to make a gesture that would defy their emperor's will.

The guards and their followers passed into the slums, where Zano found a reinforced pity for the deprived Scaldor who resided there. They were muddied, with expressions of forlornness. They were uncared for, forced to live through performing the jobs the wealthy never dreamed of doing.

The group reached the western side of the towering wall, which wore a hat of snow but appeared as sturdy as a mountain. The crosshatched gates of iron stood firm to the ground, impossible to lift with simple, brute strength.

"Here is your exit, Blood," one of the guards said with a supercilious tone, then arrogantly walked away with his partner.

Zano stared at the massive gateway. It began to rise by the revolving of an enormous wood wheel. Gears turned with creaks and snaps, and the iron gate lifted into a slit in the stone. The Diarii he had left with the gatekeeper was no longer present. He assumed it had been stolen or returned to the Scaldor.

So, without dispute, he crossed the threshold of the Bronze City with his stunning love embraced beneath his burly arm.

The sun's warmth enveloped them now, without the shade offered by structures. Farm land was still vacant, and before them laid endless fields of snow, punctured by icy rocks. It was infrequent that a day without precipitation passed in the land of the Scaldor, and a gentle wind swathed him. He gazed out into the azure horizon, his bare feet sinking forward into the deep, arctic white.

•

Back at the Bronze Tower Sila sat on his grand bed of silk sheets and curtains. In his personal chambers, he could not be bothered. He could only be pacified by the presence of such abounding luxury and affluence. The bronze- and gold-crested walls, silk banners bearing the symbol of his sovereignty, and the ornate window that looked out upon his city from its lofty perch with the sound of rushing water outside. His eyes were glazed as he remembered the blood which once stained the now glossy, marble floor. He stroked the smooth edge of his sapphire dagger, tossing it to the side hurriedly as he heard a knock at his elaborate gold door.

"My Lord, the concubine has arrived," a guard announced.

"Send her in," Sila said and rose to his feet, his white night-robe unfurling to the floor. He gazed out the window at the twilight sky with the sun just falling beneath his great walls. A woman stepped quietly into the room, and he turned to behold her.

"You are beautiful," he said, and smiled compassionately. She was young, but he had a fancy for girls who hadn't yet been corrupted by the world. Her face was gaunt, her lissome frame worthy of an emperor, but she had yet to fully develop the features of a woman.

Sila scanned her naked body with a grin and invited her over to his bed. Without a quarrel, she sat, carefully eyeing the glinting dagger against the gold-trimmed pillows.

"It is an honor to be before you, esteemed one." She bowed subserviently, but Sila hushed her and laid her down with his palm. She breathed rapidly as he caressed her slender legs and began to kiss her. Slowly, he stripped off his garb and placed himself over her, ready to perform the profane action she hadn't yet experienced in her short life.

"Gedima…" he groaned in a trancelike state, but just before he could consummate, she yelped and slapped him across the face. Quickly, he stirred from his daze, glaring at her.

"What are you doing to me?" she yelled, but then she realized what she had done. Sila held her down and continued as she screamed in pain, yelling for him to stop, but the emperor could not be dissuaded until she slapped him again. His eyes seared with rage, and he tossed her off of the bed.

"You bitch! How dare you deny me!" he roared and sprang up, wielding the dagger in his right hand. She crawled, crying, up against the wall beneath the window.

"Forgive me, my Lord," the girl sniveled as Sila hoisted her up and glared into her eyes. Through the blue of his pupils, she noticed a dormant fury—a deep-seated loathing that had been sealed away. Once she realized this, she knew that death was not far away. The dagger was rammed into her thigh, and she shrieked before tumbling backward out of the window. Her cries stopped with a soft splash of water.

"Gedima… Gedima…" Sila sobbed, throwing the dagger

at the wall in a huff. He ran his fingers through a pool of scarlet blood. His head fell back against the wall, his eyes staring ahead.

"My Lord, is everything all right?" a guard outside questioned worriedly.

"Everything is fine!" Sila bellowed, caressing his temples, which were lined with bulging veins. He glanced at the sapphire blade jutting out from a painting on the wall. It had pierced a portrait of a beautiful woman directly through the eye, and there it remained. He pulled himself up by the windowsill and shuffled over, his tense breathing beginning to calm.

"Gedima," he said, stroking the hair of the painted woman. She was exceedingly elegant, fit for the hand of even the most prestigious of lords. With a snarl, he ripped the dagger out and held it before his gaze, looking into the reflective surface. There was a splatter of blood on his scaly cheek. His lambent eyes were drawn back, his hair messily swept over them.

"Is this how you felt too, father? To be so near to Brazdor...Now I understand." The emperor sighed and shut his eyes, obsessively fondling his dagger's sleek blade as he paced across his chamber.

Zano and Suvia were well on their way when Merasu ascended the illustrious Bronze Tower. The emperor's hall unveiled itself through the masterful gates, and there sat Sila in all of his infinite glory. There was pain in his countenance. Halos of black were traced around his eyelids, and a few specks of crusted blood were sprinkled on the side of his face.

The masked general walked impressively down the aisle of shimmering guards, his black robe flapping and tossing around his unseen frame. Sila nodded with the pomposity of a man of divinity, refusing to look into the eyes of his subordinates. He opened his mouth to initiate conversation but was interrupted by a frantic guard bursting into his serene hall.

"I bring news!" he yelled, panting heavily. It was one of the guards who had escorted Zano out of the city. Merasu wheeled around to see the intruder, and Sila's expression quickly grew irate.

"Spit it out, knave!" he roared, his sapphire eyes fuming with rage over the sudden interruption. The guard gathered his breath, and after a deep inhale answered his enraged lord.

"I passed by the Great Temple of Brazdor and overheard the Archpriest speaking *treacherously*," he said, then stopped out of fear of the emperor's wrath. Beckoned to continue by Sila's stern look, he went on. "He said that you are a traitor for allowing foreigners to peacefully walk these streets. That ... that you are an imposter to the blood of Brazdor." The guard awaited the reaction with a wince.

The emperor steamed, his fists clenching. Uncontrollable energy seemed to be bursting from his eyes, but he collected himself.

"You speak the truth?" Sila demanded with an unruffled, staid tone.

"Every word, my Lord. On my life," the guard stammered fearfully, though he appeared to be honest.

The emperor pensively stroked his chin, attempting to find a solution to the insubordinate words of a religious official. Merasu gazed at him intently, having already predicted the impending verdict.

"Merasu, I believe I have a solution to this recent ... dilemma," Sila said bitterly.

"Go on," Merasu coerced, with a witty glint in his spheres of lavender.

Sila peered around the room, meeting the terrified stare of the guard. He wished to aggrandize his prestige in the moment, before announcing his decree.

"Religion gives those without it hope. If we are to secure our position, then we must grasp it by the throat. We must hold dominion over every facet of the temple. Akul has held his position since my father ruled this kingdom, but the winds have changed, and so must the Temple of Brazdor. Merasu, I have a task for you. Come closer," Sila demanded. By the gesture of Sila's hand, the masked general advanced until no other inquiring ears could hear.

"Take a company of soldiers to the Great Temple. The Archpriest Akul has lived long enough. Slaughter him and his entourage of priests. Then, I will name you in his stead. I cannot have these dissenters swaying the minds of my people any longer. Can I trust you with this?" Sila whispered directly into his general's wary ear. His orders were without remorse—callous toward a priest who had served properly since his father was young.

"Yes," Merasu responded hastily and heartlessly while he blithely fingered the black hilt of his menacing blade.

"Leave none present alive."

Merasu bowed. His eyes were no different than Zano's when he returned to those who had enslaved him. With his ironclad hand around the handle of his sword, he took heavy steps out of the throne room, nodding cruelly at the intruding guard. Sila held an iniquitous smile as his reaper departed to further augment the power he hungered for.

Merasu stood camouflaged in the dark lift, staring up toward the roof of the tower. "Oblikaron, forgive me for my service to a false god," Merasu prayed, showing a sense of repentance, which he rarely expressed. "Yes, you are right. The Temple of Brazdor will only serve to further our cause." He spoke to an unheard voice within his mind.

Night shrouded the great city. Stars flickered above its infrastructure, the moon illuminating the blackened sky with its jade hue. The streets were silenced, especially on the eastern portion near the Temple—a structure superior to every other in close proximity. It was plated with garlanded bronze, reflecting the many anomalies of the night sky. Sculptures of Brazdor were impressed into the walls, which were littered with fabulous stained glass windows. They depicted scenes from ancient battles and of the god himself, who was always shown encased by water. The bronze, tiled roof was sharply-pointed, with a bell tower protruding from its center. Stealthily, a black wraith creaked through the massive golden doors that held the same design as the entrance of the extraordinary tower, which over-shadowed the temple.

Inside was a place of redemption and of utter serenity, with a vaulted roof lined with an unmoving sheet of shimmering water. On the right and left were gold statues, figures of lesser importance pressed against the vast murals of painted glass. At the other end, across a scarlet-carpeted aisle, through marble benches, was a small set of stairs. On its crest stood an ornate, bronze sculpture of the god of water himself, garbed in an orna-mented robe. It was so finely chiseled that it appeared to be a real man frozen in metal, though it ascended to a height no mortal could attain. It stood upright, its eyes peering off into some unknown expanse of celestial wonder.

The shadowy shape stepped across the polished, white, mar-ble room, made visible only by the dim light from scattered can-delabra. A spiked blade rested in his fist as he stepped up behind the man who knelt before the towering bronze statue. The kneel-ing man was the Archpriest Akul. His hair was gray with wis-dom, and his burdensome robe rolled down an emaciated frame. It was pure white with embroidery of cerulean that looked to be a crude drawing of flowing water. Each edge was trimmed with gold, and the cloth was as thick as an animal's hide.

Hearing the scraping of metal behind him, the archpriest turned nervously. His face was wrinkled to such an extent that he appeared near death, and at the sight of the wraith, his stare detached from existence.

"It appears my time has come," the old priest realized with a withered voice. His sapphire eyes went gray as the vision of death met them, and his heart discerned that his release from Isinda impended. Purple orbs of hellish intensity glared into his terror-plagued face from beneath the dark mask of death's hand. A demonic blade rose to his thumping chest. He was thrust to his feet, and, without compunction or hesitation, the blade tore through his heart. Blood showered the feet of the heavenly statue as holiness was forsaken in this place of worship. Whimpering, the priest collapsed to the ground, the blade sliding out of his flesh. He breathed his last blood-filled breaths as life absconded his physical being, and he was left to be judged by the heavens.

The dark mask exuded fiendish exhales as the phantom clenched its sword with rugged, iron-encased hands. His lavender eyes were smoldering like those of a demon, pleasured by the granting of death. Blood dripped from the tip of his claymore, which scathed the glossy floor. Wisps of candlelight dithered over his mask and black robe while he hulked over his helpless prey with bloodthirsty gasps.

"The others have been quietly slain, Lord Merasu," a black-garbed Scaldor said as he entered the main chamber through a bronze door that led into the living quarters. "My Lord," he repeated again, seeking an answer from the general.

"I understand," Merasu said brutally, without removing his glare from his victim. The soldier moved forward, and before he could speak again, an iron grip grasped him by the throat.

"My ... my lord?" he begged as his eyes lit up in trepidation. Swirling purple flame seeped out of Merasu's hand and wrapped around the soldier's throat. The flame hissed and drowned out the guard's whimpers as his neck dissipated, and his head went tumbling to the floor from the charred tip of his spine. The other soldiers stared frightfully as they realized what had happened. The soldiers began to scurry toward the entrance, but the massive doors were sealed shut by a film of violet flame.

"S ... stay back," one of the six soldiers stuttered as they all wielded their blades.

Merasu chortled, his eyes flaring with satisfaction. A soldier thrust at him, and without hesitation, he grabbed the blade mid-slice. The sword turned to ash in moments, and Merasu's fist sent the soldier crashing into the gate, where his body split in half. The others dropped their weapons and fell to their knees, sniveling like frightened dogs.

"Fools! Following every order without question. Are you so naïve?" Merasu laughed wickedly as his blade scraped across the floor.

"Spare us!" they cried, their eyes moving back and forth between their slain brethren.

"The weak cannot be spared. The foolish must suffer. Arm yourselves. The last one standing shall live." The masked general rested with his arms on the hilt of his menacing sword.

The guards wielded their weapons and stood, waiting for Merasu's move, which never came. It didn't take long, however, for them to realize what had to be done. Each of their savage natures was revealed as they began to fight amongst themselves, falling prey to the scheming of an agent of chaos. Merasu watched happily until the last drop of blood was spilled and the remaining soldier approached him. The man's face was numb. Any civility in him had been stripped away as he murdered his own people.

"I … can live?" the soldier begged, then crumbled to his knees.

"No. I am still standing." The Scaldor's mouth dropped and tears filled his eyes. "Tears will not save you from Oblikaron's bidding." He grabbed the guard by the chin and heaved him up. Purple flame enveloped him as he squealed, and then a pile of blackened bones plummeted downward.

Satisfied, Merasu walked over to Akul and wiped his blade against the slain archpriest's hefty robe before sliding it back into its sheath. His unlawful deed was complete, his emperor's will satisfied by the blood of an honest man of pious servitude.

Dawn came by the splendid rising of a great sphere of boundless light. This was met by screams of distraught horror and howls from frightened townsfolk and devout temple-goers. The carcass of their beloved head priest lay in a bloody pool at the foot of the water god's shrine, and his disciples were murdered in their sleep, their throats slit before they could raise alarm. At least fifty lay dead, along with their master, reaved of life beneath the vast twilight.

The news met Sila's ears, and he received it with a fallacious remorse. Kneeling over the celebrant's corpse, he forced a tear to his cheek and clenched his fists in loathing. Then, in all of his eminent glory, he walked outside to the foot of the entrance of the temple, where a crowd of his roused people gathered on the streets.

"My people, today we have lost a devout servant of my ancestral line." Sila went silent with his arms stretched outward, his exquisite robe draping elegantly about them. Thousands of Scaldor stared at him in silence, awaiting his words as though they were his own children. Bronze gleamed at his rear, tracing his outline as an angelic figure derived of light. Guards formed a disciplined line in front of him, their weapons anxiously facing the mob.

"Who is to blame for this atrocity?" he continued indignantly. His people erupted into chaos, desperately seeking to condemn the culprit of the revolting act. "It is the Humans! In a night without honor, they have sent assassins to weaken our resolve!" He divulged a blatant lie, yet his people accepted the scapegoat with ferocious animosity. They jeered and cursed the Humans with disregard for the truth, simply accepting to fault a race that had long been despised. Sila needed not to offer any proof, for his word alone was enough to shape an empire's train of thought.

"We will not be distraught! The Humans will pay dearly, my people. The time has come!" The crowd exploded like a field of geysers, their condemning hollers echoing to the very crest of the Bronze Tower.

"It is time that the vehemence of the faction of Brazdor matches that of this illustrious new empire. The new Archpriest must be strong, willing to spill blood in the name of Brazdor! He must lead for the prosperity of the Scaldor and forsake the passive notions that the temple has represented for far too many years. This act calls for a changing of the tide, for my hand to exist with sublime vigor!" Sila's attentive people watched with impassioned gazes, craving to view their new sacred minister. The shimmering doors of the temple crept open, and a figure adorned in black paced out from the shadow. Lurid purple eyes radiated from beneath an ominous iron mask, overflowing with emotion and discernable lust.

"Your new archpriest!" Sila proclaimed fervently, his voice reverberating with godly magnificence. Merasu stepped forward, a sanctified demon, his robe fluttering and eyes fuming beneath his death mask. His portentous blade hung in its sheath at his side, reinforcing the verity that he was not a priest these people would recognize.

The crowd raved with deafening approval, both from their staunch adherence to Sila's will and their dread of the masked general. The deception went unnoticed, even to the educated, as the throng was overwhelmed with ardor. Merasu outstretched his palms, basking in the brilliance of his moment of ovation. The passing of a high priest was a once-in-a-lifetime event for these people, and they disregarded their fallen mentor at the news of his replacement. It was a changing of the guards—a man of compassionate beliefs replaced by a mystifying black wraith who was a commander of armies.

"Any guards who had any insight to these actions are no more. Now, we control all facets." Merasu's mask rose a tad, as though there was a heartless smirk forming below its veil. It did not matter that the Scaldor knew not whether the masked general was one of their race. Fear can achieve tremendous ends if it is utilized to supreme effect. Dread can affect any courageous man into dedicated servitude, and the man of darkness beside the dazzling emperor was indeed a lord of dread.

ARROW IN THE DARK

*"So, I meet my end here by such
cowardice. The heavens will tremble
as I drive my blade through the heart
of their gods."*

Ushtar the Barbarian

There was a legend in the east. It was the story of a man who held no equal and whose vigor has lasted centuries in the annals of history. Ushtar the Barbarian, as he was called, was a Deimor said to have collapsed a fortification with naught but his fist. He was a champion who towered over even a Sarnon and whose frame was sculpted as only fables could tell. His heart was black, yet brimming with virtues of the honorable Deimor. Horns rose from his head, stained with blood and as menacing as his sword, which spanned two-thirds of his height.

Ushtar was a barbarian because he killed mercilessly and without reason. They said his eyes could set flame to a village, and his might could repel thousands. For years, he and a band of Deimor preyed on the Scaldor. They were undefeatable and ruthless. He was the plague of the north. He would not subside, and so, on his behalf, blood spilled in rivers.

As many great men do, he grew bold and arrogant. He decided to lead his cohort of no more than two thousand men before the great walls of the Bronze City. The truth is unknown, but legend has it he reduced a section of the impregnable stone wall to rubble, allowing him to plunge into the city. With his followers at his back, he left a wake of unjust carnage. There, he ravaged bodies of any Scaldor who stood in his path—innocent men, women, children, and soldiers alike. Though vastly outnumbered, none could stand before his wrath. He weaved a blood-paved street until the force of the Scaldor was holed up within the glimmering tower of bronze.

King Shorn, the lord at the time, sat patiently on his throne, awaiting the destruction of his kingdom. To Brazdor he prayed, pleading for a small chance of survival while his oldest son, Kuldar, stood far below, facing the ornate entrance to the tower, a bow in his hands. A mob of terrified men shivered at his rear with their weapons and armor rattling.

"It is unwise to enter. The corridors are narrow," a Deimor cautioned the great warrior outside.

"We will slay them like dogs!" Ushtar roared and cleaved his own follower's head from his shoulders.

The gate bashed open, and the legend swept in, surrounded by his barbaric horde. Candles plummeted, lighting cloth aflame, and iron clashed in a flurry of sparks and chaos. Ushtar swung his blade mightily at his helpless foes, unable to be assailed and devastating the Scaldor force. He was on the path to greatness until an arrow from Kuldar's bow met his unarmored throat. A savage roar erupted from his mouth, his neck too thick for the strike to kill him instantly. He charged, piercing Kuldar through the abdomen and rending him to the ground in a bloody heap.

The halls were too narrow for him to dodge the projectile safely, and his overconfident storming of the tower was foolish. Seeing their leader wheezing and slashing blindly, the Deimor attempted to rescue him. Scaldor soldiers flooded through doors on the right and left behind the force, which had advanced too far into the trap. They were slaughtered without their godly chief, though Ushtar continued to fight on wildly, his naked body bathed in blood, and his blade continuing to slay any who neared him. A nervous soldier wielded the fallen prince's bow and fired again into the warrior's chest, causing blood to spew from his mouth as he fell to the ground, laughing maniacally all the way.

Corpses lined the long, slender hall, which was packed much too tightly, as fires tore through the cloth on their backs. The Scaldor waited far from the barbarian, still in fear of his illustrious might. Ushtar continued laughing, as though he had no troubles. It was then that he uttered his most famous phrase.

"So I meet my end here by such cowardice. The heavens will tremble as I drive my blade through the heart of their gods," he chortled with a mouth full of blood and a painful rasp in his voice. Then, with a bestial snicker, Ushtar the Barbarian lifted his menacing blade and punctured his own heart. The flame in his eyes refused to dissipate as he subsided to the ground in a gory mound. All Deimor are taught to die by one that they love, and he did not stray from that creed. In the heart of the barbarian, he loved nobody more than himself. He refused to fall by the shameful arrows of his enemy.

The legend ends with a gruesome hall and Ushtar meeting his defeat, not by blade, but instead from yards away, by the string of a bow. He was a man unparalleled in physique and strength, who to any other, appeared to be immortal. In his final moments, though, it was his arrogance that defeated him—the well-aimed shot of a clever prince. He became known as the crimson warrior, a name which Zano would also share.

•

The dense obscurity of night swathed Zano's resting face, his arms wrapped firmly around the fragile body of Suvia. Moonlight glistened off of her alabaster skin as if she were a part of the white snow encircling her. Beneath them, the snow was melted, leaving behind a patch of grass. Zano had thawed this bed for them and now acted as a flame to her body.

She had yet to come to the realization of who her savior was but was unopposed to the warmth he offered. Rolling hills of gray spanned around them, unblemished with structures or stone. A fascinating green shimmered faintly off of the snow, as if Silarion himself had blessed the land with his color.

Zano's heart beat steadily and unalarmed, matching that of the body with which he twined. He was oblivious to the shadows that crept toward him, shuffling through the snow in silence.

Still, the crimson warrior slept harmoniously, his fatal blade resting tranquilly within its sheath as gleaming eyes of sapphire skulked nearer, going unnoticed until they stopped a bit away. A string was pulled taught, and a faint whiz sent an arrow through the ridge in Zano's armor, piercing his back.

The Lord of Blood howled fiercely and sprang up, panting in pain, and just avoided the second arrow, which would have punctured his skull. Suvia gasped in horror, unsure of her surroundings, but roused by the menacing roar. Zano dashed toward the shadows, unsheathing his blade as he bounded through the snow. His eyes smoldered with twisted ire as he roared mightily once more. Two more projectiles flashed toward him, but he warded them off with a dexterous slice, then pounced in rage toward the Scaldor assassins, who revealed foot-long daggers. They swung blindly at the incensed warrior, who came down with a slash across one of their legs. Blood spurted, along with a chilling scream, as Zano rose up with a twirl and sent the other's head tumbling in a messy heap onto the snow. The fuming warrior then glared down at the whimpering Scaldor who wheezed heavily, blood oozing from the wound on his leg.

"My lord is a fool. Death to the Bloods," the assailant grumbled. With chilling silence, the Blood Scaldor fell with his weapon and brought the beak of his eagle-shaped hilt into the man's mouth. Red gushed up, and the attacker could speak no more.

Moaning in pain, Zano heaved the armor off his torso and tossed it to the side. His blade stood in the head of his enemy at his side, doused in the fountain of blood that had erupted. Gently, he removed his robe over the arrow and discarded it atop his armor.

The wound was fairly deep. He cracked the projectile in half with a cringe. His arm gave out, causing him to plunge into the snow, gasping for a breath that eluded him. When all hope had escaped him, he felt the angelic brush of a familiar hand across his scarred back. The swift fingers grasped the broken shaft, and Zano flinched at the contact.

"Be still," a soft, enchanting voice uttered.

Without delay, the arrow was torn from his flesh, and the crimson warrior let out a howl that could make wolves cower.

"Lie down," a tender woman's voice ordered.

"Suvia!" Zano gasped. He was so short of breath, his voice had lost its fervor.

Fluttering fingers swept across his back as she voiced enchantments. They were words of a cryptic language, mystical in such a way that they echoed through the night.

"Your lung is punctured," Suvia said under her breath. An air of distress was about her, though she remained utterly composed.

"At least I may die for you," he panted so weakly that any tone of longing was indiscernible.

"Be still, my love." Her hand palmed over the wound, and she continued on with her incantations. Spiritual energy of white, swirling radiance flowed into Zano's back. It traversed his gash with a lambent pulse compelling Zano to scream in agony as blood spurted from the wound. Then, by the Blindar's magic, the injury began to dissipate. Tissue fused together, and skin closed up as though mended by expedited stitches.

White light flashed, and all of a sudden there was no gash,

only a scar and a splash of crimson liquid on a scaly back. Air filled the crimson warrior's lungs once more, and a heavy cough expelled from him. By the fantastical touch of his love, there was no more pain, only a dull sore where a fatal injury had once thrived.

With a relieved sigh, Zano rolled onto his back, his eyes toward his beloved. He sensed her mind probe his; her thoughts were entangled in his own. Abruptly, his arms extended and hauled her onto his chest, where he squeezed her with rigid passion. Their lips pressed, and their hearts were fused once more, the snow against Zano's back beginning to liquefy under his extreme heat. Her pearly skin glistened in the night, lustrous from the beads of sweat running down her smooth back.

"I thought you had forgotten," Zano spoke softy as their wet lips detached.

"I was blind without you," Suvia answered, luring him once more toward her luscious turquoise lips.

There were no more words to be said, as both souls were ensnared by the extreme emotions of souls reunited. Their unclad bodies rubbed in an action in which they had not engaged for many months. Jade moon overhead, gory corpses beside, and all defenses put aside, they consummated their love so fervently, so passionately, so primitively, that even the animals of the dark strayed away. Their bodies were again one as they were promised to be, and their hearts smelted like the most enduring of metals.

The sun resurfaced, its warmth caressing the weary bodies of the beloved. Zano rose and stretched out his bare frame, enjoying the gentle touch of a warming breeze. He stepped through the thinning snow and reclaimed his attire. Attending to the growl of his stomach, he grasped the bag of rice he had taken and began to unhurriedly consume it. His eyes gazed upon Suvia as she roused from her deep sleep and walked toward their decapitated foe. Her exposed splendor was flaunted under the dazzling rays of the sun as she knelt at the torso of the exanimate and groped in order to find the right spot. She displayed her unsuspicious canines, and forthwith appeared long, tubular fangs fashioned to pierce flesh. Carefully, she dipped her head and sunk them ravenously into the artery on the headless man's throat.

Zano observed, not with panic, but with curiosity. He wondered how it must feel to hunger for blood as opposed to rice or bread, to be without need for water and merely require a portion of life fluid every few days.

Her head bobbed as claret liquid flowed up the tubes and down her throat, but this no longer appeared undesirable to Zano. Her uniqueness, compared to this world's growing conformity, was reassuring. It was bizarrely reminiscent of his own individuality. After a few minutes of feasting, they had both completed their meal. Zano tossed his empty bag to the side, and Suvia lifted, her mouth dripping with blood.

The crimson warrior, along with his brilliant maiden, began to make way at a leisurely pace across the white landscape. There was no onslaught of snow, for in these days of late Frigusa, the Scaldor lands met their only lapse in precipitation. Halfway to their destination, Zano slung Suvia off of her drained feet and bore her atop his broad shoulders. The majestic man displayed his trophy for all to see.

It was near dusk when they reached the gorge town, and the sight overcame the Lord of Blood with delight. He gazed down below to see Blood Scaldor and Scaldor living amongst each other in peace. His people now wore clean, tidy tunics of comfortable tan cloth, and the warming air implored them out of the cave. He witnessed children frolicking together, as well as men and women strolling over the frozen earth. Scaldor walked amidst them, holding conversations, some attempting to improve the former slave's dialects.

The crowd looked upwards to see the crimson warrior encircled by the sun's red aura, with a radiant woman slung over him. He began to make way down into Sotto as passing people paid heed to his presence. The Scaldor, who had earlier pardoned him, bowed as he treaded through the cluster of houses. Men gawked at the beauty he wore on his shoulder, their eyes studying each slender curve of her lithe body. As he readied to enter the murky cavern, Carthago greeted him at the entrance with Verana clasped to his side.

"I distribute clothing. I get people leave cave. I do as say," Carthago spoke up, eagerly trying to prove to Zano that he did not fail.

"Easy, my friend. You have done well," Zano said. He smiled warmly and placed Suvia on the ground in order to embrace the boy.

"Who this?" Carthago questioned with enchantment, his eyes unfolding upon the strange markings and beaming elegance of the Blindar. Verana, too, eyed Suvia, but with an expression of jealousy.

"I am Suvia of the Dresvario," she said with dignity, and from that point on, she was like a goddess to the people. Their lord was now matched by an equal mistress, one of a derivation that not even the present Scaldor knew to exist. She was mysterious and intriguing, her powers hardly comprehensible to the former slaves.

Days passed after their arrival, each bringing greater warmth to the climate and to the relationship between the races. Zano fueled the bond upon his return with endless tales of his adventures throughout Isinda. He told them of his exploits in the unforgiving dark of the Dresvario and in the renowned arena of the Akai Desert. Each night, they gathered round in attention, absorbed by his romances across Isinda.

Suvia entertained them with tricks of her mind. She read their thoughts like books, by which even the hardened Huldra was astounded. The eldress was a woman of few words, and her face was worn more from experience than age. They marveled at how Suvia found her way around the world, and she chose to identify with them by garbing herself in an identical cloth tunic.

Zano assumed Carthago's duties and distributed the rice just as he said he would. He took no surplus amount for himself, thereby demonstrating how he and his people were on equal terms.

The snow gradually liquefied, and, after a week, it was no more than scattered blotches across the land. Amber grass was unveiled, eagerly waiting to soak up the sun's rays and grow to its full extent. It was this day that a caravan from the Bronze Kingdom arrived carrying additional rice and bread, as well as leather, wood, and armaments for a new legion of soldiers.

By these days, new Blood Scaldor began to flock into Sotto by the hundreds, stemming from the many villages of the Desolura. They were as ignorant and afraid as those already present, their nights plagued with nightmares as well. Each member of the budding town assisted in the assembly of tents, but still many of the Blood Scaldor had no choice but to sleep in the cave or on the grass, allowing the Scaldor to sleep in their modest dwellings. However, even the Scaldor occasionally allowed sickly children to enter for the night.

The rainy season of Forunhor arrived, and crops of rice were planted and tended to on the moist, terraced slopes of the valley. Most inhabitants farmed, but out of the exponentially growing Blood Scaldor, nearly five hundred men and a handful of women chose the path of the warrior. They wore the newly burnished suits of the Bronze Empire and were trained by Zano with *katana*, for Sila chose to send the weapon at which Zano was expertly proficient.

In the nighttime, the Lord of Blood, Suvia, and the Scaldor educated the former slaves. They taught them how to speak correctly and read. Zano also lectured on history and the ways of each race. He strived to rid them of their horrid dreams, as his master had done. It was not long before he even took Carthago as a sort of protégé.

Weeks turned to months, and the town began to define a sense of self. It developed uniqueness as distinctive as that of its inhabitants. The Scaldor grew less and less skeptical of their scarlet cousins until, to them, the difference was imperceptible. The people of Sotto became a single unit, bent on the completion of whatever task they pursued. The soldiers hunted, along with Zano, tracking packs of Bilo—woolly creatures of immense stature with longs tusks extending from their jaws—and boar. The tranquil ponds became baths, where all eyes always moved toward Suvia as she entered, though none dared touch her, for she was the woman of their uncontested leader. The Scaldor women taught the red-scaled women how to wash and sew clothes from animal furs. Fields of tended rice stretched out of the valley, fed by the bombardment of heavy rain.

Another month passed, and the town grew to be self-sufficient. No longer did it need supplies from the great city or help from its emperor. Zano united the town into a closely-knit group. He imparted his ways of respect and honor onto his people, and their diligent work won the hearts of the Scaldor. As the blue-scaled prayed to the statue of their god Brazdor, they cared not that the Blood Scaldor followed in Zano's steps of godlessness. There was no mistrust; religion took a side seat to the well-being of the town they had all grown to love. Suvia also followed the way without prayer, for her people had forsaken the gods long ago.

Zano preached to his people never to beg or ask for forgiveness and help from the heavens. He said that for forgiveness, they must look deep within, and that for their problems, they must find their own solutions. He spoke of how, in his opinion, prayer was a weakness, that it crafted men to be more dependent on omnipotent beings who had been abstinent from mortal affairs for centuries. Still, just as his master had, he presented them with the choice to practice whatever ideals they desired, and some Blood Scaldor chose to join the Scaldor in their worship.

Daily training groomed the five hundred warriors to be skillful with their blades. Carthago clearly was emerging as the most able, and he quickly became the unnamed second in command to Zano. Each day he trained until his body seared with pain, then spent most of the night under the personal tutorship of the crimson warrior or Suvia. His words grew as eloquent as his blade, and his lean body filled in stunningly.

Just as Zano had been at his age, the boy was energetic and zealous, always eager to undertake a new task, no matter what the difficulty. The Lord of Blood treated him like a younger brother, seeing himself in the glint of the boy's eyes. In consciousness, Carthago's mind was cleared of terror, for he had begun to join Zano in his meditation, and in sleep he rarely shuddered.

One day, Zano and Carthago strolled together through a small forest nearby. Rain trickled down through the canopy of round, amber leaves. Branches were intertwined above them, wrapping and curling with each other in the chaotic fashion of nature's cohesion. Thin strands of sunlight peered through, stirring animals from their dwellings in the trees. Birds chirped pleasantly, carrying pink flower petals through the air with their sweet melodies.

They sat on a fallen trunk overlooking a small pond. The placid water glittered with the reflection of the leaves and gently rippled as water dribbled in from a stream that coursed over tiny pebbles. It was surrounded by gray rocks, on which a lush, golden moss flourished, and tiny insects skipped over its lustrous surface. Carthago stroked a stick through the loose dirt, watching as the tiny brown particles collapsed inward in its wake.

"I always know you return, Zano." He turned to the crimson warrior and smiled broadly.

"To the Desolura?" Zano asked, ensuring that he did not misinterpret the young Blood Scaldor, who had improved in his speech but was not yet fully literate.

"When you disappear. I know that you come back later. And you did. Why did you come back to save?"

"Do you remember that night?" Zano saw Carthago's reflection in the liquid. Carthago nodded. "Not a day goes by that it doesn't repeat in my mind. I cannot dream any longer, and I may have learned to put the horrors of my past behind me, but no matter what I can do, I will always see the face of the little girl."

"The one who lost heart?"

"Yes. I wish I could have saved her, but time has taught me that I cannot mold the past. I can only see it in a different light. I can only accept what has happened and allow it to provide me with purpose."

"I do not understand . . . "

"When I looked at her and held her gaze, I rid her of her tears. I purged her of her pain, and before she died, she smiled at me as if not the smallest thing were wrong. I always thought I loved her, but it was not the girl I loved. It was the smile. I gave her hope when there wasn't the slightest, and for once, she was at peace. She gave the same to me, though at first I did not realize. If that is not worth fighting for, my friend, then, by the heavens, what is?"

"I think I understand . . . Why did you do what you did to high priest?"

"I longed for that moment for many years. I pondered every day over what it would feel like, whether it would soothe me or not. We may all fall prey to rage, Carthago, but some men deserve more pain than can be dealt to them in a single lifetime." Zano reflected intensely, but not a tear came to his eye.

"I hate him, too." Carthago grimaced. "How did it feel?"

"It was as though I was cleansed of all my hatred in a single moment. His blood tasted like the sweetest honey on my lips, but anticipation can misconstrue even the most profound of undertakings. Now that it is over, it does not feel any different than any of the other hundreds I have killed. I am not proud of what I have done, but I am not ashamed . . . I did exactly what my master would have wanted." He paused as he realized this was true. "I followed my heart. However, in that moment, I was lost to fury, and it is this that scares me. Vengeance can cause the most virtuous of men to lose sight of their aspirations. A warrior should always know for what he is fighting, for a warrior without a purpose is simply a sword—that is all."

"I hope one day I can understand." Carthago smiled as he eyed a mosquito that had just landed on his thigh.

"You will," Zano laughed. "You will."

Carthago went to swat the insect, but just as he did, a gentle hand grasped his arm and stayed him.

"Even the tiniest creatures must feed to survive. We cannot curse them for it." Carthago looked up to see the ever-beautiful Suvia speaking. She spread open her hand, and the mosquito landed on her palm. It pierced her skin with its minuscule mouth and slurped the blood from her veins.

"Forgive me, Suvia," Carthago said, and he lowered his head shamefully.

"There is nothing to forgive," she said. Suvia grinned. "I knew I would find you out here, Zano. Come back with me to the village. We miss your presence already." She gazed at the insect as it finished its meal and buzzed off to the backside of a leaf. Then, she pressed her sumptuous lips against Zano's, and with this he could not deny her request.

"You're right, my love," he conceded with affection. "Come, Carthago. We will speak again another day."

They departed the tranquility of the forest, Carthago tagging along and observing all the nuances of nature.

"I've been meaning to ask," Zano broke the silence as they strolled, "how did you come to be a servant in the Bronze City?"

"I could not live without you any longer. Against my father's will, I fled. I hiked across the Narsano peaks with a vial of blood until I collapsed of fatigue in snowy fields somewhere within the Scaldor domain. I awoke in chains at that bar to be used for my beauty. I starved for days before convincing the owner I required blood. Live rodents became my nourishment. That is before you came," Suvia explained, before kissing Zano.

"You could have died! You know I would've come back for you."

"I know, but even my elongated life was too short for me to wait."

She smiled, and their hands clutched tightly, their hair tangling as a slight breeze whistled through the trees.

Many months had passed, seemingly in the blink of an eye. The last of the Blood Scaldor had arrived, and there were now well over three thousand populating Sotto. Hundreds of tents were erected from the gift of leather and wood, as well as the hides of the animals Zano and his warriors had slain. The Scaldor and Blood Scaldor were now as kin, though they still held differing beliefs and were of unlike coloration. Scaldor doors were no longer prohibited to any, and a few of the younger men and women chose to sleep with newfound partners of another race. Some of the Scaldor had even discontinued their prayers to Brazdor and found faith in the crimson warrior's path.

In a world of hatred and war, Sotto became a secret, glowing beacon of hope for peace between races. The inhabitants learned of Suvia's unnerving needs but came to accept her. When a man of blue scales looked upon a man of red, there was no longer disgust, only amity. A spiritual serenity pervaded the valley, which was defended on either side by hulking crags and dotted with two glimmering ponds. One could almost feel it— the conformity of the Scaldor with a people who had conquered the oppression of that very same race.

These things were raised above any statue of a god or loyalty to an emperor. They were the meaning of a newfound life, a life of a tolerance and compassion that could be found in few places within their vast world. It was a minute slice of the colossal dream that flooded through Zano's very being.

On a rainy day in mid Forunhor, the season following and preceding Frigusa, an envoy of Sila, garbed in golden silk, arrived at the summit of the terraced slopes of Sotto. Zano met him with his usual respect, and the messenger held a simple request, "My lord requires you." He then went on to enumerate the circumstances.

Since Sotto began blossoming, the east had changed drastically. The last of Sila's armies returned, and all other Scaldor kingdoms were subjugated. By blood and by bronze, all of the eastern forests and grasslands came under Sila's sphere of influence.

As the messenger spoke, Zano found the man's vision trailing with awe toward the coexisting peoples. The envoy observed smiles exchanged interracially. Upon his departure to Sotto, he had expected the races only to be wary of each other's existence, but nothing more.

Continuing, he imparted onto Zano Sila's order for him to muster a regiment and hastily make way to the southern border of the Akai Desert. The emperor sought to extend his authority into those harsh lands by means of an alliance. Elated at this offering of unity, the Lord of Blood humbly accepted and sent the envoy off.

Zano brought the news to his legion of soldiers, who were training on the amber fields outside of the gorge. Their blades had grown swift, just as the Bronze Armies' were. However, their scales were that of blood. They received the news just as Zano had, eager for adventure, to hold purpose, to fight.

The Lord of Blood fervently awaited their morning departure, choosing to allow his men to say their goodbyes. Most of those who were to stay behind were somber over their families leaving for the very first time, but the Scaldor were pleased to hear of the eastern campaign. Most held quarrel with the Arikarnon. Centuries of war with the desert people had made them untrusting and unbelieving that the Arikarnon could change. Zano, in his compassion, swayed this thought, and now it was naught but a whisper—a fleeting idea that had been replaced by harmony.

Tears flooded from siblings and lovers. Verana clasped Carthago's hand as if for the very last time. Suvia was not flustered or dismayed. She slept soundly at her lover's side as she always had, knowing that Zano was a survivor, and that, by his promise, he would return unscathed.

After a long, gloomy night, daybreak arrived with a torrent of rain. The soldiers were rationed with bags of rice and crude canteens filled to the brim with water. Zano was exhilarated, raring to return to adventure and brandish his thirsty blade. With Carthago by his side and an army of four hundred ninety-eight men at his back, the Lord of Blood blissfully began to march. Thousands bid them farewell with solemn cheers and kisses. Before they knew it, their army had vanished, lost in the endless grass and rain.

ENTER THE SAND

"There is a land where colossal Scorpions prowl,
where geysers of flame erupt from the earth,
and where sand spans like a sea across
the horizon. I call it home."

Acosta, first king of the Arikarnon

It had not yet been a year since the Blood Scaldor were freed from the chains of slavery, since their hands ran red with their masters' blood, and their eyes were filled with unprecedented hatred. Surely, they were still inundated by horrid dreams, but as they walked and farmed and trained, their minds grew clearer. This was eased by a new home and by the acceptance of a race that had at one time beleaguered them. Their town grew in size, but also in ideal.

In their troubled hearts, they believed as Zano did: that this land cursed by war could have peace. It was a dream he imparted upon them, but it was still only a murmur in an earsplitting clamor, too delicate a belief to openly present. Entwined within their very beings, it laid dormant, residing in the way that they lived and in how they felt. It was inconceivable how far they had come in so short a time and how they reflected their leader with such sublimity. The Blood Scaldor held an unalterable history of blood, a trait they shared with the land on which they slept.

The Lord of Blood now led an army of zealous Blood Scaldor. The trek to the desert was long, more than a week's time from the peaceful cliffs of Sotto. Thunderous clouds soared overhead, flooding water down onto the helpless terrain. At first it was unbearable, the constant batter of rain atop their heads. This is why some would compare the Scaldor to fish, for they shared a sheet of scales and lived in a water-doused land. However, in the Scaldor's case, the scales proved to exist not only for insulation, but also as a natural armor.

Rolling fields of amber grass, glimmering on the tips with dew, trailed around them, dotted by glossy, gray rocks and small forests off in the distance. There were forests of Okura trees, which were of a modest height and held bright golden, oval leaves stemming from the black branches of a rugged trunk. Forunhor brought them dainty flowers of pure white, much like snow. On a rare day without rain or clouds, it was said that these trees sparkled like yellow flames under the midday sun. They were of no amazement to the Blood Scaldor, however, because it was these beautiful trees that sparsely made home in the valley of Sotto.

In nearly twenty days of travel, there had only been one day of clarity, where the sun's illustrious warmth stroked the faces of those below, and a vivid blue sky was visible, speckled with few blotches of white. On the dawn of the eleventh day, when they had already consumed half of their rice and water, they came before a phenomenon unlike any other. Before them, with a vicious organic swirl, stood a wall constructed by neither the Scaldor nor Arikarnon. It was a barrier not of stone or mud, but of the very elements of Isinda herself. Whirling sand and dust rose like a tempest, towering upward as high as the Bronze

Tower. The discreet waves of heat were visible, radiating forth from the restless sand.

Zano's men gazed up in trepidation, but it was not foreign to him, though even he was startled by its presence after so many years. As they neared it, the rain began to evaporate before it could reach land. At its base, there was no rain at all.

A Scaldor scout crept up on the captivated army and said, "His lord awaits you on the other side."

Zano turned to him and nodded, his hand resting alertly on his hilt, distressed by the figure's ominous creeping. He scanned the faces of his people. They were afraid; he could see it in their eyes. Even Carthago held an expression of apprehension about him. The barrier was imposing, a forceful vision of nature that Zano had feared those many years ago. It seemed that by entering, they would be swallowed whole by a swarm of particles and heat.

"Enter slowly and walk straight. I have passed through before. You shall be fine," Zano assured his men with a comforting smile.

Their leader's reassurance put the army at ease. They watched intently while he plunged his hand into the gale. His body was enveloped, but a call back implored his followers to pursue. Intense heat overcame them, an abrupt alteration of temperature that dynamically increased. The brisk air of the Scaldor lands was replaced by sweltering heat. Sweat instantly dripped down from beneath their scales as they traversed the tumultuous cloud of brown. The ground grew granular and unstable, the bare feet of the Blood Scaldor sinking into the sizzling sand. Legends say that if passed through too quickly, the drastic fluctuation of temperature could halt a man's heart.

They emerged through thin wisps of sand and wind, and before them, sparkling beneath the sun's concentrated rays, was a sea of sand—never-ending dunes with streams of sand drifting above them against the crimson-tinted, blue sky. There were no clouds or rain. The air was arid, making each ensuing breath more difficult to take in. Flame-spewing geysers erupted from mounds strewn across the dunes, emanating distant auras of translucent red. The Arikarnon Desert was a harsh land, parched, churning with fire, unforgiving to the unprepared souls, and possessing of a heat so intense that the milky, supple skin of a Blindar would scorch in its wrath. It was a place where the oasis was the key to survival and where only the hardy could sustain life.

To the left, they spotted a mottled fortress of no extravagance, its walls constructed of weathered stone. It appeared out of place in the vast emptiness—a random protrusion of gray in a sea of auburn.

"There!" Zano shouted, pointing to the structure.

His men answered with a nod, and they began to trudge through the ground which caved in around each footprint. Sand brushed across their faces, stinging with contact into open eyes and burrowing under their scales. They panted like dogs, the merciless heat shooting up their nerves as brilliant sun rays beat upon them with uncomfortable warmth.

Zano took a swig of water from his canteen as the walls of the fortress climbed before them. The archway was open and awaiting their arrival, so without hesitation, the army of Blood Scaldor entered. The yard around the bastion greeted them with hostile glares. Hundreds of scowls rained down from bronze-clad Scaldor, but they went unnoticed. Zano had taught his people to ignore these empty threats and win others over through actions.

"Just in time to join us, Lord of Blood," Sila jested through a curl of sand, garbed in a velvet robe of nacarat, which was garlanded with gold. His sapphire crown glittered, each ruby like a tiny sphere of flame. A servant walked by his side, docilely fanning him with an ostentatious fan.

"For what?" Zano questioned.

"Wait your people at the wall and come."

Zano motioned his followers toward the fortification. He

was nervous that the Scaldor would be far less than hospitable, but he remained unruffled, for he knew that they feared their emperor.

He and Sila exited the stronghold and were surrounded by dozens of guards. Three officers hastened up to their sides. One was Merasu, who offered Zano a friendly bow. One was a chiseled, veteran soldier who wore nothing but a loincloth, and the last was near Zano's age. This one held a fervent stare and wore a tight silk tunic of scarlet and gold. The two who were unfamiliar to Zano peered at him snobbishly. They had heard news of the Lord of Blood but were still flustered that their master allowed such a man to hold a standing of nobility.

The group walked out into the compact sea until the fortress was no more than a brown haze at their rear. Sand swirled about their feet. All were silent. Sila held a smug grin on his face, and the unfamiliar officers continually glanced toward the unwanted presence. Suddenly, there was a quick thumping of limb against the land that coursed through the vibrating earth. Silhouettes emerged on the horizon, gleaming with golden armor.

A colossal scorpion loomed in the distance, no smaller than the size of a seafaring vessel. Its eight extremities flurried across the sand, leaving behind a dusty wake, and its back swished rigidly with each forward movement. Two chilling pincers extended to the right and left of the two black orbs, which were its eyes. Each piece of its segmented rubicund carapace was plated with solid gold. The beast's needlelike tail swished with a menacing stinger fixed onto the last segment. Its pincers were enhanced with fixed iron spikes, and on its broad back sat a figure of imposing stature. His skin was gray as charcoal, as though he had braved a pit of fire and lived. Eyes of gold glared across the dunes, lustrous with hostile concentration. His jaw was wide, with two tusks extending from his bottom lip to the height of the tip of his capacious nose, and atop his hairless head was a circlet of gold, embellished with flawless topaz.

The men of the Bronze Empire reared as the creature

halted with flaying pincers. It let off crackling noises as well as unearthly low growls and hisses. Sila stood pompously, his back erect beneath his extravagant garb. The man on the back of the creature rose to his feet as sand puffed up from the Scorpion's many appendages, and its gold plated carapace imitated the sun's radiant glare.

"Why have you come here, Scaldor?" he demanded harshly, with a brutish voice that was common to the Arikarnon. His armor was no more than a circular plate of gold, encrusted with a hefty topaz, which expelled chains of the same metal that wrapped around his hunched back. His arms were elongated, like those of a primate, and strengthened with long muscles. His tall, husky legs were sheltered with a skirt of thin metal plates down to his knees.

The Arikarnon forcefully leapt from the beast's back onto a flare of boiling sand. Even with his arched back and bare feet, the man still hulked over all those present by at least a foot. A battle-axe of thick iron hung from a loop in a chain on his back, hoisted upright so that the blade protruded from either side of his cranium.

"I come bearing gifts and the exchange of words," Sila answered calmly.

"We have spoken. Now be gone!" the Arikarnon roared, his voice lingering on the empty air.

"Please heed my words," Sila said, unperturbed by the Arikarnon's discourtesy.

"Speak then, but be careful what you say, wretch!"

"I am Sila, emperor of the Bronze Kingdom, which now controls the greatest of all armies in Isinda. I come bearing many tons of bronze and an offering of union between our two great races," Sila explained, clearly speaking down to the Arikarnon.

"Do not come here with your empty threats, Scaldor! I am the king of these lands, and we will not be bought out by your ruses and lies!"

"Do not tempt me. I offer my hand in friendship only once," Sila dealt his ultimatum.

"The sun will sear your men's scales! My lands roar with flame and death, so do not threaten me with war! Come with your 'vast' army, and see as they crumble beneath mine. The dunes will swallow you, Sila," the king remarked, spitefully.

"You will regret those words, king. Do not force my hand. Accept my offering, or bring suffering to the dunes you hold in such high regard," Sila extended his hand out for the final time.

"As you may see, we hold all the gold we need. I suggest you depart before morning." The king spit at Sila's feet and defiantly mounted the bestial arachnid.

"Very well. You have sealed your fate," the emperor said, then bowed before the foreign king with civilized respect. The gesture was not returned as the Arikarnon wheeled his mount and snaked off into the distance. Sand spit into Sila's entourage before the group began to make way toward the castle.

The emperor refused to move, his elegant robe fluttering as he was fanned, gazing at the withdrawing figure. He had rarely met such defiance, such insubordination to his godlike status. The rest continued to depart him, but Zano glanced back. He was unaccustomed to Sila's arrogance and studied his bearing with each passing moment. Granules swept about him. Fields of golden brown cascaded, layered by a thin sheet of sand, and Zano also stopped in his tracks, to which none paid any heed. The world swirled in a vortex. Memories flooded through him, and suddenly Sila vanished, and a younger self stood where he had.

• • •

From the northern plains of amber grass, Zano and Tarak had made their way into the blistering dunes of the Arikarnon. By each night, they sparred with sticks or blades, and while the sun still shone, they walked under the shade of the Okura trees.

They had passed the wall of sand that mesmerized Zano, just as it would do to his people nearly five years later.

Zano took cautious steps across the sand, which scorched his scaly feet. These were his fledgling steps into a new land. His dagger lay dormant in the folds of his master's robe. Never had he imagined a land of such uniformity, where not even a stone broke the subtle rolls of the earth. The heat was sweltering, as proven by the sweat that poured from his frame. His tongue panted like a dog's, and his muscles grew fatigued with each passing step. Tarak slid his feet through the heated particles unaffected. It was clear that he had braved this wasteland before.

They hiked for hours without uttering a word. Zano's mind was too lethargic to both walk and speak simultaneously. Streams of sand continually blinded his squinting eyes, wedging up under each scale and the nails on his fingers. His throat ran arid, parched as a loaf of dry bread. Then, as if by some miracle of the gods, a blemish appeared over the sheet of gritty auburn. Tarak pointed toward the anomaly, ridding Zano of the thought that it could be just a cruel trick of his listless mind. Particles exploded into the Deimor's face as Zano collected the last of his energy and sprinted toward what appeared to be an oasis. His feet slid out from under him as he reached the basin with exhilaration and gazed ravenously upon the crystalline water, surrounded by sparse amber grass and by trees with golden palm leaves. Ripe, shaggy coconuts grew in clumps beneath them, instigating the freed slave's drool.

Scaly hands disrupted the water's smooth sheen, as they dipped into ripples and siphoned handfuls of liquid. Parched lips rejoiced in the pleasure of the oasis, and Zano was quick to leap into the somewhat shallow water without discarding his clothes. His feet barely touched the shifting bed, for which he was fortunate, because he knew not how to swim. He waded through the tepid water with delight, taking frequent sips. Small fish zipped away from the foreign presence, not wish-

ing to investigate the mammoth that intruded on their terri-
tory. Tarak came to the edge laughing, his eyes brimming with
compassion. Gracefully, he scooped up a few mouthfuls, then
propped his back up against a palm tree.

They held neither a map nor any sense of where they were
in the expanse of sand, only that there, encircled by hell, was a
sliver of paradise. The sun began to set, and the two sat side by
side, gazing out onto the scarlet hills. Flares of fire emanated
orange flashes across the horizon, and as the sky grew black,
heat manifested beneath the blanket of jade-hued sand. The
stars twinkled brightly, flickering like tiny fireflies off in the distance. Streaks of opaque purple ran across the plethora of black,
blending with the celestial marks of ethereal white.

As Zano sat beside Tarak, he realized the mystery that
shrouded his new master. His past was uncertain, and his reason
for freeing the young Blood Scaldor still unclear. He had yet to
even remove the black hood from his head. All Zano knew was
that he was a Deimor, a race that was feared and misunderstood
by all of Isinda. He was wise, and, above all else, he had taken
his place in Zano's consciousness as master. With each passing
hour, their relationship tightened. Tarak had become the face of
approval in the Blood Scaldor's eyes. Here they slept, mislaid in
an unforgiving desert, but the freed slave was unafraid. By the
side of his dignified master, he could receive no harm.

Day came by a splendid sunrise, and Tarak decided to fashion two sticks of wood from the bark of a tree. With these crude
weapons, they trained for hours on end. Always Tarak came out
on top of their duels; however, the old Deimor saw the glint
of greatness in his apprentice and sought to unearth it by any
means possible. He did not have the energy that Zano did, but
it was his experience that made him a master swordsman. His
blade was not exceedingly swift, yet it always seemed to find
its strike or its parry. It was his grace, like that of a renowned
dancer, which kept his apprentice's blade at bay, for the young
Blood Scaldor was rash, too eager to lay that finishing blow.

RHETT C. BRUNO

Days passed without dilemma. Tarak fished the inhabitants
of the oasis with his diamond-tipped blade. The sun cooked
them and blessed the travelers with hearty meals. Not only did
they train with weapons, but the Deimor also instructed Zano
on how to stay afloat without ever entering the water himself.
Their nights consisted of stories, mostly legends of ancient
warriors and battles. No matter how hard Zano pried, the past
of his master remained a secret. Instead, Tarak told him of far
off lands, of a jungle that far surpassed the splendor of his old
home, and a labyrinth of jagged ice and rock where barbarians roamed. By the sun's glare, they habitually sparred, Tarak
desiring to impart his virtue of patience onto the young man,
whose uncontrolled zeal was not only deadly to others but also
to himself.

Weeks passed incredibly quickly, with only one moment
of danger. A pack of Sadrul ambushed them as they sparred.
These were creatures that baffled Zano, for they swam beneath
the sand as though it were water. They stayed shallow, with sea
green fins jutting from the parting sand. Serrated teeth gleamed
within their wide mouths, and, while visible, they appeared as
savage fish the size of half a grown man. With ease, Tarak eradicated the beasts before their ambush could cause harm, and
they made for a lavish feast once baked by the sun.

Over time, the heat's effect on the Blood Scaldor was less-
ening, and his visits to the water reduced. His muscles developed their resilience, and the temperature no longer swindled
his mind. His nights were still plagued by nightmares, but here
in the unending desert his conscious mentality was free. Meditation became a daily event for him, where he would clear his
thoughts and enhance his focus. His path to freedom from his
past ensued no differently than it had with his people in the
unforeseen future.

After more than a month, the inhabitance of master and
apprentice in the deep desert was finally noticed. Silhouettes of
Arikarnon warriors appeared through the sandy haze. Zano was

alarmed, feeling as though a fight was looming, but Tarak eased him as the gray shades closed in.

Silent steps brought three of them before master and apprentice. Their skin was like coal and their eyes like gold. The vision caught the gaze of Zano, who hadn't before seen a "Grayman". They were giant and naked but for white loincloths and an iron battle-axe in each of their hands.

"A Deimor and his pet here? Shall we send them to Agoge's flame?" one of the men mocked with a loutish, almost barbaric accent.

Zano clenched his fists, but Tarak dropped to his knees and submissively placed his hands to his head.

"Why now?" one laughed. "Their death will profit the Arena."

The group snickered and approached the two foreigners with caution. Zano was poised to brawl, though he held no weapon.

"Sit, monster!" an Arikarnon snapped.

Tarak's hand gently grabbed the Blood Scaldor's ankle to reassure him, and, ceding to his master's will, Zano knelt. The last thing he saw were six golden beads before the blunt edge of an axe fell on his skull.

He awoke in darkness, huddled in the corner of a dungeon. His vision was blurry, but he recognized the robed figure of Tarak sitting across from him.

"You awaken," Tarak said with a grin.

"Where are we?" Zano asked dizzily.

"You will see."

"Why didn't we fight?"

"It was the only way for foreign men like us to enter here."

"Where is here?"

Zano rose to his feet, stumbling for a moment and then walked toward the iron grate that blockaded him. The prison was hot, littered with scraps of rotten meat and bones, perhaps not of animals. Zano noticed that the ebony sheath still hung from his master's side, but he did not question him, for a noise caught his ear.

The shadows of two towering men wavered across the russet wall. They came before the iron bars, water dripping down their fearsome lower fangs. One unlocked the confinement. A spear point held steady at Zano's throat as he was hauled out, and Tarak followed closely behind guarded laxly by another. They were pulled through a labyrinth of dark halls, the sound of clashing blades echoing around them. Shiny blood stained the walls and dripped from the low ceiling.

They entered a narrow, winding staircase of discolored stone and were shoved through a crude door. Sunlight blinded them as the door was locked along with the Arikarnon behind them. A cheer from a massive crowd erupted, feet slamming against the ground in seemingly ritualistic chants.

"What is this?" Zano shouted above the deafening noise, which originated through the gate of spiked iron bars at the end of the arched tunnel where he stood beside his master.

"The Heart of Agoge—the great desert arena where warriors and criminals alike must battle for their lives," Tarak stated in a glorified manner.

"We're criminals?"

"Be wary. We shall survive this and win over these brutish people," Tarak unworriedly advised.

"I get no weapon? Where is my dagger?"

"It is their custom for criminals to fight for forgiveness with whatever they are caught carrying. However, the dagger could easily be concealed, and so it was confiscated. In time, they will return your weapon, but worry not—one is better than none. You must learn how to kill, or we will both be no more than jesters here."

Tarak stepped forward, and Zano mimicked, distraught that his prized dagger had been taken from him. They traversed the short tunnel and waited with their hands on the bars.

"Today, Agoge is pleased to present you with demonic

intruders to our desert. A mutated Scaldor and a Deimor!" a voice roared, and was followed by an eruption. The iron spikes lowered into the sandy floor, and the crimson men ran out into the arena. Zano spun in awe of the great structure. They were in a shallow pit, enclosed by unsettling spikes. A tremendous stadium of sandstone rose around them. Rows of benches sat between elaborate gold statues, and gold-plated walls were filled with crowds of shirtless men and women. The Arena soared toward the sky, each row extending outward farther and farther. Vibrant cloths embroidered with ornate gold patterns fell over the spiked wall. Great fires outlined the gold crest of the Arena, which had taut chains connected to the center fixture. Directly above the pit was a complex gold chamber, which held an eternal sphere of flame. It was bright as the sun, brilliant and still—an anomaly of an element held by no natural means, as it simply suspended in midair within the golden cage.

The throng jeered and stamped, cursed and roared as the outlanders whirled in the pit's center, observing the stunning structure of death. Demonic hisses spewed through the iron bars across the way. This gate, however, was wider than the other. Zano could not fathom what spawn of the underworld the entrance detained. The crowd of Arikarnon greeted the noise heartily, but nerve grew upon the criminals—fear of an unknown fiend.

"Your lord Kalo is pleased to bring you the Scorpion!" the same stately voice shouted to the eruption of all around him.

The gate released upward, and, fleeing in rage from the jabbing edges of spears, a monster burst through the darkness in a cloud of sand. It was a Scorpion, massive and crying toward the sun with outlandish animosity. There was no gold plating his carapace, only the naturally impregnable shell of black fire. Its jagged pincers snapped, and its tail lashed, each movement drawing the thrill of the crowd.

"Be steady, Zano, and Desara Norrath! Strength and glory!" Tarak yelled and ripped his sword from its ebony casing. Sunlight sparkled along its keen edge, drawing the glance of all viewers.

The creature reared its long torso and crashed across the arena. Tarak and Zano dove out of the way, rolling as the Scorpion wheeled to make its next move. The Arikarnon spears had infuriated it. All that it now knew was to kill; all that it desired was blood.

The beast came bounding toward them, its pincers thrashing wildly. Tarak readied his blade, and as the monster passed, he swiftly slashed its many limbs. In the thick, natural armor, only mere cuts of no major harm were left. Zano sprawled beneath the Scorpion's segmented belly to the crowd's delight, though they groaned when he arose unscathed and leapt back to his nimble feet.

The beast was relentless, its onslaught of rabid charges steadily tiring its prey. Its pincers lashed zealously toward Zano, but he evaded them. Tarak took any open chance to slice the hard outer shell but met no success. The creature had an endless supply of energy and began to batter the ground with its lean stinger. One jab of the poisonous tip would leave the gladiators limp on the ground in an instant.

Ten minutes passed, leaving the master and apprentice wheezing. None in the crowd expected them to last this long, so they were eagerly watching from their feet, waiting for the foreigners to meet a gruesome demise. To their dismay, there was a stroke of brilliance in Zano's actions. As a pincer nearly crushed his ribs, he leapt up and wrapped around the spiky appendage. Tarak took notice and kept the attention of the other pincer by brutally hacking at the unbreakable exoskeleton. With dexterous grace, Zano climbed up the limb, dodging thrusts from the stinger, and dove onto the beast's back. The precise attacks of the poison tail could not land on the Blood Scaldor, who rolled adroitly back and forth.

"Tarak!" Zano frantically screamed.

The Deimor quickly understood and tossed his sword to

Zano, while dodging the clamp of both pincers. The handle landed in the Blood Scaldor's hand, and without delay he shoved the diamond tip between its death-black eyes. The creature cried in hellish agony, swinging wildly. Zano held tight to a spike on its back, with the beast's great strength nearly tearing his muscles to shreds. Tarak sprinted to the blade and tore it out with a spray of green goo. He jabbed the jade eagle into each eye and continued to savagely chop at its head. The ground trembled from the stinger's smashing, the crowd roaring as each pincer slashed through the air.

The stinger plunged down near the warriors in a few futile attempts, but the scorpion only wound up deeply puncturing its own back. Poison quickly coursed through its body, and with one last screech, it collapsed to the ground, absent of life.

The crowd was silent. The only sounds were the heavy gasps of the fighters. Zano stumbled off the fallen beast's back and found his footing on the dry sand. His eyes met his master's, and there they were held, a new bond passing between them—an intertwining streak of destiny, which unified them. The vanquished beast lay docile at their side, but this feat was greeted with no applause. Empty glares rained upon them, looks that illustrated disappointment and disapproval.

Tarak said nothing, but spat upon the monstrous carcass before he began to walk toward the gate, blade in hand. Zano looked around, from one side of the quiet Arikarnon mob across the sphere of flame to the other. He didn't understand why they shunned him. He had slain a tremendous beast; he should have been considered a hero. A film of water formed over his glaring eyes as he took up behind his master, weary and disgusted.

The gate opened, and more armed guards escorted them to the dreary prison. The chambers held no more echoes, only silence. It was a hush as unwelcoming as the gates of the heavens would be to a demon. They were tossed into a dungeon like worthless dogs.

"Why are we not cheered?"

"You must understand, Zano, that wherever we go, we are outsiders. I am of a race that conquered all others, and you are an abnormality. They will reject us, perhaps even hate us, but it is up to you to sway their stance. Did you see it in their eyes? The astonishment. It was as clear as day."

"Yes, but I saw disgust as well."

"Of course. They believed we would die. They desired it because we are outsiders—men not intended to survive their harsh culture. Shock can take the breath from the coldest of men, Zano," Tarak sniveled. "However, you must not grow disillusioned. Whatever they throw at you, you must press on. This is your first test. Win over the favor of the Arikarnon. Gain their cheer by your success and their ire in your defeat."

Zano sat attentively, taking in the wise words of his master with compliant ears and a pensive mind.

"It is not easy to become accepted. I know," Tarak continued. "It is precisely why the Deimor failed. You cannot rule a people that detest you. You can conquer their lands, and you can bleed their hearts, but war, as well as life, is more than a battle of wit and blade. It is a battle of ideas and minds. You can kill an army of men, but the eradication of a belief is the test of true greatness. They think me to be evil, and they believe that you are an abomination. You cannot win them over simply by spilling blood in an arena. You must make them see the greatness within you—the greatness that I see, the promise that lies within you to open your heart and mind to all, and the ability to abstain from a senseless hatred that so few on this world hold."

"What must I do, master?"

"Be who you are. Be a sun in an ocean of stars, my friend. Life will bring you all of the answers you need," Tarak responded, then tossed his elegant sword to his apprentice.

Before he could respond, Zano caught the weapon and examined it. Green blood drenched the blade, but the hilt felt comfortable in his hand, as though it were fashioned specifically for him. It was custom for the Arikarnon to allow their prisoners to hold whatever they were caught with. It was an incentive for the prisoners to try and escape, a way to keep the guards active and always vigilant. Still, their taking of the dagger illustrated a slight nervousness and distrust.

"You will need this here more than I will," Tarak said, as the sound of metal boots clanking against iron echoed down the dull hall. Zano placed the blade down and pounced to the iron bars.

The man walking down the aisle was one of great girth. He was tall, as was every Arikarnon, with eyes that emanated lust and greed. His head was bald and his face tattooed with dramatic white streaks. A loosely-fitting robe of sparkling gold fluttered down from his shoulders, kept tight by a long belt around his fat belly. Circlets of gold chain adorned his long tusks, which appeared threatening but were essentially useless.

"Under normal circumstances, you two would be free to leave, but I do not desire the hatred of my fans, so that simply will not do," the Arikarnon spoke to himself.

"We killed your beast! Let us go!" Zano demanded defiantly.

"Do not bark at me, scaleface! Even your blue brethren apparently shun you. Our customs apply to us, not you, therefore I will do what I wish," the man shouted. "You two are skillful warriors, so I have an option other than instant death."

"Speak," Zano hissed.

"The Grand Tournament of Agoge will begin in but a few days. My people desire to see you and the Deimor die before their eyes. What better way than by one of my people?" he chortled. "However, I have room for only one of you. Who will die for my profit?"

"He will fight," Tarak voiced from the corner, "but he will not die."

"Will he not?" the man laughed. "If he is, in the rarest of circumstances, to win, then I shall allow you both to leave our lands in peace. If he dies, then the pain you will suffer, Deimor, will be unbearable."

Zano glared at his master with overwhelmed eyes. So abruptly he was being thrown into a barbaric gamble, where his life was the prize. He had never even killed a man, and now he had no other choice.

"Good. Follow me to your chamber, demons, and don't try anything rash. The only escape is up," the plump Arikarnon mused.

The rattling of keys opened the cell, and Zano grasped the sword before following the man down the narrow passageways. Tarak was close behind, reflecting on his choice to entrust his apprentice to the callous sand of the Arena. An old wooden door was pushed open, and the foreigners were sent in. The door slamming behind them signaled the silent retreat of the Arikarnon, who seemed to run this entertainment industry of death.

The room was small and dark, furnished with nothing but two sheets of leather, a torch, and a crude wooden dummy. Sensing the discomfort on Zano's young face, Tarak praised him and rubbed his shoulder before collapsing onto the bed. The Blood Scaldor then realized how exhausted he was and soon joined his master in slumber, though his was, as usual, filled with horrid nightmares.

Three days passed with nothing to eat but tough, raw meat and a scarce amount of lukewarm water. The chamber was dry and hot, parching the tongue and lips of its inhabitants. Had the heat of the desert not trained Zano earlier, he would be in no condition to fight.

The days were filled with guidance. Tarak swung his sword at the young man to build his agility, sometimes nearly shaving off a piece of a limb. Zano slashed and practiced his footing, advancing all measures of his skill.

At midday, Zano was to be set forth before the crowd to battle, and only minutes remained until his moment of fate. The fear in his manner was evident, and in their last moments, alone his master attempted to ease him.

"Are you afraid, Zano?" Tarak asked empathetically from the comfort of a leather cushion.

"I have never killed a man before," Zano whispered.

"When you look across the way and see your opponent standing there, envision somebody or something that you hate. It is simple really—battle, that is. Drive your blade into the heart of your enemy, or he will claim yours. It is a natural part of life to kill. In a fight, you must become an animal, savage and ruthless. Whatever death means to you, you must fight with that in mind," Tarak said, comforted by clear knowledge of the experience. A knock at the door indicated that the time had come.

"Thank you master," Zano said with a humble bow. "I will return."

The Blood Scaldor exited the chamber to the smile of his beloved master and was escorted by heartless guards to the same door as before. He took a nervous gulp of desiccated air and pushed the crude door open. Light lapsed across his crimson face as he came to the iron bars and peered out through the slits. The crowd was roaring in anticipation just the same. Dust sprinkled off of the tunnel's ceiling, and the blood-stained walls taunted Zano. In his right hand, he held his master's sword, and on his body, he wore his tunic as a loin cloth. The contestants could wield whatever weapon they chose, but were forbidden from wearing armor, though the scales of Zano's hide offered him the advantage of a natural armor that no Arikarnon possessed. His body was youthful but strong, and his frame was lean from slave labor and constant training with Tarak.

"Agoge is pleased to bring you the first fight of his tournament. You all know the warrior Asul," the familiar voice of the plump Arikarnon shouted to the erupting fans. "His opponent today is a man spawned of Pregarus. He intruded our borders but showed his will to stay by conquering a mighty Scorpion. I give you ... the Blood Scaldor!"

The crowd jeered harshly, they cursed and spat, taunted and

threatened as the bars slid down. Zano was pelted by bits of food and rocks as he jogged out into the Arena. The structure was packed to full capacity, filled to the brim with people who desired to see him die. Yet, showing more poise than his age would allude to, Zano ignored the rash hatred that surrounded him. He gazed intensely across the sand at the massive man who stepped out from the darkness.

Asul shared the usual features of his people, save that he was built strong as a Bilo. His muscles nearly tripled the size of Zano's, and this was attested by the massive axe he wielded with both hands. The weapon was almost the size of the Blood Scaldor, and its blade was as sharp as a razor.

Heeding his master's advice, the young warrior's mind transformed the scene. Sand turned into the apex of a stone pyramid, and the Arikarnon's face became that of the High Priest. The hallucination laughed menacingly with the bloody head of the little girl in its heartless hand. Zano's eyes smoldered, one like blue coal and the other hot fire, as he wished he could have his dagger back if just to slay its original owner. Suddenly, he reviled the man before him, though they had never before met.

The roaring crowd became like thunder and their tapping feet like a torrential downpour of rain. In reality, the gold-eyed gladiator bowed with conceit to the crowd, but in Zano's eyes, he cruelly tossed the girl's head to the side. Her frozen face longed for justice with a smile that warmed Zano's heart and eyes that gave him hope. His fingers tightened on the jade hilt, and his heart raced as he began to charge with a bloodthirsty scream.

Caught off guard, the Arikarnon hastily raised his weapon as Zano bolted past and cut his leg with a swift strike. The massive man bellowed and wheeled with a mighty swing of his axe that nearly crushed Zano's skull.

The axe thrashed in rage, and the Blood Scaldor could no longer find an open shot. He dodged and weaved his way around the slashes, each time to the cheers of the crowd. In frenzy, the

Arikarnon rushed him, and with an overhead smash, sent him soaring to the ground even though he parried the blow. The crowd went into uproar as their favored fighter's axe came down toward Zano's chest, but he rolled out of the way and sprang up with a slice across the hulk's arm. Asul took a careless hack at his opponent's chest, but the Blood Scaldor slid to the side and brought his blade down, slicing off the warrior's good hand. The axe dropped, and with a howl Zano's arm was clasped by Asul's remaining hand, and he was tossed across the sand.

With panther-like reflexes, Zano landed on his feet and slid across the ground until his tough soles halted him. The Arikarnon grasped his weapon, still able to wield it with only one bulky arm. Zano bolted toward him, flourishing his blade, and deflected a swing from the axe. The strikes were nowhere near as powerful, but they were feral, so the Blood Scaldor continued to defend his body. A lucky thrust impaled the Arikarnon's functioning forearm, but a strong kick caused Zano to lose grip of his weapon. The massive man tossed his axe aside, screamed, and tore the blade from his flesh. Blood leaked from his arms in streams, but still he wielded the sword. Unarmed, but alert, Zano began to evade the haphazard strokes of his lost armament.

The crowd was upright, desperately urging their fighter to make a killer blow on his opponent, who stood a foot shorter and was a great deal weaker. In desperation, Zano dove to the axe and lifted it. The weapon was cumbersome, so instead of fighting with it, he twirled and flung it at the Arikarnon, who was taken off balance by the blow. He then leapt and punched him directly in the wound on his working arm, causing Asul to howl and drop the sword, stumbling back as though he were intoxicated.

Sand trickled to the ground as Zano gripped the sword again. Swiftly, he pounced toward the Arikarnon and shoved the diamond tip through his throat. Tissue shred and blood gushed onto his face as the massive warrior crumbled to a heap on the ground.

The collapsed gladiator's eyes lost their color as Zano received the dousing of a shower of blood. His eyes flamed like the blazing sphere above, and the silence brought him joy. It was as if the energy of his fallen enemy transferred to him. Even in his clouded mind, he now stood with his hands grasping the hilt of the blade, which had impaled his opponent, in an arena of sand within a foreign land. No longer was he within the Desolura. Remorselessly, he ripped the sword from its fleshy sheath, the glossy iron trickling blood.

Silence empowered him as he took victorious strides toward the iron bars that opened upon his arrival. It encouraged him to go on, to fight until he may win over these people. He did not beg for applause but simply strode out with success in his own heart, leaving behind a corpse that was his first kill. It was then, as he traversed the dark halls of the undercroft, that he realized he was born to be a warrior—that the blade was all he innately knew.

The door to his chamber opened, and Tarak sprang up in jubilance. His withered face lit up with the vigor of a child. He saw Zano leave clean and return saturated with blood. The honor of battle was evident by his manner, and the experience of killing emanated from within his pupils.

"Now you are a man," Tarak stated with a heartfelt smile.

"I will make this crowd realize the foolishness of their hate." Zano said earnestly. He did not smile. His face only showed a sort of seriousness that few men of his age should harbor.

"Blood suits you," Tarak jested, trying to change the subject.

Zano cracked a smirk as a knock at the door revealed a bucket of fresh water, or at least, that is how it appeared in the darkness. He lifted it and began to drench himself, cleansing the blood from his body. Then, he scraped the damp blade and placed it on the sheet of leather. Realizing his apprentice's exhaustion, Tarak did not contest his lack of words. Though he appeared to be undaunted, the taking of a man's life is no easy endeavor. To drive iron through muscle and tissue to the sound of its tearing can unnerve even the heartiest of souls.

"You have killed many men Master?" Zano broke from his silence.

"I wish I knew how many..." Tarak closed his eyes as if in deep concentration.

"What happens when they die?"

"Most people of Isinda believe that we rise to the heavens after our death. And that the wicked are damned to spend eternity in the foul pits of Pregarus."

"What do you believe?" Zano leaned against the wall, deciding to take advantage of this rare moment to pry into Tarak's mind.

"I believe that this faith in a tranquil second life, in a sublime afterworld, was developed mostly to make the taking of life an easier task. Slaying a person whose soul will be reaped from his being, only to subsist eternally in nothingness, is a horrible thought. The Deimor believe that the heavens are reserved for gods, and so I am not sure where I will go when I die. I only hope that my mind is left to dream and have everything I never could in life. Tell me Zano, what do you believe?"

"I... I never thought about it. I suppose being lost to dreams would not be so bad, as long as they were nothing like mine." He shirked, thinking of how he tremored in fear throughout most nights.

"Death is not a nightmare. Whatever you believe Zano, it does not matter. What we do in life is how history will remember us. Take comfort in sending those you kill to a better place if you must, but know that most of them would gladly see you rot for eternity."

"Well then I guess I hope that in death we go wherever we most desire. That our minds take us to a place and a time where we can be happy."

"That sounds like a wonderful notion," Tarak smiled warmly,

"Perhaps when you see more of this land your ideas will change. Never believe something simply because it is expected or you are told to. Promise me that Zano."

"Even if it is you?"

"I can only guide you. I am not divine."

"Well no matter what, I trust you master."

"I hope that never changes," Tarak wiped a splash of blood off of his apprentices shoulder and patted his back. Fatigued from battle Zano laid down and closed his eyes with a faint smile painted across his face.

The day was young, but it did not matter; the light could not penetrate here, and Zano fell asleep with ease. That night, he dreamt of blood and death, of falling without any means to get up. Tarak observed him soberly as he trembled in a perturbed slumber. His past flooded through him, spawned by his most recent venture, as he scratched the floor in search of his dagger.

The Blood Scaldor envisioned himself roaring, finally freed of his chains, the rain pounding on his armor of naked scales. The fanatic Scaldor ravaged the girl with whom he had shared his heart, and blood seeped from the High Priest's mouth. Deep in the recesses of his latent mind, he desired more than all other things to mangle the priest—to gain vengeance for the lifetime of slavery his people suffered through and for his own suffering, which continued to plague him. The image of himself plunging his oppressor's dagger into his heart pleasured him, and then, he awoke.

Another day had passed, and again, he was scheduled to fight. There was no more time left to train or to talk, only for rest. Though Zano was young, an instinctual ferocity flowed through his veins like that of a wild animal. With an encouraging pat from Tarak he was off to fight once more.

This time the opponent wielded a bow and two long daggers. After a hard-fought battle of agility and reflexes, Zano

212

came out on top by jabbing the Arikarnon in the eye with his own arrow and slicing the head from his shoulders.

Again, Zano rested, and a day passed him by. This time, he spent at least an hour sparring with Tarak and then there was another battle. Quickly, he shred his opponent's leg with his sword. He found it more fitting to leave him weaponless and writhing in pain. His brutal showing won a few cheers from the crowd as another bout of combat passed, and still, he lived. His master grew elated that he had chosen this boy out of sheer chance and had uncovered a skillful warrior.

Six more encounters went by in an instant, and in each, Zano came out on top, suffering hardly a scratch. The audience grew to respect him as they realized he was there to stay. It was hardly a matter of adoration or love, but it seemed that the crimson-scaled warrior was all that was spoken of. The other gladiators desperately sought to butcher him, embarrassed that such an abomination could have lasted this far in the tournament.

Soon, there were only eight contenders left standing, fighting for an unknown prize. All full-bred Arikarnon of strapping physique, they were speechless that Zano could conquer their fellow warriors. As overpowered as he was physically, he was remarkably quick and masterful with a weapon he had only recently begun to wield.

Now that the final battles had arrived, there was a break in the competition, and Zano awoke only to find himself bored as he consumed his daily meal of an unknown vegetable and tough meat with his master. The Arena was being used for criminal fights and entertainment by creatures or exotic dancers.

As he and Tarak simultaneously sipped water from a dish, a loud knock on the door signaled the entrance of the plump Arikarnon. Rarely had he returned to speak to Zano, so this visit was unforeseen, but welcome.

"You have surprised me in many ways scale face," the man stated in an indiscernible manner.

"Do you need something of me?" Zano questioned.

"Agoge's Hand desires to meet with you," he explained with a slight bow.

"Who?"

"Foreigners," he murmured under his breath. "He is the king of the desert, lord of me and now you. The mortal hand of our beloved god. This is an honor one rarely receives, so do not deny him."

"I will come."

"I suggest you come alone; a Deimor will not be well received."

Zano glanced at his master, who shook his head and then smiled in approval.

"Go. I'll be here," Tarak said comfortingly.

With a nod Zano stood, leaving the sword behind, and followed the organizer of the Arena out of the chamber. There were no escorts this time; the Arikarnon had come to realize that this Blood Scaldor had too much honor to try and flee. Through a maze of hallways they walked, passing guards and gladiators who all skeptically eyed the outsider. After minutes of traversing bends and sharp turns, they emerged through a wooden hatch into the light. Hot sun licked their faces with intense rays, and for the first time, Zano saw the city in which he fought.

It was spectacular, like nothing he had ever seen before. Only the distant glimmer of the Bronze Tower paralleled its splendor. The buildings appeared to be a disorganized jumble of meager shanties fashioned of mud brick and more affluent houses of sandstone and limestone, both housing gardened, flat roofs. The streets were lined with vivid green cacti, which sprouted blood red flowers from each needle. The more prosperous houses held fenced gardens of varying desert flora and had windows plated with gold. A few of the luxurious houses had elaborate designs carved into white marble panels as well as gold ones. All of these dwellings circled around the numerous, scattered oases that provided for the city. The Arikarnon may have been well adapted to survive long periods without water, but they were not free from its clutch.

Zano followed the plump man through the wide streets, which were littered with citizens and trade carts. Merchants sold weapons originally purchased from blacksmiths, as well as water and foodstuff, from common to rare. Untrusting gold eyes battered Zano; however, all now knew who he was. Perhaps not by name, but his crimson scales distinguished him. Children frolicked, toying with wooden weapons, and adults flocked back and forth. Women transported clay jugs of water, on their heads, to the bazaars, and men worked and strolled for differing motives. Most, including the women, wore only loincloths; however, the wealthier were adorned in vibrant, flowing robes, much like the Arena's organizers, with turbans atop their heads.

Behind them, in all of its wonder, stood the great Arena, like a beacon of Arikarnon glory, its gold and white outer frame glistening in the sunlight. The folds of its inscriptions and the statues within the openings of its pointed outer rows of arches were even visible from a long distance, perfectly engraved by the Hand of Agoge himself. The many columns along this wall had fluted shafts wrapped in gold, with elaborate capitals of pure white marble. Roaring flames brought attention to the peak, which towered above all else, reaching upward to graze the sky and uncover the heavens. The Heart of Agoge was its name, implying the very emanation of his strong will and might. Indeed, it was the heart of the Akai Desert, and the desert, in the eyes of the Arikarnon, embodied Agoge.

Guards, dressed no differently than civilians, armed with scimitars and spears, eyed Zano like a criminal, waiting for him to make one wrong move and to take his head for themselves. Together, he and the Arena organizer passed colorful vendors until, above the roof of a mudbrick hovel, the palace of the desert king could be seen. There were four white marble spires topped with golden domes that thinned out to a point at the top. Flawless rubies lined the edge of each one, wrapping around to a flame at the sharp point. Streams of red cloth draped down the towers, which were engraved with swirling embellishments. The square structure encompassed by the spires was coated with marble as well, except this marble was beautified with elaborate depictions of the ancient legends of the Deity of Flame. Each pointed-arch window was outlined with topaz, and a panel of polished gold lined the main structure, around its area, just beneath the flat roof. Atop the roof was a lush garden of flowers and vegetation, most of which seemed unnatural to the region.

Just as it did when he witnessed the arena for the first time, Zano's mouth gaped at the sight of the palace. He could not begin to fathom how beings so small could construct such a mammoth wonder—a building which lasted through wars and coups, through storms and the fury of the heavens, and which should long ago have been decimated. He came to the great gate, which could easily fit four Arikarnon stacked one on top of another. Two rows of guards readied their weapons and checked Zano to make sure he did not have any. By the wave of the arena organizer's hand, one soldier nodded and tapped the great gate of solid gold, which was painted and carved to appear as a churning inferno. The bulky doors creaked open, and Zano followed into the hall.

The hall was long and narrow. A red carpet, threaded with golden designs of spiky flames, was unfurled down the long passageway. Along it on either side were shining pits of roaring fire with a gold-clad guard armed with a spear beside each one. Iron chambers hung from the ceiling, which held immense candles. Fantastic stories and legends were painted down the room's length, with colors as vivacious as the golden floor. Doors of detailed marble protruded along the paintings, leading into the many quarters of the palace.

Across the way was the great throne, which was like nothing Zano could have envisioned in his young mind. The gray figure of the king sat within the outstretched palm of the hand of a giant, which was sculpted masterfully, each ridge of the skin finely detailed. The arm extended up into a smooth pillar of swirling white marble, and three more pillars of the same formation stood on each side, with golden candelabra jutting along the length of them. Directly on either side of the palm were pits of fire that spiked to about knee-high. There was no lift necessary to witness the extravagance of the room—only the invitation of the most powerful mortal in the desert's entirety.

With each step there was a lengthy echo, and with each forward movement the great king's figure grew more apparent. His bald head shined, and his eyes held an inert significance and strength. He wore the same topaz-embedded gold plate and the same gold circlet atop his head. As if meditating, he sat, legs folded, in the center of the colossal palm with his hands outstretched to each side. A subtle smile formed on his face, and his eyes sparkled with a visible hospitality. As soon as Zano approached, he knew in his keen mind that this was a kind king—a man who, despite all the wondrous conventionalities of a lord, cared immensely for the well-being of his people.

The organizer of the Arena subserviently kneeled at the foot of the throne, and, unknowing of any other course of action, Zano followed.

"So this is the red Scaldor I hear of?" the king asked with a brutish voice that harbored a hint of compassion.

"Yes my lord. This is he," the plump Arikarnon answered with a *kowtow.*

"Good. You may leave, Orthal," the king said, then bowed.

"Yes, my lord," Orthal responded nervously and exited the room with as much silence as was possible, leaving Zano, the Lord of the Desert and at least 12 guards alone inside of the great hall. Ill thoughts filled the minds of the present soldiers as the foreigner approached their beloved lord.

"I am Kalo, Lord of the Arikarnon. Agoge's Hand. It is rare that an outsider may kneel before the palm of his holiness. What is your name?"

"I am Zano, and I am a Blood Scaldor," Zano uttered softly, in awe of the grandiose man who peered down at him.

"Well Zano, tell me. What brings you to my desert?" Kalo said as he rose from his illustrious throne. He was tall and mighty, more with the appearance of a warrior than a sovereign.

"My master sought for me to learn about the desert people."

"You did not expect the circumstances that now enshroud you?"

"No. I was a slave in my hometown. My master freed me and desired to educate me on the history and present of Isinda."

"A slave! Yet you speak and fight so well?"

"Some slaves refuse to surrender," Zano answered after taking some time to formulate a response.

"I see," Kalo said as he ran his hand through the flames of one of the pits. "I have invited you here to inform you of my dilemma."

"Dilemma?"

"Yes. You see it is not against the laws of the arena for an outsider to compete; however, it is not written that he may. People have begun to question whether or not it is lawful to let you fight. Most thought that you'd have already died. Ultimately, as the Hand of Agoge, the decision is mine. So tell me. Why do you fight?"

"I was tossed in the arena against a beast I did not imagine to exist. I was given the choice of fighting for my life or dying— to either win and be free or bleed before a mob that hates me for reasons I do not understand!" Zano explained, his eyes searing and his nostrils flaring. The guards brandished their weapons, but Kalo halted them with a wave.

"You have scales like our age-old enemies and coloration like those who conquered us. You are a race that even I am not familiar with, and people fear the unknown. Arikarnon are distrustful of the other races, which is the reason you were forced to fight in the first place. Nobody wants to see a foreigner make a mockery of our most esteemed competition—"

Zano cut the king off with a hasty remark. "That is why I fight. To win over your people, so they might look upon me with love."

"Do you not have a home of people who love you?"

"I am a product of rape and slavery! Should I return to my shackled people who will forget my existence? To the Scaldor who will chain me or sacrifice my life for their god? I have no home!" Zano abruptly sprang to his feet and roared with the rage of years of slavery swelling up in the forefront of his mind.

"Forgive my ignorance," Kalo sighed. "Though I do not know the consequences should you win, I shall allow you to fight. You are brave to scold me in my own hall, Blood Scaldor."

Zano remained silent, though the expression on the king's face emitted an earnest apology. "Perhaps your bravery will win over my people. It has certainly won me. Never in all my years as king has a man reprimanded me in my own hall. I now see how you have come so far," Kalo said. He smiled warmly and rose to sit once more on the great palm. "You may leave with my blessing."

"Thank you, king of the desert," Zano said calmly and showed gratitude with a slight bow. He wheeled and began to cross the elongated hall, the flames swaying toward him like a message ordained from the heavens.

"May Agoge guide your hand, Zano. Thank the heavens that your sapphire kin are not nearly as courageous as you," Kalo shouted across the hall, his voice reverberating through its emptiness. Zano did not turn around, but the subtle praise of him over his former masters did not go unnoticed. The king's ignorant remark failed to overshadow the respect that Zano now held for him. Most lords would have had a man executed in the wake of such actions, but this one realized his blunder. A rare trait for a ruler to hold is humility, and if not for it, Zano would have lost his life without delay. Unlike with Sila in the future, he was of no real benefit to the Desert King—in fact, it was precisely the opposite. Only for honor was he spared, and that made Kalo's favor a mutual feeling.

Zano had entered the palace without the slightest idea of what to expect. Now, as he left, he had won over the king of an entire race. Bold and young, he bellowed at Kalo, discounting the magnitude of his actions. The thought crept into his mind that if he could gain the favor of the Lord of the Desert, then he could acquire the same from his people.

CALL OF HONOR

"From the sand and gold of
my desert, I construct this Arena.
Here will my subjects fight
for my heart, in my honor."

Agoge, the Lord of Flame

What is it about death that can bring a crowd to its feet in exhilaration? The battle may have no sway in their lives, but the thrill of witnessing an animalistic endeavor drives them to utter ecstasy. It can be just as addictive as an opiate or a tankard of ale. Can man's desire to observe the savage nature of his kind truly be explained by words? For who is more savage, the warrior with the sole skill of killing, or the crowd? The gladiator fights for survival; once he enters an arena, it is all that fills his mind. The observer is in attendance simply to choose a favorite and root for the other to die. How far can that possibly be from unprincipled? Should the audience not aid their fellow man, rather than perpetuate the death of one? Did the gods curse us at our inception with the desire to see violence before our very eyes—the desire to see blood spurt onto sand? Or have we done this to ourselves? Have war and battle become so much the culture of the races of Isinda that it has taken over everything we are? So much that a gladiatorial battle draws a throng of thousands, and an execution becomes the day's affair?

Perhaps death's amusement exists out of man's fear of it. That seeing warriors defy their dread boils man's blood so that he lives vicariously through them. If the fighters could be revived, how thrilling would an arena's practice actually be? As a viewer watches, he stamps his own fears onto his favored contender, hoping that he may defy the odds and become greater than life, or die trying. If he is to die, the observer does not join him, but simply awakens from his fantasy and chooses another to applaud. All that is certain is that the industry of death will never ruin. There will always be those of us with a fear, and we will look for others to put it to the test, so that we may be free of death's clutch.

The day of reckoning had arrived. A choice of three armaments was arrayed on a table before the spiked iron gate: a circular shield, the wooden face about the size of a man's head, which strapped around the forearm; a short bow along with a quiver of ten arrows; and the stone dagger of the High Priest, which the Arikarnon had confiscated from Tarak. Zano was forbidden from utilizing his master's sword in this battle, so he eagerly chose the stone dagger, which he had, for whatever reason, missed. Since he was not proficient with a bow, he also wielded the undersized shield. Then, he peered through the wide slits of the entrance, out into the Heart of Agoge.

The Arena was as it never had been before, deafeningly loud. The Arikarnon were so riled that their stamping feet knocked stone shards from the tunnel in which Zano waited. There were drums echoing throughout the structure, being pounded in brutal, tribal beats as the eternal flame glared fiercely, as if ready to deliver Agoge himself from the darkness.

"From the east gate, I bring you a warrior from the province of Ekal," Orthal announced and gazed around the stadium, his resonant voice gaining the crowd's silence. "A man of nimble feet and a true shot. Agoge bids welcome! Yuru!"

The audience exploded with a slew of voracious applause. Dust and stone bombarded Zano's head as the onlookers frenzied, trilling their tongues and slamming the ground. He was astonished that a structure could withstand such abuse, but if any could, it was the Desert Arena.

"Next, I welcome a man who has surprised us all. Through all of your jeers, he has persisted and now stands in a position in which no other has stood. Agoge is pleased to welcome the Blood Scaldor—Zano!" Orthal roared, and the crowd doused the name with taunts and hateful cries. Food and rocks battered the sand before Zano as the derision was amplified to a level he could not have fathomed.

The gates of Pregarus slid open, and the Blood Scaldor stepped out into the hot sun, suspended straight above. Every inch of the Arena was crammed with Arikarnon who had flocked from the outer provinces for this grand spectacle. Time seemed to slow as he came before his opponent. Each moment was extended. The kicked sand dangled in midair.

Yuru was tall, yet he didn't appear exceedingly powerful. His muscles were long and lean rather than bulky—built for quickness and agility. A bow and a quiver of ten arrows were slung over his back, and a poignard was tucked into his tight loincloth. Their eyes met with vicious glares. There was not a bit of compassion, for they were both well aware of the reality of the situation. One of them was going to die, and the crowd desperately willed it to be the bold foreigner.

"Kneel before Agoge's Hand, warriors, and let the flame of our lord be with you," Orthal beckoned. From the shadow emerged King Kalo. The audience went into a frenzy as the King settled within a gorgeous viewing chamber of solid gold. He sat beside a gold-adorned woman of wondrous beauty with a long, slender frame. She was obviously his queen. To his other side was a zealous man, just a bit older than Zano, with fiery eyes. He was the apparent heir to the throne of the Arikarnon. By the stretch of the king's palms, the crowd grew silent, and Yuru kneeled, placing his weapon on the ground. Zano followed, stabbing his dagger into the sand, and then rubbed the loose particles between his rough hands. He gazed at the king intensely until a nod signaled them to rise.

"Stand before your gates warriors and Agoge be with you!" Orthal yelled from beside the Lord of the Desert. The mass remained silent as the contestants stood at either side of the arena. "You all know of the fires that lay dormant beneath this arena. My people! Today I bring you … The Warren of Flame!" he shouted to the crowd's undulating delight.

The arena seemed to be rocking as the sound of chains and gears crackled. Patches of the ground began to fold down in a puff of dust, and after a few minutes, the flooring of the Heart of Agoge was reduced to a maze of narrow pathways surrounded by black pits. Within the pits were roaring infernos that would consume any who fell from the treacherous walkways above. The flames flared up like the ravenous tongues of elemental beasts.

The ground had just transformed before Zano's very eyes into a labyrinth that hungered for his life. The sound of the audience was like nothing he had ever heard, too boisterous to drown out. Peering across the way, through the hazy smog of gray smoke, he saw Yuru stringing an arrow into his bow.

"Warriors … fight!"

With a pluck, an arrow was sent whizzing toward Zano's head. He raised his shield and deflected it, but the impact threw him off balance. Losing his sure footing, he leapt off of one foot across a blazing hot gap and landed on another sandy path. He gripped his dagger and sprinted toward his enemy. The turns were sharp and slippery, wrapping like snakes of sand and stone across the fire-donned ring. Another arrow sped toward him, but this time he was prepared with his shield and was unfazed by its shock.

Dexterous feet had brought Zano halfway to his prey, but now there was a wide pit without a crossover before him. Following a deep exhale, he dove across the break with an arrow just grazing his leg, peeling off a scale as he rolled to safety. Just as he gained his footing, another projectile zipped through his hair. Out of instinct, he recoiled, but he slipped off of the path, catching the edge with one hand. Flames seared the soles of his feet as Yuru shifted his position in order to gain an advantageous shot. Swinging upwards with his dagger, Zano jabbed the ground and heaved himself up. His head spun until he found Yuru, but another arrow sent him sprawling onto his back. The shot pricked the tip of his nose, and the proximity of his death exhilarated him as well as the crowd, who groaned. Finally, Zano found his footing and continued his advance. The sixth arrow zoomed futilely into his shield as he rounded another corner. Rage and instinct fueled him as he bounded hurriedly down the meandering paths.

Yuru sent an additional arrow speeding at his opponent, but the Blood Scaldor betrayed the will of the crowd with a twirling evasion. Then, fate brought the two of them standing face to face, an inferno between them. Zano's eyes smoldered, cold and heartless as a snake that had cornered its prey. Yuru smirked and strung a projectile through his bow, then pulled back the string. At the sound of a high-pitched snap, the arrow zoomed at the Blood Scaldor, but it was met with a crash. It splintered in pieces onto the ground, and Zano effortlessly hurdled the gap. The Arikarnon tossed his bow away and unsheathed his poignard, meeting the vicious slash of his enemy with a parry. The opponents brandished their weapons skillfully. Clashing iron flashed, and blades whirled atop cautious feet. One wrong step could lead to a fatal plummet into an agonizing abyss.

Seeing he was outmatched in close combat, Yuru fled down a path, and Zano hastily gave chase. The Arikarnon's nimbleness was unfaltering. With long strides, he easily gained a distance from his enemy and halted, but his plan of exhausting Zano, whose youth and exhilaration were peerless, failed. Yuru slashed high, and the Blood Scaldor tackled him to the ground. A cloud of dust blinded them as they thrashed violently. They writhed and punched through the sand, coming dangerously near the perilous edge as each struggled to pin down the other's armed hand.

After minutes of toiling, a fortuitous blow to Zano's hand sent the stone dagger skidding across the sand, out of reach. In rage, he struck Yuru in the head with his shield and lunged over him. The Arikarnon wriggled his body as the Blood Scaldor plucked an arrow from the quiver on his back in mid-air. He slid across the loose ground until finally finding his footing. Yuru staggered toward his adversary and thrust at him. As if able to anticipate his actions, Zano grabbed the assailing arm and fell backward, driving upwards with the arrow. He rolled to get on top of the Arikarnon, who collapsed to the ground in anguish and then twisted his body around.

As Yuru came to face the sky, his poignard propelled toward Zano's throat, but fortunately, Zano caught his enemy's arm and tore the weapon from his clutch. With callous eyes, he sunk the blade into Yuru's heart, and the tumultuous crowd was hushed. Blood squirted from the gashes as the Arikarnon struggled for his next breath. His lips whimpered as life fled his being and ice traced his veins.

Zano rose to his weary feet with his chest heaving. His mighty frame hulked over the corpse beneath him as he shed the shield on his forearm. His hair flapped wildly, the sapphire strands glistening under the sun. In this sublime moment, he was immortal, a legend of his own making. And then, suddenly through the reigning silence, a single clap prevailed. The powerful hands of Lord Kalo smashed together, until another followed, then another, and another after that. Zano lifted his arms and roared toward the serene sky. His voice echoed like a beast vastly larger then he in signal to the audience. They erupted in appraisal for his triumph, and as deafening as the ruckus was, it was as harmonious to him as the notes of a flute. The cheers poured on him as though he were a conquering hero, and it was like nothing he had ever dreamed of. Pillars of flame spouted on either side, recognizing him as the victor. The fire was that of Agoge, and in essence, he was proclaimed victorious by the grand God of Fire himself.

Zano retrieved his dagger and left the grand Arena a champion; for what reason had the Arikarnon to hate such magnificence? As he was escorted down the murky corridors, he could not help but feel that he had won this significant tournament, though in truth it was but the beginning. The door opened, and spheres of swirling red greeted him. Arms clamped around his bloody frame, and he returned the grateful squeeze.

"So you shall go unchallenged to victory?" Tarak smiled, brimming with excitement.

"Did you hear them, Master? Did you hear them cheer?" Zano stuttered in excitement.

"Aye Zano. You have won them over. If a king shall clap, so his people shall follow."

"With blade and words, Master," the ecstatic Blood Scaldor said, reflecting on what Tarak had said to him.

"Never forget it," Tarak advised as Zano sat upon the leather sheet.

The Deimor congenially joined and placed the brilliant sword by his apprentice's feet. He watched as the young warrior grasped the handle and examined the glossy blade, running his fingers up to the malicious diamond tip.

"I see so much of the Twin Blades within you," Tarak praised sincerely.

"You knew the Twin Blades?"

"Knew them? I was one of their trainers. I watched them grow side by side since they were shorter than the sword you wield."

"As a slave I looked up to them. I read that they were invincible warriors." Zano's eyes trailed out into his unbounded imagination.

"That is how it goes. Unfordive was so masterful of the art of swordsmanship that they say he stood an army by himself-"

"Is that true?" the Blood Scaldor interrupted.

"To an extent. But he was beside his brother Seekoras, whose strategies were unprecedented, and together, they conquered Isinda. They were two pieces of one extraordinary whole. Apart, they were shards, one of strength and one of wisdom. Combined, they were the dread of millions, faulted with only one weakness," Tarak said, pausing.

"What?" Zano questioned, believing them to be the embodiment of perfection.

"Their love for each other. Either one of them would rather lose a battle than see the other come to harm—a trait rarely seen in those of pure Deimor blood."

"I read in a legend that they were impure. I didn't believe it though."

"It is far from false. They were born half of Deimor blood and half of Suvrarian blood, yet though they appeared different, their people loved them more immensely than they loved their king. I loved them. Though their senior, just being in the presence of their brilliance sent a tingle down my spine. It was surreal. I thought them to be unparalleled in all ways until I came across a raw warrior of blood equally as impure," Tarak eulogized and looked at his apprentice with watery eyes.

Zano gazed back, not knowing how to respond. Such an extravagant appraisal was something he had never experienced.

"Tell me more of the brothers," Zano whispered.

"We have many months left of travel, and you have already far surpassed me. Without my tales or legends, what use would you have left for me?" Tarak said, grinning.

"You praise me too highly, my Master," Zano spoke modestly.

"No Zano, in fact it is just the opposite. You will come to recognize your greatness soon enough."

"I'll never conquer Isinda like they did."

"By the time the luster flees your eyes, you won't have to."

That was the end of their conversation, and those final words would stick in Zano's mind for the years of life to come. They would lead him to ponder whether the Twin Blades truly did conquer this land. What was the purpose of all that spilled blood if they could not retain what they had gained, he thought to himself, *they may have indeed subjugated Isinda, but without the hearts of its people, what was truly accomplished?*

These thoughts filled Zano's mind as a bucket of water was placed before his door. He thoroughly cleansed himself and handed Tarak his dagger to conceal as he heard the steps of Orthal echo down the passageway.

"You do not cease to amaze me," he said admiringly as he entered the room.

"What do you require?" Zano questioned hurriedly as to avoid an unwanted lecture.

"I cannot say whether I agree or disagree with his lordship's decision; however, your presence brings me great fortune."

"I am pleased to see that I make you content," Zano responded sarcastically.

"Yes, well it is customary that at dusk on the morrow the final four warriors assemble for a feast in Agoge's name," Orthal said.

"I will attend." The Blood Scaldor did not hesitate a moment in his acceptance.

"No foreigner has ever attained this honor, Zano. I cannot tell you how the others will receive you, and I do not wish for a death before—"

"Do not worry. All of the fights will occur appropriately. All of the gold you can desire will be yours at the end of this spectacle of death," Zano grumbled.

"Do not mock what I do!" the Arikarnon shouted and then

breathed to calm himself. "Very well. I will assure the lords that you will be present. I *hope* that no harm comes to you."

Zano merely replied with a bow. After the plump Arikarnon left in a huff, he wearily collapsed to the ground.

Tarak broke from his silence. "Be wary of the others, Zano. They will surely detest you," he warned.

"I know, but all he cares about is that I am able to bring him gold. I have only been free for a short time, but I already see what men like him are," Zano asserted.

"And what is that?"

"He is greedy—a man with no more honor than a sick rat. Men like him don't love brothers or women. They love gold. If my death at the feast was to profit him, he would surely send me with open arms," Zano explicated.

"He sees all of the fighters as coin. It is your uniqueness that yields him revenue, so I couldn't see him taking any audacious course."

"I would love to see him do what he gets paid to make others do."

"Do not fret, Zano. Fight for yourself, and let him have all the plunder he desires. The pride and glory that victory brings is gold enough for men like you and me," Tarak responded in a comforting tone. He rose to his feet and moved beside his apprentice, placing an affectionate hand on his shoulder. They grew silent until Zano fell into slumber, still drained from battle. The Deimor watched over him as a father would, securing him from all who might attempt to bring him harm.

Dusk of the next day came with a fluctuation of silence and cheers for spectacles above. Zano was escorted through the doors of the city's grand, domed temple to the God of Flame. The structure gleamed scarlet under the rising sun, its gold polished and unblemished. Present was a circular table, which was clearly transported for just this occasion; the wood did not match the ornate walls. Glittering statues lined the holy sanctuary. Servants laid an elaborately-decorated crimson tarp over it and slid four cumbersome seats of solid white marble up to the edges. The chairs matched the sleek floor, and the sheet corresponded with the crackling torches and candles that littered the room.

As Zano approached his seat, three pairs of repulsed eyes stared him down. They belonged to the stern faces of his opponents, whose features were stalwart and shoulders were broad. They too wore nothing but loincloths, though unlike Zano, their skin was like charcoal and their builds more developed. Servants departed hastily; as the foreigner shifted his chair to sit, there was an eerie sullenness about the room. He sat, but still the only sounds that could be heard were the rustling of his scales and the soft hiss of the flames.

Minutes of hushed silence passed, until the servants provided each man with a golden plate, fork, and knife. Ignoring the insolent glares, Zano raised the fork and studied it. He had never seen or used a utensil such as this, and it baffled him. Still, all he could think about was jabbing it into the trio of hulking Arikarnon.

Food by the heap came flowing in, from fruits and vegetables to the carcasses of small animals, then larger ones. Chewy meat of the colossal Scorpions came in segments of carapace, as well as other nourishments, of which Zano could not guess at the identity. Everything about the event made him uncomfortable. Unknown food and other items were flung at him and the loathing in the Arikarnon' expressions was far from discreet.

The serving plates were quickly cleared of victuals. It was a feast the likes of which Zano had never experienced. He was so overwhelmed with delectable food that his stomach was near exploding. The others ate civilly with forks and knives and scowled at him for eating as he knew how to—the way a man instinctually desires to consume. The Arikarnon to his right whispered into the ear of a servant with a culpable smirk on his visage. This one seemed to be the most venerable warrior of the bunch. His jaw was more pronounced, and his muscles refined to perfection.

Soon, the servant returned with four crystal glasses of a translucent liquid and placed one before each combatant.

"It is customary for the final four chosen by Agoge to indulge a glass of water in his name. For you foreigner, it will be your last," the man on the right snickered.

Zano did not respond; he didn't even offer a glance. He simply lifted the water and took a sip. Irate at the young man's arrogance, the Arikarnon rushed out of the temple and, with a smile, the Blood Scaldor followed, drink in hand, no longer interested in the meaningless ceremonies.

Darkness overtook him, the orange light of scattered torches wavering over his face. The streets were bare for the most part, save for the guards who escorted him, until Zano saw the frame of a child huddling in the corner of a structure. The boy clutched his stomach and whimpered in agony. He was naked and emaciated, simply left to die. Seeing his own torturous past in the suffering boy, Zano, against the will of his escorts, placed the glass of water near the boy's head and let him be. The guards pushed him forward as he looked back to see two golden slits peering up at him in unspoken gratitude.

They continued to walk, when from the shadow of an alley, two wrinkled hands grasped Zano by his shoulders. The soldiers whipped around with their spears aimed steady at the figure, but upon seeing who it was, they knelt admiringly. Zano gazed curiously through the shadow to discern an aged woman. Her face was marred by creases and blemishes, and her back was hunched over, making her his height. She was frail, and her hair hung loosely like thin, gray wires, but within her there was untold strength. Behind the web of red veins coursing through her gold pupils, there was a knowingness that could not be denied. A crown of thorns rested atop her head with colorful beads draped off, and around her chipped tusks were beaded gold circlets. Her rags fell down her lean frame as though she were a beggar. For some unexplainable reason, Zano knew she should not be underestimated.

"You..." Her sharp voice dithered with wisdom and age. "You hold great promise, but with that promise comes the inevitability of possible failure." She reached out and placed her trembling hands on his cheeks.

"Who are you?" Zano questioned dubiously as torchlight wavered over her craggy face.

"She is the Fire Seer, foreigner. Respect her wisdom," one of the guards demanded from his *kowtow*.

"Yes, I sense a flicker within you. I will gaze into your future. Ease your mind. Feel mine meld with yours." Her eyes rolled back in her skull as her lids began to shudder. She shook violently, squeezing Zano's temples with aberrant power. He felt eldritch energies streaming through his mind. There was a piercing pain, and suddenly he screamed the Seer's eyes sprang open with flares of ethereal flame. Both panted as they glared violently at one another.

"What did you see?" Zano gasped.

"I saw... I saw a sky. It is dark and stormy, but inside of it..." She walked out into the street using a gnarled cane for support and glared at the sky, in somewhat of a trance as she motioned to the vision in her mind with her hands. "There is a city of gray stone and arcane enchantments. It suspends at unreachable heights as the coldness of the upper sky laces it with ice. From it rings a mighty roar that shatters the heavens. Then, it plummets to the ground with a splash of rock and dust. The world quakes and shudders. Then there is silence." As she finished, she fell to her knees wheezing. The guards rushed over to brace her as her eyes rolled back to their normal state.

"What does that mean?" Zano was perplexed. None of what she said applied to anything he had yet experienced or understood.

"I can only see. I cannot give meaning. My sight spans from birth to the extent of your influence on any who remain. What

I see is an ephemeral glimpse at the scheme of your impact and existence. Your path will always be illuminated, Zano of the Blood Scaldor," she said, then retreated to her alley, pointing to Zano with her cane as she shuffled backward.

"What does it mean?" he shouted desperately as she melted into the darkness.

"Her predictions can at times be … erratic. Now keep walking!" one of the guards advised before pushing Zano, who could not take his eyes off of the alley, along.

The next day came through a tumultuous sleep, which Zano felt he would not survive. It was not dreams that haunted him, however. He instead trembled and sweat from a sharp pain running down his veins. His battle was approaching, and Tarak realized that he was not well. He tried to speak with him and dissuade him from fighting, but Zano showed an incensed manner that was not in his nature. With a scowl, he pushed past his master and was escorted to the gates of the Heart of Agoge.

Each breath he took was troubled. His heart felt as though it would sink from his ribs, and his feet faltered as he grew woozy, the sword in his hand becoming his only support. The world swirled around him. Echoing shouts of Orthal could not be discerned. Cheers pierced his eardrums, and he released a scream from his blackened lips. The gate slid open, and he stumbled out in a state of vertigo like a drunkard. Black vomit spewed from his mouth, and without a word, he crumpled face first to the ground.

The entire crowd was silent; they had awaited the moment of Zano's defeat for so many days but could hardly believe it had arrived. The warrior across from his vulnerable body was the man who had sat to his right the night before. His eyes gleamed with bliss as he brandished his large axe and approached Zano with the desire to slay him. None in the crowd opposed the motion, for awe had inundated them. It was the wise words of the great King Kalo that broke into this serene moment of Arikarnon triumph.

"Do not go near his body, Arkul!" he bellowed in a commanding tone. Orthal observed him with shock. He could not understand his lord's act of compassion toward a foreigner.

"My lord, it is not my fault that he is too drunk to fight! A man such as he deserves death. This crowd wills it!" the warrior Arkul pleaded upward with his case.

"They are silent, as you should be!" Kalo demanded with a force that struck the imposing fighter into stillness. The king glistened in the sunlight between his gold-clad wife and child. His eyes were like a torrent of golden flame, swirling and vehement as two smoldering stars.

"Yes my lord," Arkul desisted and knelt obediently, though against his own craving.

"Does this look like the deed of ale? The Blood Scaldor has been poisoned! Do you hate him so much to see him die by this dishonor, or have you none? Outlander or Arikarnon, no one deserves this act of cowardice. You have your victory, Arkul, but it is a hollow one." The King's vigor commanded respect and wonder as guards flowed onto the sand and lifted the limp foreigner.

His body was transported to the underground chamber, where priests and healers were sent to sustain his being. Tarak could not believe his vision. His eyes teared as he uttered to the heavens in the Desthoroth tongue. Priests hummed while spooning what seemed to be antidotes into Zano's mouth. They also rubbed burning herbs across his forehead in an unearthly ritual. Kalo stood, displeased, in the room in order to observe the working of his subjects. It was just then that the old Deimor saw the effect his apprentice had on the king; he realized his own boundless adoration for the young man he had taken in as his own.

For hours, they waited in a hush, begging for the first sign of a gulp of air. Zano's pulse throbbed meekly, but its existence was hope for all. Finally, the crimson of old flushed his scales, and he gasped. Tarak brimmed with excitement, as elated as he had ever been, and Kalo joined him. The weakened warrior attempted to speak, but one of the priests instructed him to rest.

"What happened?" Kalo questioned the healers respectfully.

"He consumed a small portion of Scorpion venom. Slowly, it coursed through his body until it claimed him. Had we not gotten to him in time, and had the favor of Agoge not been with us, he would surely have died," the healers explained with feigned grins in order to please their lord.

"I thank you. You may leave," Kalo dismissed them, receiving a bow from each as they passed.

"I have spoken with Orthal, Deimor. You may leave this place when he is able," Kalo stated and turned to depart.

"You are a kind king," Tarak praised with a motion of appreciation.

"No man deserves this injustice. Not I, not he, not even you," Kalo refused to look at the man to whom he spoke, and exited. Tarak could see that his past dictated many years of loathing toward the Deimor race and did not question the disrespect. He only valued the fact that he and his apprentice still retained their lives.

For a few days, the old Deimor sat at Zano's side. It was the first time that the Blood Scaldor had appeared frail. It chilled Tarak to the very bone. He knew that had any more of the poison been consumed, his apprentice would not still be breathing. Yet, in his quiet mind, all that Zano thought about was that the boy to whom he had demonstrated generosity was surely deceased.

Zano's body ached, but a brooding hatred developed inside him. It didn't escape his intellect that Arkul had arranged the placing of the venom; however, he desired to know why. He wondered how any man could partake in such dishonor. It vexed him more than all of the other anomalies he had witnessed since his liberation.

Tarak waited until Zano was rejuvenated enough to begin to walk and speak with the same verve as before. His young body was hasty in its recovery. Where others would be incapacitated for a much longer period, the Blood Scaldor was swiftly rejuvenated. When Tarak deemed him ready, Orthal arrived at the door with a sufficient jug of water to escort them out of the great desert city. They shared no words while sluggishly moving throughout the labyrinth. It was an awkward quiet, but Zano could tell how ashamed the Arikarnon was.

They passed through the brilliant city, which was bustling with activity. The celebration ceremonies for the champion of the tournament were in progress. A spectacular parade doused the crowd with red flower petals and was speckled with twirling torches. It brought a tear to Zano's eye. The crowd, in their exuberance, did not take notice of the outlanders, who gazed across the sea of Arikarnon. Atop a black Scorpion sat Arkul in an illustrious robe of gold. The blasphemer absorbed appraisal like a conquering hero, but what had he conquered? Unlike all others, he glanced directly at the foreigners with a spiteful smirk. There was not a hint of regret in his eyes, and it drew Zano's lasting malice.

After a long, slow walk across the vast capital, they had reached the low sandstone wall that encompassed it. The iron gate opened, and Orthal did not offer a word. He simply handed over the water, bowed, and walked away for Zano never to see again. The raw sand was searing under the pulsing rays of sunlight, as together master and apprentice walked out, until a clamor of pounding footsteps halted them. Behind them, with a small regiment of clothed guards, came Kalo in his elaborate adornments. Tarak told his apprentice not to arrest, but he disobeyed. He waited as the grand king approached, and like a gleaming star fallen from the heavens, the Lord of the Desert came before them.

"Now that I have the foreigner Zano within my grasp, shall I let him go as a just man should, or kill him as should be the result of his loss?" Kalo wondered out loud.

"That was my deal with Orthal, not you!" Zano protested, offended by the King's words.

"The heavens tell me that I shouldn't let you go; that you will one day pose a threat to my land. For the first time in my life, I find myself compelled to disobey," Kalo smiled warmly.

"I do not know much, besides what I have managed to read and see. Perhaps there is more to this world than devotion to the unseen. You are a good king, moreso than your people."

"Those are your beliefs. Agoge is my lord and my champion, but our hearts cannot always follow our lord's will, as the man who poisoned you has contravened my own. Trust me, Zano, not all of my people share that dishonor," the great king said defensively.

"Yes, but, I wish that you and your people would listen to the advice you just offered me," Zano replied cunningly. He did not elaborate on the thought, but his words clearly struck Kalo at his heart, for he said nothing as the Blood Scaldor bowed and began to depart.

The king remained still, long after the outlanders were out of view. He was in shock. A man, who had just recently been freed, cut down to his very inner sentiment. His lingering distrust and often hatred of foreigners, especially the Scaldor, was unearthed. They were words that would dwell within him for the rest of his life, even those many years later at the feet of Sila.

"You have stunned a king," Tarak said and grinned tenderly as they continued on across the endless sea of sand.

"Was I not right?"

"You are already a wiser man than me. You will be great; I know it. Bards will sing of you. Legends will talk of your splendor," Tarak praised, his mind tracing out into the infinite possibilities.

"I always dreamed of being a hero. It was hard to imagine while I was in chains; hard to free my mind," Zano spoke with childlike excitement.

"That is what separates you from all others. You didn't surrender. You fought for your sanity. You learned and adapted, and now you are free."

"Because of you," Zano smiled.

Tarak laughed and continued on, "Let me tell you about how we Deimor conquered this unforgiving wasteland."

The old Deimor unveiled his story as they walked across the hot sand. The time had come for them to leave the desert with the favor of its lord. A golden vista was unfurled before them, assembled of gentle rolls and a blanketing haze. With the jug of water that was bestowed upon Tarak before they left, master and apprentice began their crossing of the folding sand, of the fire-breathing dunes of Agoge.

THE CHAMPION
OF AGOGE

*"You can hold on to your past. You
can allow it to clasp onto you like
the jaws of Pregarus. Or you can do
what seems like the impossible ... let go.
Release all that haunts you, for that
is true freedom."*

Sagu the Oracle

Justice is a rare phenomenon in this land called Isinda. In a world where death prevails, who defines one death as just and another as unjust? Revenge can be as scornful as cold-blooded murder. Death by the dagger in the secrecy of the night can be as vile as the slash of a sword by day. Can one act of violence be forgivable while another is punishable by yet another death? Are there truly opposites in killing? Death by searing flame is surely no different than lungs clogged with water, though these elements oppose one another. In this land, honor is an infrequent discovery, far more uncommon than diamonds and gold.

Perhaps it is these few men that hold the only comprehension of what justice really is. Is it the slaying of a master of slaves, or of a king who slaughters his own people without relent? Wouldn't any man like to believe so—that the execution of a petty criminal who stole a loaf of bread to feed his starving children is just the opposite? In fact isn't his act one of just cause? Men such as Zano would hold this true to their hearts, for only the honorable can dictate what is just and what is not. That is the unwritten code by which all should reside; otherwise, all killing has essentially no grounds.

Back in the time of the Bronze Empire, Zano walked through a hallway of the aged Deimor stronghold, scratching the stone with his invaluable dagger. The wall had been crudely painted and carved by long-dead Deimor artists, a rarity at the time this fortress was constructed. The artwork told the story of this structure as well as the Deimor conquest of the desert.

Having already subjugated the Scaldor, the brilliant Seekoras devised a plan. Over many months, this castle was built at the outer rim of the desert. Deimor would train in waves, one contingent moving in as another moved out. They trained under intense temperature, adapting so that they were able warriors within the desert climate. Each time the Arikarnon sent forces, Unfordive defended the fortress with fervor until his enemies were forced to retreat. Finally, King Malum used his influence to persuade an army of Scaldor, who long despised the Arikarnon, to invade a small town. The diversion was a success, as the vast forces of the Deimor flooded into the dunes. They moved leisurely with a steady supply of food and water at their rear. The Arikarnon tried to cut off their supply train but were thwarted by Scaldor and a group of Deimor concealed beneath the land. To avoid the same kind of ambush as he used, Seekoras sent small regiments of soldiers to trigger ambushes. When attacked, these groups retreated hastily and were reinforced by the blade of Unfordive the Sublime.

The Deimor cut straight through the desert like a bloody river, deflecting even the calvary of scorpion riders. Not weakened by an effortless invasion of the Scaldor, who chose to surrender quickly instead of sustain massive casualties, the Deimor went on an offensive against the heavily-guarded capital city of Agoga. Spears flew down from the low walls, but could not penetrate the shield phalanx. Arikarnon reinforcements approached from all outlying cities but were too late. An array of ladders and crude siege towers encompassed the city, and Unfordive had already entered, bringing with him a wrath that the desert people had never encountered. They thought him to be a descendant of the heavens.

As Arikarnon reinforcements arrived, they found the Deimor occupying and defending their own deity's city. Disillusioned by their inability to gain the walls, the King of the Desert, Lokal, father of Kalo, yielded to Malum, who stepped into his throne. Unlike the Scaldor, the Arikarnon suffered massive loses against the stream of horned warriors. The "Trail of Blood," as the invasion was called, was a heroic victory for the Deimor who now held dominion over the powers of eastern Isinda.

Zano, of course, knew this story by the tongue of his now-fallen master, but the crude, yet gruesome depictions fascinated him. Each image of Unfordive held an encircling, radiant aura brighter than the present torches, while Seekoras always wore the vivid robe of a master strategist. Passing the images, the Lord of Blood came to the chamber that was his. It was bare as the desert itself, furnished with only a worn strip of cloth for a bed. It was not much different than in the Arena undercroft, except the stone here derived from Scaldor lands. He sat on the material, removed his belt, and began to twirl his dagger in his palm. He eyed the blade with curious intensity, for it held an intrinsic value to him. His sword was the bestowment of his master, but the dagger retained his dreadful past within its very existence.

There was only a brief moment before Merasu walked through the door. The dark room, lit only by a livid beam of moonlight through a narrow window, enhanced his mystery. Smoldering purple eyes screamed death, and an unflinching mask hid a history too agonizing to imagine. Somehow Zano found trust and comfort with the ominous figure.

"What does the dagger mean?" Merasu asked pensively, though with an imposing voice, as he sat down.

"My freedom. My people's freedom. My rage and my darkness," Zano stammered, overwhelmed with passion. Merasu noticed the troubled look of loathing and decided to pry no more.

"Bold of the Arikarnon to deny us," he shifted the subject.

"Indeed," Zano cleared his throat.

"My Lord's generals do not trust you, but they will soon realize your strength."

"I don't need their favor. Until your lord allows my people to rest inside, that is all I will petition for."

"It will take time for them to trust the Blood Scaldor completely. You are different. Surely you must understand this."

"Aren't you?" Zano questioned tersely.

"Aren't we all?" Merasu responded with a smile under his mask, for it rose just a bit with his cheeks.

"If only they saw that."

"The king's goodwill shall win the blue-scaled over. Trust me," Merasu assured in a way reminiscent of Tarak.

"Well, if it could win them over to you," Zano jested, prying a rare laugh from the masked general. "Tell me Merasu. Is Sila a good king?"

"He holds a troubled past just as you do, but as far as kings go, I believe that he is. Have you heard the tale of how he was crowned—how he became the reincarnation of Brazdor?"

"No," Zano leaned forward in anticipation.

"Well. Years ago ... " Merasu began to weave an elaborate

story that enthralled Zano enough to visualize it happening before him.

> Following the annihilation of the Deimor, the Bronze Kingdom was in a steady decline. King Lordral, father of Sila, was one of the ninety-seven survivors of the Battle of the Deadlands. He was tainted by the death, by the curdling screams of all those around him. Like a poison, it coursed through his veins and crowded his mind, depraving him into a creature dominated by fear and dementia. He grew enamored with the arts and music, often disregarding his duties as king in favor of heartwarming parties and feasts with the nobles. Outlying kingdoms began to prey on towns and villages, but the king refused to send any troops. He desired an end to bloodshed, which was an impossible feat in his time. As enemies drew closer and closer to breaching the very gates of his city, he neglected them. Always in the past, the Bronze City boasted as the most powerful Scaldor kingdom, and all the others yearned for its endless water and metal. But, under Lordral's crazed rule, soldiers and guards were relieved of duty, sending the city in a downward spiral toward desecration. Crime flourished as all production of goods and trade with other kingdoms ceased to exist. Desperately, Sila attempted to talk sanity into his disillusioned father, but to no avail. The closest towns were breached, and the Army of Bronze was hardly sustained.

> One night, Sila stood within the Bronze Tower's lift beside a grizzled, veteran general. Verun was his name, and he, too, was a survivor of the Deadlands, though to him the battle remained only a horrid memory. It dwelled within him but failed to become a plague. Instead, it was precisely what made him the hardened warrior he was.

> "Do what must be done, my Lord," Verun willed somberly as the lift came to a halt and the chains stopped clanking.

> "Yes," Sila whispered with a detached expression.

> The prince stepped through an ornate bronze door and into the sleeping chamber of his father, the King, one floor below

the throne hall. Tarps of vibrant silk, from all spectrums of the rainbow, dressed the marble and bronze room. A bed too large for any normal man, of golden embroidery and white drapes, rested on the side of the space. Verun had it prearranged that no guards would be present, to which the manic king paid no heed. The walls were as ornate as the outer structure, with candelabra of crystal along them. The king gazed out of an arched window and beckoned his son to approach. A tear slid down the prince's cheek as he joined his father.

"It's beautiful, just like your mother was before she died," Lordral said as he observed his city. Water sparkled in the circular pool that outlined the tower on their level. Liquid cascaded down the side, splashing on either side of the opening and causing profound ripples that reflected the moonlight. The thousands of bronze roofs below emitted a jade glow, encompassed by luminous fortifications. The stars glittered in the clear night sky, streaks of vibrant anomaly giving it a surreal appearance. Sila took the vision in. It was the finest work of art he could imagine. A construction of the gods greater than any painting a mortal could reproduce. He desired now more than anything to defend it from the enemies that loomed at the apex of his sight.

"One day, it will all be yours," Lordral said and smiled innocently, with no more understanding of the present circumstances than a child. Sila eyed him in his lavish robe of vivacious red. The crown of sapphires and rubies on his head shimmered like something not of this world. The prince's eyes swirled with the passion of a raging storm and were filmed over with a sheet of liquid. The king held not a worry in the world. In fact, he was quite oblivious as his son removed a dagger of pure sapphire from his robe.

"Yes, father. One day," Sila gasped. Then, before he could change his mind, the prince let out a heartbreaking cry and plunged the blade between his father's shoulder blades. Tears flooded his cold cheeks as his king fell backward into his quivering arms. His legs buckled from the weight, and he collapsed to the ground, embracing the dying Scaldor with all of his love.

Winds of change caused the elaborate drapery to gently flap and the robes of the two men to billow. Lordral struggled for words while blood leaked through his trembling lips. His eyes grew bright as reason flowed back into his mind, and he realized all the wrongs he had committed.

"Be at peace, father," Sila whimpered with a stinging throat as he slid the dagger from his father's flesh. The king's eyes were frozen open, staring at his traitorous son with ghastly conviction. The dagger plummeted with a loud clash to the floor, blood trickling onto the glossy white marble. Sila's hand quivered violently along with his lips as he clenched the body of his beloved father, blood staining his hands.

"He died long ago, my Lord," Verun asserted as he stepped through the door, with a trail of water down his stern visage. He approached the body solemnly and removed the brilliant crown. "My king," he praised and placed the divine article atop the mourning prince's head.

Sila peered through sticky tears at the general who knelt before him. Their faces were both of sorrow, but they knew that this was necessary. The man who once ruled this kingdom firmly, who guided his people lovingly through suppression from the foreign Deimor, had long been astray.

Sunrise had just begun to commence as Sila walked through the luxurious doors of the Bronze Tower. The sky was painted scarlet and blue as thousands of Scaldor, both rich and poor, gathered at the foot of the stairs amongst lush vegetation. Verun had informed them of the King's passing due to illness, and the city was present to witness the crowning of a new lord. They lined the streets in mobs, so far around the city that the prince was not visible to most.

"People of the Bronze Kingdom!" Sila began with a booming voice, tears still streaming down his rigid countenance. Verun was on his right and his stunning wife stood at his left. The

Scaldor listened intently as he began to speak, most realizing that their anarchy was about to come to an end. "The winds of change are coming. My father's passing is both a blessing and a curse to this kingdom. He will always be remembered as a great lord and man, but our enemies now close in around our walls. We have grown weak, but that time is over!" Sila's eyes twinkled with passion. "We have disillusioned our eminent Lord Brazdor with our failure to make use of his blessing. My people, there is hope! He has spoken to me. He has named me his reincarnate on this mortal world," Sila claimed as the mouths of his people gaped in astonishment. The High Priest Akul stood at the back of the mob. It was traditionally his place to crown the king, and Sila's proclamation sent a fearful chill down his back.

"He has promised this kingdom a return to greatness. The time for lawlessness is over! A new world births on the horizon. A land of Bronze! The heavens have mandated that I take this crown. Brazdor has mandated that I take on his title. Long live the Bronze Kingdom. Long live the Scaldor!" Sila raised his arms toward the brightening sky, as his people went into an uproar. They chanted the name of their god and honored the man who was now more than their King. He was the acclaimed mortal reincarnation of him to which they all prayed. Verun gracefully placed the sapphire crown on the new king's long, blue-streaked, black hair and affirmed Sila as the Lord of the Bronze Kingdom.

"He killed his own father?" Zano asked pensively.

"Sometimes, doing what is necessary is the hardest endeavor a man can face," Merasu asserted in a self-reflecting manner. "Well, I am going to go check the gate. Shall I pay a visit to your men?"

"Please."

"Of course. Farewell, Zano." Merasu bowed and stood up.

"Farewell," Zano bid goodbye as the dark figure exited the chamber.

The Lord of Blood found himself in deep thought. His legs were folded, and the dagger lay across his lap. It was as though he were meditating with his eyes remaining open. A beam of light ran across the fire-eyed side of his face. It wavered, unsure of its presence, not decisive in its decision to remain or depart. Zano and the ray were not unlike at this time, for he too wavered. His mind was jumbled, though he could not decide why. The night was quiet and peaceful, but something undetected troubled him.

His eyes began to close due to fatigue, and, as he prepared to lie down, a deafening crash shook the fortress like an earthquake. He sprang to his feet, dagger in hand, and bolted to the slit in the wall. Shouts echoed from the base—battle cries and screams of fear. He saw trails of fire spring up outside of the ramparts and then great, flaming projectiles were heaved at the fortress with tremendous force. Zano shuddered, grasped the belt that held his sword, and sped out into the hall.

Soldiers were roused in their bronze armor and began to sprint down beside the Blood Scaldor. They flocked by the hundreds and took him up as their leader, despite the color of his scales. The wall before them exploded into thousands of pieces, some stabbing fatally into the soldiers and leaving a gap in the floor too wide for any normal man to jump.

"Find another way!" Zano roared. He cautiously judged the distance before leaping over the gap with the nimbleness of a cat.

Down below, a battle raged on. Flaming rocks pounded the sealed gate of the fortress, which was slowly giving in. Javelins and arrows rained down upon the soldiers at the foot of the keep, and boulders of stone smashed them from behind. They hid beneath large planks of wood that served as defensive shields, with the Scaldor occupying most of the grounds and the Blood Scaldor crammed into a corner. Spheres of fire bombarded the battlements without relent from the very creatures of Isinda itself. Colossal Scorpions, shielded by gold and iron, launched the lethal projectiles from the end of their whip-like tails.

The Scaldor were caught by surprise in the dead of the night, unprepared and without defenses placed atop the fortifications. Archers scrambled to the makeshift barracks for their bows and were placed by Verun behind the gate, ready to let loose a barrage. Merasu stood, as promised, at the front of the Blood Scaldor regiment, beside the young Carthago, who appeared meager in comparison.

Zano sprinted through the halls, which were pounded by merciless waves of fire. Shards zipped past him as he ran, constantly changing his route through a maze of senseless turns. His dwelling was at the fortress's top level, and even his animal-like sense of direction could not guide him to the base with ease. Soldiers met with him and scattered into separate hallways to find an alternate course.

The gate burst from its hinges, and, through a smoky film, a mass of armed Arikarnon stormed in. A wall of arrows met them, building a pile of dead in the narrow passageway, but an endless number continued to swarm through. Verun roared for his army to charge, and they smashed into the wall of gold- and ironclad Arikarnon, who wielded spears or great axes and shields for defense. Sparks flashed, and iron rang as blood spurted out onto the hot sand. Double-sided *naginata* twirled with deadly wrath while more assembled from within the castle to repel the attackers.

The Blood Scaldor were prepared to jump into the fray when the wall beside them came crashing down. They fled behind Merasu as rubble poured like rain from the black sky. Through the dust emerged a horde of vicious Scorpions with spear-wielding riders. The cries of the beasts were unearthly. They had never seen creatures of that size, and their eyes brimmed with trepidation.

Merasu laughed deeply before flourishing his blade as the arachnid cavalry bounded forth. The Blood Scaldor could only observe as the shadowy figure gained eldritch power. He leaped toward one Scorpion and beheaded its rider, then flipped onto another and did the same. Swirling orbs of dark, purple energy flung from his iron-plated hands, searing the flesh of the Arikarnon in a way more gruesome than fire, so that bones were visible after but a few moments. His tremendous fury was unleashed until the Scorpions stopped flowing. He then urged the Blood Scaldor to charge the ensuing force with him, and, with courageous hearts, they followed.

Zano was just a level below where he had begun. He gazed out at the raging battle with ire, desperately craving to jump from this height. Suddenly, Sila came running toward him with the fervent young general from earlier supporting him.

"Zano, they come!" the king shouted urgently as the wound on his belly became visible. A group of Arikarnon, who had infiltrated the structure, darted hastily down the hallway in pursuit.

"Run! I will take them," Zano bellowed. Sila nodded and the man supporting him grinned arrogantly before they escaped through an opening to the left. The crimson warrior sheathed his dagger and brandished his stunning sword. He snarled viciously, desperately yearning for battle. By a quick incantation, a ball of flame erupted from his palm and struck his assailants. Their eyes depicted fear in every sense of the word as Zano came toward them, slashing through the smoke and ash. He tore through the group of nearly one hundred with ease, blood spilling onto his armor and cloth, until a trail of bodies screamed in agony behind him.

"It has been a long time, Zano," a brutish, familiar voice stated as its holder stepped into the gory hallway. There was a moment of silence as a gust of wind rushed down the passage, the fumes of death upon it.

"Arkul," Zano realized scornfully. Hatred was on the tip of his tongue in a way that it had not been since he drove his dagger into the heart of the High Priest.

"Finally I will have a chance to test your strength, my old friend," Arkul mused.

"Don't use that word with me!" Zano snapped.

"You have grown since last I saw you squirming in the great Arena, on top of your own bile."

"Have you no honor! You were too much of a coward to face me then, so face me now!" Zano boomed.

"I have spared you these long years of life. I would have killed you then; I will kill you know. Do you see this red-jeweled crown?" Arkul gestured to the circlet of gold fixed with a hefty, flawless ruby. "This is the symbol of a champion. You cannot stand against me."

"You do not deserve that crown for what you did! I will reave your soul to the pits of Pregarus!" Zano barked.

"The Arena was no place for creatures such as you! Now, we will see!" Arkul grunted as he flourished the two unnerving battle-axes in his hands. His body was bare and glistening, veins piercing through his flexing muscles. A loincloth was all that he wore, but his height and brute strength appeared to hold advantage over Zano.

The Lord of Blood roared, and with it came a flare of flames from his scales. His eyes smoldered with intensity as he rushed his foe, blade in hand.

The taste of defeat was in the mouths of the weary Scaldor. They were not well-adapted to the temperature and could hardly hold off the rampant waves of charcoal warriors. The only section of the defense that held strong was the ardent Blood Scaldor and their present leader Merasu. They unleashed years of hatred and torture onto their assailants, fighting like animals, undaunted by their first moment of true battle. Just as Zano did, they saw the faces of their loathed masters on the Arikarnon. Just as his eyes flamed passionately, so did theirs.

Ferociously, they tore a fracture into the enemy's lines through the break in the wall. Realizing this, Verun focused all of his effort toward the foreigners, creating a path for retreat. Sila emerged from the stronghold beneath a shell of guards.

Projectiles swarmed them, but each time a soldier died another took up his place in defense of the wounded emperor.

Another section of fortification caved from constant pounding. Arikarnon poured in, and Verun signaled the full retreat of all forces. Scaldor dispersed from the castle, carving a bloody trail toward perceived freedom. The people of the desert funneled into the battleground while their opponents channeled outwards. Spheres of blazing fire were launched toward the fleeing troops, but none gave chase. Merasu took up the rear but halted as the Blood Scaldor stopped before him.

"We must return for Zano," Carthago voiced proudly.

"Oblikaron be with you," Merasu bowed and followed the trail of his King across the dunes.

Zano and Arkul were engaged in an epic battle. Since his victory at the Arena, Arkul had become a general and was hailed as the finest warrior in the desert. Zano had become the unsung swordsman who had built fame as the crimson warrior across Isinda. Their blades moved with such mastery that neither could prevail. It was a perfect battle—a *katana* that moved with blinding quickness versus two mighty axes swinging precisely. Had only the Arikarnon demonstrated honor to the foreigner, a crowd of thousands could have witnessed the spectacle of Isinda's finest warriors.

Arkul swung high, forcing Zano to duck, then came upward with his other axe. Zano flipped backward out of the way, and the desert warrior charged forth in rage. The Blood Scaldor parried every stroke effortlessly until a crushing blow from both axes sent his sword sparking across the stone floor. Arkul chortled and slashed at Zano, who took hold of his dagger and rolled behind the giant. Speed was his gift, and as blow after blow sped toward him, he evaded them as though he were a ghost. To any viewer, it would have appeared that each strike found home, but in truth, Zano dodged them by naught but a hair. He flipped and twirled acrobatically, out of the way of relentless swipes.

"Come here!" Arkul snarled impatiently and thrust forward. Zano caught the impending arm and sunk his dagger through the Arikarnon's wrist while evading a slash aimed for his neck. A cry rang out as an axe plummeted to the cold floor. Zano was without a weapon, and his enemy bounded toward him, swinging violently with one axe. The Lord of Blood, however, was as elusive as the air. He pounced, and the axe slightly scratched his arm as he punched the dagger further through Arkul's wrist and out the other side. There was a horrific snarl as Zano spun, caught his weapon, and rushed upwards with the dagger into his enemy's heart. He drove the blade through hardened flesh, blood spraying onto his already-dripping face. The second axe fell harmlessly to the ground, followed by a tremendous thump from the weight of Arkul's body.

Zano breathed heavily, glaring down at his opponent, who lay outstretched on his back in a heap. Arkul's eyes spun in disbelief that the life was flowing from his once ardent veins.

"Take the crown," he whimpered through quivering, blood-drenched lips.

"No. You will die knowing it is yours," Zano answered abhorrently. The words stung Arkul, who realized his dishonor just before he died. His skin morphed to a lighter shade, and the gold of his eyes went dull as rusty iron.

The Lord of Blood retrieved his sword and collapsed against a wall. Battle had fatigued him, and all he desired was rest, believing that there was more fighting to come. The reverberation of a regiment of footsteps sounded down the hall, and he was about to spring to his feet, until he saw a familiar face staring at the grand corpse. It was the face of a lord, and it was the king of the desert.

"I see you have had your revenge, Zano," Kalo exclaimed as he drew near to the slouched warrior.

"This is the man that poisoned me," Zano claimed in his own defense.

"I know. I always believed that this day would come when

you would claim your rightful spot in the Heart of Agoge. He was one of my finest generals, but a man without honor deserves a death no less fitting." Kalo stopped a few feet away from the carcass and gestured his men to stay behind.

"Now I am in your grasp again," Zano sighed exasperatedly.

"Yes, and now you are my enemy. Shall I strike you down? My men will it. It would probably be essential for the continued existence of my kingdom."

"I would rather die by no other hand," Zano offered his head.

"And I you. But perhaps I do not hold the ability to do what is necessary. I cannot stand to see such power disappear. You are a hero without equal, and you are the greatest threat I've ever known. You could be the ruin of my kingdom, or you could easily be the opposite. How can a mortal man know? The empire you serve is strong, but be wary of the emperor who rules it," Kalo warned with a grim frown.

"You speak only of its lord. What of its people?" Zano tested his response.

"Your words have never left me. I am a wise enough man to release my ignorance and realize that all Scaldor aren't the same. If you are willing to serve the Bronze Kingdom, then there must be some good in it."

"You have me in your clutches again, and you are just going to let me go?" Zano questioned in disbelief as he rose to his feet.

"We all die Zano, but trust me, I will die much sooner than you."

"You speak solemn thoughts. You are a generous king, Kalo. We shall meet again, though I hope on better terms," Zano bowed appreciatively and humbly before the lord who spared him again.

"My people will permit you to leave. I have already ordered it. Your followers await you down below. Now you are the champion of the Heart of Agoge, Zano. Farewell, and may his Lordship be with you." Kalo returned the bow, and as Zano walked past, their gazes never met.

Just as he reached the parted rows of soldiers, he wheeled and glared back at the frozen corpse, realizing that his dagger still remained. Since his freedom, he had held onto it as a memento of a horrid past. It was a poison that lurched onto him—a parasite that clung onto his lingering hatred. Cries of torture and images of forsaken slaves crept into his usually clear mind. Pain shot through him, no differently than when a man relinquishes a drug. The image of his master Tarak came to the surface, and he recalled his words.

"One day," he said, "you must learn to let go, to rid yourself of a troubled past and realize that it is no longer so. You must learn not to hold, but to press on with the zeal and vehemence that I know you hold—that all the heroes to bless our beloved land of Isinda have held."

The dagger was the last relic of Zano's profound hatred. It was a symbol of his life of slavery, and it was all that remained of the priest who bound him. For years, it remained at his hip, always returning, even when he attempted to pass it on to Carthago. Always it haunted him with its silent wickedness, serving as a reminder of all he claimed to despise. With confidence, Zano turned away from its gory temptation without ever looking back. He vanished from the room and there the dagger remained, plunged into a dead man's chest, where it had always found comfort, yearning for a master to wield it, but there were none to heed its call.